DEATH COMES KNOCKING

DEATH COMES KNOCKING

A THEA KOZAK MYSTERY, BOOK 10

KATE FLORA

ONE

Most people would think the soft gray-green we'd chosen was an odd color for a baby's room, but it was peaceful and soothing. The baby I was carrying was an acrobat. A night owl. A perpetual motion machine. I didn't yet know whether when MOC —our abbreviation for Mason, Oliver, or Claudine—appeared Andre and I would have a son or a daughter. What I did know was that whoever we met in the delivery room, the child would need peace and soothing. Or we would.

I was prying the lid off the paint can and wondering whether it was safe for a woman shaped like a whale to climb up the stepladder when the doorbell rang. I hesitated before heading for the stairs. We didn't know many people in our new town, which meant it was likely one of Andre's siblings. I like them well enough. They're family, after all, but they have a different sense of time from mine. Their visits go on too long and their sense of personal boundaries seems nonexistent. I wasn't keen on a discussion of my girth, or my birth plans, or whether I was planning to breastfeed, never mind whether MOC would be baptized. Or was it christened?

Still, family is family so I headed downstairs and opened the door. The woman I found on my doorstep was no one I'd ever seen before. I'd remember her if I had. Anyone would. She was absolutely stunning. She had long, straight black hair and piercing blue eyes and alabaster skin. She was wearing bright red lipstick and a dress that looked like she'd stolen it from hippies—a flowing multi-colored extravaganza that screamed exuberance. I've never in my life owned something that bold. Tall women with big chests try to minimize their physical footprint, though those who know me would agree I'm no shrinking violet.

She smiled at me and held out a hand. "Hi, I'm Jessica." She gestured back down our sloping lawn toward the street. "I've just moved into the cottage. Jeannine, down at the library, said you were my neighbor and that we should meet."

Ah. Small towns. You hardly had to mind your own business because your neighbors were minding it for you. I shouldn't complain, though. Andre and I had looked forever for a house, and this was as close to being our dream house as a piece of real estate could be. I never expected having a house could make me so happy.

At my skeptical glance toward the cottage, she nodded and turned back toward the small, shabby house mostly hidden behind a hemlock hedge. "Yeah. It needs work. A lot of work. But it will be cute when I'm done."

It was only when she turned sideways and gestured toward the hidden dwelling across the street that I realized the crazy dress was hiding a pregnancy about as advanced as mine. Maybe more, given how short she was.

"Thea," I said. "Come in. Welcome to the Whales Club. Would you like some tea? Or coffee? And I've got some lovely Finnish coffee bread."

"I would love some coffee," she said, following me into the house, "but I've given it up. Do you have any herbal tea?"

I did. Andre calls it 'gerbil tea' and says it tastes like a cup full of straw, but I've grown rather fond of it since I've cut down on coffee. Anyway, hibiscus and berry didn't taste like straw. Neither did blueberry. In the kitchen, I put the kettle on, got out the bread, and sliced it. For a woman who often forgot to eat and usually had a depressingly empty refrigerator, I was becoming awfully domestic. Maybe having a house was changing me. Not a house. A home.

Jessica took a chair and studied my kitchen. "Wow. This is lovely. I've always wanted a place with tall glass cabinets like this."

"Me, too," I agreed. "Although it means there's no way of hiding the mess. We looked a long time before we found this place. So you've moved into the cottage? It looks like a place with possibilities from the outside. Is it nicer inside?" In truth, it looked like a shabby wreck, but I didn't want to daunt her optimism.

She hesitated before answering. "Like I said, it needs some work. Well, a lot of work. But it will be nice and cozy when that's done. Hope I'm not overestimating how much I can do before the baby."

We chatted in the way women do, comparing our babies' antics and what we surmised about their personalities. As our talk went on, I realized that while she was a pleasant conversationalist, whenever I asked about her background, where she'd moved from, or why she'd chosen Stover or pretty much any question that might give me insight into who she was, she deflected the conversation to a different subject. I've interviewed a lot of people, many of them reluctant to talk to me, so I recognize those deflections. It was odd, since she'd chosen to visit me, but I had no reason to pry. After a pleasant hour, during which we, mostly Jessica, managed to eat almost the entire loaf of bread, I realized that she knew a lot about me, and all I knew about her was that her name was Jessica and she was expecting a baby girl. There had been no mention of husband, boyfriend, or significant other. None of family or work. I didn't even know her last name.

Her deflections were so skillful that I wondered if she was hiding something. Or from something. For all her attempts to appear casual and easy, once or twice, when Andre's dad and his cousin, who were working out on the barn, roared up the driveway in a truck, or dropped something with a clang, she was instantly alert and on the edge of her chair.

"My father-in-law and my husband's cousin," I told her. "They're fixing up the barn so we can put the cars there in the winter. And so Andre—my husband—can have a workshop out

3

there. He loves to make things. He's made a beautiful cradle for MOC."

"Mock?" she said. "Is that what you're going to name your baby?"

"M.O.C. It's a nickname. Short for Mason, Oliver, or Claudine. We decided not to learn the baby's sex, so it will be a surprise."

"It will stick, you know."

"That's what everyone says. What about your baby. Do have a name?"

Jessica smiled and patted her roundness. "Amaryllis. Amy for short. Her dad picked it out."

Then she went silent, her small teeth biting her lip, like she'd said something she hadn't meant to say.

"What does her dad do?" I asked. I didn't want to say 'your husband' because she wasn't wearing a ring, and anyway, relationships these days were often undefined.

"Oh," she said, giving little Amaryllis another pat, "he's not in the picture."

I've been reading people for a long time, and it was clear to me, from her wistful tone, that his absence wasn't her choice, and that it was very possible his absence was permanent or his return uncertain.

I waited for more. When it didn't come, I changed the subject. "I'm a consultant to independent schools. Private schools," I said. "My partner and I run EDGE Consulting. Right now, I'm working from home. Actually, this morning they said I was making them nervous and threw me out of the office. Told me not to come back until Monday. I think they're hoping by Monday MOC will have debuted, but it's too soon. This kid needs more cooking. Maybe they just knew I needed some time to paint the baby's room." I shrugged. "I can't help it if I can't find a comfortable position, and my shifting makes them nervous. I'm still getting plenty of work done."

I looked over at the clock on the wall. In fifteen minutes, I would be calling in and Sarah, my secretary, would be updating me on all the crises that needed my attention. I might be gone, but I wasn't forgotten. "Do you work?"

Yes. A rude question. But I was too curious to hold it back.

Jessica smiled. "I'm a consultant, too. To...uh...it's a government job. Something I can do remotely. I just need to get the cable people out to get the cottage updated. Which, so far, seems like a difficult task."

She looked around the kitchen, finished enough to give a deceptive sense of the house, some of which still felt like a construction zone. "Have you had trouble getting service people in?"

She'd almost given something about herself away, though I had no idea what. I wasn't going to learn it any time soon, though, because abruptly, she was on her feet and heading for the door, saying, "Got to go. Sorry. Thanks for the tea."

I followed her to the door, answering her question with, "Yes. It can take a while to get phone and cable out here."

I had no idea what I'd done to upset her, maybe nothing, but she was definitely done here. So much for another new mother in the neighborhood. Maybe she was just shy or had something in the oven that would burn, so I tossed out, "I'm going shopping tomorrow to get some baby stuff. Want to come along?"

She hesitated, like it was a big decision, then said, "Sure. I'd like that. I've pretty much done nothing to get ready and I don't know where to go. Though I expect Amazon delivers here, right?"

"They always know how to find us."

For some reason, that remark made her nervous, or was it the idea that Amazon might need her address? I plowed on, unsure why I was doing so. Maybe that she seemed lonely? On a shopping trip, spending more time together, she might be more forthcoming. "Pick you up at ten?"

She looked down at her wrist, where there was no watch, then back across at the cottage. "Sure. Ten. That would be great."

"Wait," I said, "let me give you my number. In case something comes up."

She hesitated like an animal on the cusp of flight while I went to my office and grabbed a card. She tucked it into a pocket in the wild garment. She was the one who'd reached out to me, but now she seemed to be having second thoughts.

"It's just shopping for baby things," I said. "I'm going anyway. Be nice to have you along."

She nodded and was gone.

I stood in the doorway and watched her trot down the rolling green lawn, hesitating at the road and looking around her like she was afraid of hidden bad guys. She was definitely afraid of something. Then she hurried across and disappeared behind the hedge that shielded the cottage from the street.

The rest of the day went quietly. I opened all the windows and finished painting the baby's room. I may not be the world's best painter, but it looked great when I was done. As I put my painting supplies away, I wondered idly what kind of accommodations Jessica had for her baby. The place didn't look inviting, but maybe she was one of those decorating geniuses who can bring cozy out of squalor.

Decorating is so far from my thing that it is a miracle we have furniture, though I'm trying to do better. Andre is more interested than I am. He likes comfort. The color blue. And surprisingly, antique tribal rugs. To look at my handsome husband, with his firm jaw, nearly military-short hair, and fierce eyes, never mind the broad shoulders and six-pack abs, you'd never imagine he'd have opinions on window treatments. He's taught me a lot about not underestimating people, as has my work as a consultant to independent—read private—schools. I like it when the surprises about people are pleasant. Unfortunately, such is my fate that I more often meet those whose surprises are not. Often enough that I sometimes wonder if I'm a bully magnet.

I was heading for the stairs, planning to explore dinner possibilities in my uncooperative refrigerator, when I looked out the big window in the hall. From there, I could see over the hedge to more of the cottage. There was a small black Honda in the driveway, and Jessica and a taller, older blonde woman were standing beside it, arguing.

TWO

Intriguing as my encounter with my new neighbor was, never mind my curiosity about the woman she'd been arguing with, I'd pretty much forgotten about her by the time I'd checked in with my secretary, Sarah, and developed a daunting to-do list. I wondered if this was more of Suzanne and my other colleagues' attempt to bring on baby MOC. A bit of "let's stress Thea and see if it induces labor." They aren't mean, just anxious.

I left the list on my desk and made a broccoli and cheddar quiche for dinner. Maybe real men don't eat quiche, but Andre does. It helps that the broccoli is from our garden. Having some land for a vegetable garden was one thing that had drawn Andre to the house. He knew what he was doing, gardening-wise, but it was my first experiment with growing vegetables. I still consider every bit of successfully raised produce a miracle. I'm also discovering the difference when food is freshly picked.

The quiche was coming out of the oven just as Andre got home. He made a salad with our own lettuce and we spent a quiet evening without either of us getting interrupted by crises. That's not always easy since he's a detective with the Maine state police. I may think he belongs to me, but they think he belongs to them.

The next morning I worked until just before ten, when I'd said I would pick Jessica up. I might have had visions of lots of neat stores to shop for baby things, but after asking around, I figured that we would head up to Freeport and hit some of the outlets, like Carters and Baby Gap.

She was waiting in the yard. There were two cars there, a gray Volvo and a black Honda, but she was alone. Given how skittish she'd been about personal questions, I didn't ask about the cars. Maybe when—if—she got more comfortable with me, I'd learn more. Today she wore an oversized blouse with a swath of wild design and denim capris. Her hair was in a fat braid. She smiled and waved when I turned in, and climbed awkwardly into the passenger seat. If I had swallowed a basketball, she'd swallowed a beach ball.

"Whew!" she said as she fastened the seatbelt. "I've seen plenty of pregnant women but I never imagined *I'd* look like this. I was thinking, 'I'm fit. I'm young. This will be a piece of cake.' Right? And look at me! If I fell over, I'd be stuck on my back like an over-turned turtle."

I laughed. It was fun to have another pregnant woman to share these things with. I'm such a slave of duty I'm not sure I know how to hang out. "That's so true. Guess it's not something you can imagine until it happens. Who would have thought it would be so impossible to find clothes?" I said.

"You're lucky that you're tall, though. More room for Mock to grow, right?"

"Lately I feel like I'm the gym and this kid is an acrobat prac-ticing for the circus. So, today I'm shopping for basics and a car seat. What about you?"

"The same. Basics. And I need a crib or this little girl is going to be sleeping in a cardboard box. Not that she'll notice at first."

"Right." I told her where we were going as we headed out. It was another beautiful summer day and we drove with the windows down. "I love August," I said. "Farm stands. Gardens. All the green and the sky is so blue. I've spent so much time over the years at the office and on the road, I usually miss summer completely, or it's something I see through my car windows. I'm trying to reform, to practice slowing down before this kid arrives. The last thing MOC needs is a crazy busy mom."

Beside me, she sighed. I already knew she didn't want to talk about herself, so I didn't say anything. Sometimes silence works better than chatter anyway.

After a few miles, she said, "This is not what I planned."

"Coming here? Moving to Maine?"

She sighed again. "Having this baby alone, in a place where I don't know anyone."

It wasn't much, but I said, "Well, you know me now. And I'm happy to help however I can." I wasn't sure how I could help. Invite her to prenatal classes? Offer to be with her when the baby came? The more I thought about it, the more depressing it seemed. No one should have to do this alone.

I tried not to think about my adopted sister Carrie. About what her mother went through and how it had warped her. Her mom assaulted by a relative as a teenager and then shunned by the family.

Jessica went silent again and I left it alone. She was probably thinking about all the things she'd have to do on her own. I really wanted to know why her baby's father couldn't be here, but it was not my business. Because the baby's father had suggested a name and she'd accepted it, I didn't think this was a case of 'seduced and abandoned.' There was a story she wasn't telling. I focused on local things instead. I asked if she had found her way to the lake yet, and whether she liked to swim. Whether she'd gone to my favorite farm stand yet. "They have their own honey, and it's wonderful. So are their berry jams."

There was humor in her voice when she said, "Haven't tried swimming yet, but I'm sure I'll float."

We both laughed. I *had* been swimming and yes, floating on my back was kind of hilarious. "At least I don't feel quite so much like a blimp when I'm in the water," I said.

"Blimp. Whale. We sure do put ourselves down, don't we? Aren't we supposed to be celebrating our fertility? Fulfilling our womanly duty?" she said.

KATE FLORA

"I think a lot of the people who are eager for us to fulfill our womanly duty will never have to become whales themselves."

For some reason that made me giggle. I'm not a giggler, but sometimes there's just a day when everything sets me off. Going baby gear shopping with another mom-to-be was doing it today. I could already picture the two of us wrestling a baby crib onto the roof of my Jeep.

"But you don't know the sex of your baby, do you?" she said. "So how will you know what to buy?"

"Pink or blue, you mean?"

She made an affirmative noise.

"I like yellow. And green. There's orange and tan. Red and white. And silly prints and little outfits with funny animals on them."

"And those little decorated feet."

"Cloth diapers or disposables?"

She sighed. "Disposables. Right now, my hovel doesn't even have a washing machine. I'm working on that."

"Better move fast," I said, "these big box stores sometimes have a couple of weeks wait for delivery."

I felt like an idiot as soon as I said it. She was probably doing her best. Despite her secrecy, it was clear to me that Jessica wasn't here because she'd *chosen* to come and live in a decrepit cottage in a small Maine town. I wondered if she was hiding from something or someone or if she was on the run. I decided to pry a little. A bit unfair. She was stuck here with me. But if she didn't want to talk, she could just say so, or use those fine evading skills she'd used yesterday.

"What made you decide to come here?" I asked.

She didn't answer. She stared out the window and down at her phone.

I tried again. "I saw you arguing with someone in your driveway yesterday. A friend? A relative?"

She didn't bother to evade. "Not that it's any of your business, Thea, but that's the person who's helping me move. We were discussing..." She put a sarcastic spin on the word 'discussing.' "... her choice of that cottage. I'm..." A silence. "I'm pretty resilient.

10

Not especially fussy. I can live anywhere. Tent. Army barracks. Trailer park. But I am not doing that to Amy. She needs a decent place to live. Which…whatever I might have said yesterday…is not this cottage. I'm working on it, but I told her I'm not a miracle worker and she'd better find something better. I guess you could say we had a difference of opinion. She insisted this was the best she could do at the last minute."

A sigh. "I don't believe her, which I said, and then she got huffy and said she was doing her best to help me under the circumstances. And then I said that I assumed she helped people like me under urgent circumstances all the time, wasn't that her job, and she pretty much walked away. Well. Drove away in her little rented Honda, and after a while she came back with some groceries and we settled into a silent détente. For now."

I wasn't going to press her on the circumstances. It would come out eventually if she needed or wanted to talk about it, but my mind was throwing up all kinds of interesting scenarios. My best guess was that something was up with the husband, which meant Jessica needed to be hidden.

Freeport was the usual summertime scrum of tourists, but I know some secrets about finding parking, and pretty soon we were in an outlet store, oohing and aahing over adorable tiny clothes.

I'd wondered about her using a credit card and revealing her whereabouts, but she paid with a wad of cash. After hitting two stores, we put our packages in the car and got ourselves some lunch. People often think of Maine as a backwater bumpkin state, but we've got plenty of great restaurants. This wasn't Portland, but the talent has spread up the coast. We had fabulous salads with greens and lobster and fruit and an interesting sesame dressing. We had hot-from-the-oven popovers, despite it being summer. We drank raspberry-lime rickeys in lieu of chardonnay. Then we went for ice cream, sitting on a bench in the sun, people watching.

I still didn't know much about her, but she had a keen eye for human foibles and a wicked talent for description. We laughed so hard we almost spilled our cones, and neither of us cared.

"The things people wear," she gasped at one point, as an over-weight fellow in clinging short shorts and a tank top went by.

"And the things you can't unsee."

What I wanted to unsee was the man's hairy purple belly thrust out under his top and draped over his shorts. I know. We're all supposed to be accepting of every body type and fat shaming is taboo. But we didn't shame anyone, we just giggled like a pair of snarky middle school girls.

On the way home, we headed to Target to look for cribs and car seats, and giant packages of teeny newborn diapers.

The truth was that shopping for baby things was fun. More fun when there were two of us.

We were having a grand time until we came out with our full carts, stowed our treasure in the car, and drove to the loading area to pick up her crib. The guy brought it out in its giant cardboard box, dumped it at our feet, and started to retreat.

I was about to say something when Jessica said, "Stop! You hold it right there." When the man turned in surprise, she said, in a voice that didn't suggest helplessness, "Can't you see that we need help?" She said it in a deliberately loud voice, so all the other people around us who were loading grills and outdoor furniture stopped to see what was up. A woman after my own heart.

Once it became clear that what was up was two very pregnant women who needed to get that crib onto the roof of a car, we had all the brawny male help two women could ask for. Brawny men and a skinny, fit-looking woman in her seventies who produced rope and bossed our volunteers around like a pro.

We laughed about that as we rode home, until she said, "But Thea...now we have to get it off."

"Easy," I said, "we'll get your tall, blonde houseguest to help."

"She's not a..." But Jessica stopped. "Sure. That's a great idea."

She sure didn't like the other woman, but it sounded like Jessica was stuck with her. I tried making conversation about the cottage and whether the woman could find her something better. This time, I didn't get her attempt at cheerful deflection. I got tears.

"It's a pit. I'm furious that they put me there, and while she says she'll try, she doesn't seem to care that it's unfit for me, never mind my baby."

There was silence for a while and then she said, "Forget I told you that. Please."

When I dropped her off, we did tap the other woman to help unload it and carry it inside. I introduced myself, but the woman didn't reciprocate, so I labeled her 'Honda woman.' Honda woman was supposed to be helping Jessica get settled, but her standoffish reluctance on top of Jessica's meltdown made me very sorry for my new neighbor. I went home not much more informed than I had been the day before, but more certain that, in a pinch, Jessica could take care of herself. And that if Honda woman was all she had for help, she'd have to.

Interesting. A mystery in my own backyard. And a morning having fun. Most days, fun wasn't in my vocabulary.

The rest of the day was not so much fun. No more tiny socks or cute little outfits. My dance card was full. I might be working from home, but the work at EDGE never stopped. Even though we were consultants to independent schools and it was summer, the work, and the crises, real or perceived, just kept coming. The looming prospect of the fall semester always sent our client schools scurrying to get things done.

Along with reports and surveys, helping to write crisis management plans and honor codes, there were the crises themselves. That was my specialty, so it was me Sarah called to report that a school in eastern Maryland had a cheating scandal involving their summer school students. They needed our help, they wanted someone on campus right now, and I was the person for the job. Should she book me a flight tomorrow?

It was summer in Maine, with all the good things that entailed. Swimming, poking around in my first ever attempt at a garden. Working on the house. Sitting out on the back porch sipping mocktails (and real drinks for the person who wasn't pregnant) and eating salads. The last thing I wanted was to leave my little oasis and fly to a hotter part of the country. Especially since pregnancy was already making me hot, and not in a good way. But handling campus emergencies was my specialty, and expanding EDGE Consulting's reach into other parts of the country was part of the new business plan Suzanne and I had made.

I had a doctor's appointment tomorrow, so I said, "Book me an early flight for day after tomorrow and email me the details and names of my contacts. I'll call and let them know when I'm coming and get the scoop on their problem." Then, even though I didn't want to be away from Andre even for a night, I said, "And book me a hotel, just in case."

"Will do," she said. "It's so nice to be back working at EDGE again. I was never happy after you guys moved the business to Maine."

"And I discovered you were irreplaceable. How are the kids doing?"

"Loving it. Making friends at summer camp. Playing outside until dark. They are having a perfect childhood. If they miss their dad, I'm not seeing it. I think they're just grateful that the fighting has stopped."

Sarah had been my secretary back in Massachusetts before Suzanne's husband got a job as headmaster at a Maine private school and we'd moved the business. The move had made it easier for my relationship with Andre Lemieux, the Maine state police detective I met when he was investigating my sister Carrie's death. It had meant, though, that we'd left Sarah behind. She couldn't just move her husband and family. One is not supposed to be pleased about a failed marriage, but Sarah's had been pretty miserable, and I was over the moon when she told me she was divorcing, moving to Maine, and wondering if she might get her old job back.

Since her replacement couldn't be trusted to do anything right, getting her job back was not a problem. Now, with a handful of new staff, and Sarah competently running my life, things at the office were great.

With a business trip on the horizon, I went to my closet to see if anything in my current wardrobe of circus tents looked sufficiently professional. I called myself a whale, but I actually looked like a tall, slim woman who had accidentally swallowed a basketball. That should have made finding clothes easy, since plenty of summer dresses hang loosely from the shoulders. Those cute summer dresses, though, have some major drawbacks. They all seem to be designed for women with fashionably small chests, and I had an unfashionably large one. Fitting both a full bosom and a basketball presented challenges, never mind finding something that wasn't so short people would think I'd forgotten to put on pants. To complicate things further, I like clothes with pockets, which few pieces of women's clothing have.

As I stared into the closet, I wished I could wear wildly colorful clothes like my new neighbor. But getting an agitated headmaster and an upset faculty and staff to take me seriously would not work so well if I showed up looking like a hippie. It's bad enough that I have wild hair unless I straighten it with brushes and product. I settled for a sleeveless A-line jersey dress—black, of course—and a flowing black and white flowered linen cardigan. My feet hadn't swelled, at least not yet, so my smart, strappy sandals would do. Their modest wedge heel puts me over six feet, which helps to command a room.

Pressing down the chorus of "I don't wanna" that the trip engendered, I decided that if I had to be away on business later in the week, today I got to play in the garden. When Andre came home, we'd go to the lake and swim, and then he could grill some fish while I boiled corn and made a salad. My first ever ripe tomato was waiting on the kitchen island, and in one of my raised beds, I had so much lettuce I could feed a family of five. So far, the bane of Maine farmers—the cuddly and destructive woodchuck—hadn't found our yard.

I put on my grubby garden pants and was about to tie on my sunhat when duty pulled me to the desk. I printed out Sarah's email, scanned the brief description of Eastern Shore Academy's problem, and called the headmaster's number.

When a male voice answered, I said, "Dr. Kingsley? It's Thea Kozak."

I got a confused-sounding, "Thea Kozak?"

"From EDGE consulting. This is Eastern Shore Academy? I'm looking for Dr. Kingsley."

"Oh. I'm sorry," the man said. "Dr. Kingsley has just stepped away from her desk. Do you want to hold or go to voicemail?"

Sarah had neglected to tell me that Dr. Kingsley was a woman, and I'd failed to do my homework. "Can you take my number and ask her to call me?"

He took my number, still sounding confused. I could only hope that he'd remember to give it to her. Then, tucking my phone in my pocket, I headed out to the garden.

This time I got out the door, across the deck, and down the steps. I was reaching for my trowel when I was interrupted by the phone again. The caller ID said that it was Dr. Kingsley. I sat on the step and answered.

"Ms. Kozak. It's Denise Kingsley, here at Eastern Shore. Thank you so much for getting back to me. Has your staff explained my problem?"

"Not in very much detail, Dr. Kingsley. It would be great if you could go over it."

I dumped my hat and gloves, trowel and garden trug on the steps and went back inside, pulling up a fresh page on the computer so I could take notes. I put the phone on speaker and set it beside me. "I'm ready," I said. "Tell me about your situation. My secretary said you had a cheating problem?"

"A cheating problem, yes, but more like a cheating and hacking problem. Do you have much computer expertise?"

I didn't, but I knew someone who did. I knew the Sherlock Holmes of computers.

"Not my area," I said, "but I have an expert we can call on if necessary."

"Excellent. And I understand that you'll be with us tomorrow?"

"Day after tomorrow."

She made a disappointed sound, then asked, "And can he…your computer expert…join us?"

"I will see if she can. She's in great demand, as you can imagine, but she usually makes time for me."

Ha! I wasn't the only one who made assumptions.

Dr. Kingsley explained her problem—a summer school student, whom they hadn't yet identified, had hacked into an instructor's computer to get copies of tests, then shared those tests with fellow students. It only came to light when some students who had previously been struggling aced their next two tests, despite having demonstrated little understanding of the subject matter. "We've spoken with them, Ms. Kozak, but they say the test questions just mysteriously appeared in their email, and they have no idea who sent them. They figured they were supposed to use the information."

I thought the sender should be pretty easy to trace. I wondered why the school's computer people couldn't have handled it, so I asked the obvious question: "Why do you need an outside consultant, Ms. Kingsley? Is there something unusually sensitive about the students involved?"

She sighed. "I'm afraid so. This is our special summer 'catch up' program for minorities and challenged students who will be joining us in the fall. We have a post-high school year that's very popular, and I guess you could call it a pre-post high school summer program for students who are further behind. This is kind of embarrassing, but things are so charged these days that even the suggestion that we're accusing someone of cheating can become such a big deal that—" She hesitated, and added, "especially when we're dealing with minority students."

"So if there's an allegation of cheating in this population, it's better if it comes from an outside expert?"

"Exactly. Thank you for understanding. I probably shouldn't say this aloud, but frankly, it bothers me that we can't hold everyone to the same standard. That we can't be open and honest about our process as well as our rules. You work with a lot of schools there at EDGE, so you and Suzanne know how common cheating has become. It's almost like a game to some of these kids. We do our best, but sometimes it seems like they're always a step ahead."

Now it was my turn to sigh. I was about to bring MOC into a

world where often the most basic standards seemed to be crumbling. Or was this just me becoming, prematurely, kind of an old fart?

"Let me check with my computer expert, and make sure she can do the date. I'll plan to come anyway, and I'll get back to you about her availability in the morning."

We agreed on that, and I was just heading out to the yard again, hoping a bit of gardening therapy would be soothing, when the phone rang. I have developed a strong dislike for Alexander Graham Bell, and his predecessor, Antonio Meucci. The phone is a very mixed blessing.

This time it was my husband Andre. "I'll be home early tonight, and I'm bringing a surprise."

"What kind of a surprise?" I asked warily. His last surprise had been two of his sisters, who wanted to check out the nursery and my baby supplies and didn't think I was doing anything right. I was definitely not in the mood for more of that.

"I'm bringing some people for dinner."

I had the most marginal of dinner plans—mostly involving lettuce and that piece of fish.

When I hesitated, he said, "They're bringing the dinner. And don't worry. You'll like them and the food will be good."

"Can't you at least give me a clue?" I said. "Male, female? More than one? Somebody I already know?"

He laughed. "One male. One female. And yes, you already know them."

I didn't think Andre would surprise me with any of my immediate family members, but I had to check. "Are we related to them in any way?"

He laughed. "Only by friendship. And that's all I'm going to say. See you soon."

Cops. They are way too good at not answering questions. True, even when they're my own husband.

I decided not to worry about it. The kitchen was neat. The bathroom was clean. In case these mystery guests were staying over, I knew there were clean sheets on the guest bed, and I had been scrupulous about not using the room for storage. I had a couple of nice pieces of cheese in the fridge and some great crackers. I don't like surprises. Too many of mine have been of the negative variety. But Andre knew that, so I trusted him. Maybe he wanted to show off the house? He was pretty smug about having found it while I was off slaying dragons at a client school.

Since the phone was already in my hand, I called my computer expert, LaDonna Marquis, and signed her up for Eastern Shore Academy.

"Should be a walk in the park," LaDonna said. "Did you tell them I was expensive?"

"I did. Also, that you're worth it."

"You bet," she said. "Email the info, okay? And directions. Let's talk tomorrow, and I'll see you there."

LaDonna was perfect for this job. Part Black, part Asian, and looking like an exotic twelve-year-old, she was also a hundred percent genius.

"Watch out, little cheaters," I said to my empty kitchen. "You are about to get busted."

I shoved my phone in my pocket, grabbed my hat and gloves, and headed out to the garden.

A very entitled doe and her adorable fawn were snacking on my lettuce.

THREE

I ran inside, grabbed two foil pie pans, and came back out, banging and clanging them together as I rushed toward the deer. After giving me a look that was pure attitude, mama deer turned and loped away, her still-spotted fawn trotting after her. The fawn gave one last, disappointed look at the lettuce and disappeared into the back forty.

I surveyed the damage. Not too bad. Yet. But now that they'd discovered "Thea's Salad Bar," I was in trouble. The kind of trouble that required a deer fence. I'd add it to the list of chores for Andre's dad, who got restless if he didn't have too much to do. Meanwhile, I was gonna hop down to the Agway and ask about deer repellents. Dammit. Now I had to change back into something that wasn't faded, baggy, and covered with dirt and bits of grass. True, plenty of people showed up that way, but my mother raised me to be proper. Plus, we were newcomers.

Darn it! Gardening was supposed to be relaxing. That would only be the case in my life if I buried the phone in the compost.

Changed, and with my hair held back by a neat band, I went down the road to Agway, slowing as I passed my new neighbor Jessica's house. Except for the driveway, the front of the lot was lined with a thick hedge of hemlocks, so I couldn't see much. All I learned was her dark gray Volvo wagon had Virginia plates. Interesting. I knew that lots of people in Virginia worked for the government. And that Quantico was in Virginia. Did my mysterious new neighbor work for the government? Was she running from the government? I reined in my imagination before I constructed some government conspiracy or top secret mission that had forced her to hide out in rural Maine.

Inside the Agway, I consulted the wisdom of the old men behind the counter, and found what I needed. They were happy to see me and give me advice. I'm quickly becoming one of their best customers. In the course of the conversation, I learned that Jackie Bell, the assistant town clerk, had sprained her ankle, the local boys' baseball team was having a great summer, and that I really ought to bring Andre to the band concert on Friday. Mr. Blake, a farmer out on the Old Warren Road, had some really great compost if I had a truck to haul it in. I never expected to find the idea of compost exciting, but this was great news, and Andre's father had a truck. Then I really would have someplace to bury the phone.

Along with deer repellent, I picked up two flats of cosmos, two pots of cheery orange and yellow calendulas, a rosebush in a lovely shade of salmon, and a bag of enriching mulch. Hardware stores and the helpful guys who run them are fast becoming my new love. Last week it was a green flowered trowel and weeder and a pair of gauntlet gloves for pruning. Andre thinks I'm hilarious. My credit card is getting weary. But, given a choice between dealing with dishonest students and watching my garden grow, there was no contest.

I slowed again as I drove past Jessica's house. This small town curiosity was contagious. The black Honda was gone, but the Volvo was there, and she was putting a plastic trash bag in the back. I beeped the horn. She looked at me, startled, then smiled and waved. She definitely was jumpy. She'd changed from her bright colors to black jeans and a loose tee shirt and was clearly more pregnant than I'd thought. I wondered if she'd dressed up for her shopping trip with me.

On an impulse, I turned into her driveway and got out. I took one of the pots of calendulas from the back and held it out. "I thought you might use these to cheer the place up."

She looked at the cheery flowers and I could swear she blinked back tears. "That is so kind of you," she said. "It will take more than flowers, but these are a great start." She gave me a quick hug, which had to be kind of a hilarious sideway encounter because of our shapes. We both laughed. I said, "Don't be a stranger. If I can help, I will."

"I may need that help, Thea. Right now, poor Amy is going to be sleeping in a drawer. I'm trying to put the crib together, but the instructions are jibberish and I'm not very handy with tools."

"Call me if you can't do it. Seriously. I can send Andre's dad over to help. He can do in seconds what we can do in an hour."

She said thanks, and I left.

Back home, I put my new plants on the back deck, applied nontoxic deer repellent remedies to the vegetables, and then dumped myself in an Adirondack chair that I'd painted a lovely shade of blue. I closed my eyes, meaning only to rest them for a minute, and fell asleep.

The slam of the screen door woke me. The door and the sound of a familiar voice. "Wake up, Princess. We've come to make sure Andre is taking proper care of you."

Dominic Florio. My second favorite cop. Dom has been my knight in shining armor more than once. He's rescued me from idiot baby cops. Comforted me when someone tried to kill me. Helped me fight back against some crazed militia members. Even washed out my bra once so I'd have something to wear. Few men will go that far, even for a damsel in distress. I opened my eyes to find Dom and his wonderful wife, Rosie, staring down at me, each with their own particular brand of assessment. I was out of my chair in an awkward, pregnant woman's instant, wrapping both of them in a hug. Andre hung back, grinning a grin that needed no words to say, "See. I told you that you were going to like this surprise."

Once we unwrapped from the hug, Dom and Rosie finished inspecting me. Their inspection, unlike my very judgmental mother's, was delighted, caring, and mostly uncritical, though they're always looking for signs I'm not taking care of myself. They are the parents I've always wanted, and they love me like I am a daughter. A wayward one, perhaps, who tends to get herself into dangerous situations and doesn't always heed their advice.

Seeing them was lovely but instantly filled me with shame and regret that I'd seen so little of them lately. Instead, I'd filled my time with work issues: student drug dealing, a porn-collecting professor, and an unexplained pregnancy at a client school. By the time I was done with crises on top of all my other work, I had no time for the people I loved. I barely made time for Andre. Of course, he also had trouble finding time for me. This summer, we were reforming. We had to. MOC would be too young to fend for him or herself.

"I see that look. No guilt. We didn't come here for that," Dom said, wagging a finger. "We've come to insist on our right to be Godparents."

"What a great idea," I said, and Andre nodded in agreement. "You're getting a wild one, I warn you."

Dom just grinned and looked at Rosie. "See," he said. "You didn't have to worry." To us, he said, "She's always wanted to be a godmother."

She gave him a playful cuff, then linked her arm through his.

Andre moved some chairs together so we could all sit, but of course, first they had to be given a tour of the house. Before that, Rosie directed Dom to bring in the food. Because Rosie and Dom are Italian, and believe in the importance—and restorative value— of food, they'd brought enough to feed a football team. That was fine with us. Rosie is a fantastic cook. I like to eat. Andre loves to eat. And MOC is always hungry. I may be no good at taking care of myself, but I've learned that if I don't feed the little acrobat, I get kicked a lot. And MOC is nocturnal.

They loved our kitchen. Our bright and airy living room and wide front porch. Our huge bedroom with a sleigh bed and a bright summer quilt and one wall that still needed plastering. They admired our bathroom with the rainfall shower, a half-tiled floor, and tub for two. Right now, the tub for two was a tight fit as a tub for almost three.

"Now," Rosie said, "let's see the baby's room."

She'd gone up the stairs so easily my jaw dropped. When I first met Dom, who was the detective investigating my friend Eve's mother's murder, Rosie was in a wheelchair after being hit by a drunk driver. Doctors said she'd likely never walk again, but Rosie is the toughest woman I know. She beat the odds, and now here she was, looking almost like that accident had never happened. Her husband is still crazy in love with her, a model I hope will work for me and Andre.

Why had I let so much time pass without a visit?

As if she was reading my mind, Rosie said, "You've been pretty busy."

"I shouldn't let myself get too busy for friends, but yes. I've been too busy. I think Andre picked this house because it needs my attention and will keep me at home. But work never slows down. I have no idea what I'm going to do about child care."

"Andre picked the house?"

"I was working down in Massachusetts. He heard about it, looked at it, and snapped it up before someone else could. By the time I saw the pictures, he'd already made an offer. You know how long we've been looking."

"A search complicated by finding a body in your last dream house," Rosie said. "But seriously, you were okay with Andre picking the house?"

"I was nervous. But it worked out. We love this house. And we were running out of time if we wanted a place for this baby."

Rosie smiled. "I don't think I'd trust Dom to pick out a house. He'd miss some important things, like a decent kitchen and bathrooms. Just as long as my jock had a man cave in the basement and a big screen to watch sports, he'd be happy."

"Your jock is still a catch, Rosie."

"I won't argue with that." Rosie paused in the upstairs hall. "Do you have a name for this baby yet?"

"Same as always," I said. "We're calling it MOC, for Mason, Oliver, or Claudine."

"You don't know if it's a boy or a girl? I thought everyone did these days."

I shook my head. "We want to be surprised."

"Oh, you'll be surprised all right," Dom said.

"We're having an acrobat," Andre told them. "A nocturnal acrobat. Thea's mother says it serves her right. That she was a difficult baby."

"More likely," Rosie said, since she knows how my mother can be, "Linda was a difficult mother." She focused on me as she asked, "Is your mother excited about the baby?"

I shrugged. Since my experience with a student's surprise pregnancy and her toxic family at one of my client schools, I've tried to be more accepting and forgiving. My mother and I have reached a pretty good détente in our strained relationship. I thought she was excited about MOC's upcoming appearance. I was happy to be spared her criticisms and her endless queries about when I'd give her a grandchild, but I knew better than to expect her to smother me with love and attention. "My father is. My brother and his wife have a new baby, so she's pretty focused on that."

"Probably for the best," Dom said. He's seen my family get very judgy, based on their refusal to listen before rushing to conclusions. He thinks I'm better off having limited contact with them.

Dom and Andre left us admiring the baby's room while they headed out to the barn to look at the emerging workshop.

Rosie stayed with me, admiring the color we'd chosen. "It's so soothing and peaceful," she said.

"We're just not into pink or blue," I said.

"Are you doing okay? I mean really okay. You're not working too hard?" she asked, plunking herself down in my upholstered rocking chair. "Oh. This chair is so comfortable."

It was covered in a print in soft shades of gray-green and white that went well with the walls. Another unsuitable choice for a baby's room. But it fit me, which many chairs don't.

"The minute I tried it in the store, I could imagine being in it with MOC in my arms. As for how I'm doing? Except for getting tired, and when MOC keeps kicking me, I feel fine."

"You're excited?"

I'd been so busy I never thought about that. Too much of my life is reactive. But when she asked, I realized that I *was* excited. And I really didn't mind looking like I'd swallowed a basketball, except for how difficult it was to find decent clothes.

"MOC's excited enough for both of us. I'm working on calm and contented. On getting through this pregnancy without a catastrophe."

Rosie stood, shaking her head, and opened her arms. I stepped into them. She and Dom really were my second parents. This set of parents, at least, had some idea of my challenges and abilities. "That won't be easy," she said. "The calm and contented part, I mean."

She was facing the windows that looked out toward the street, and something caught her attention. "What's going on over there?" she said.

I turned, and the two of us went to the windows in the unfinished bedroom. Across the street, a black car, like the SUVs you see the FBI using on TV, was cruising slowly to a stop near Jessica's little cottage. Two men in windbreakers got out and headed rapidly down her driveway. I couldn't see whether her Volvo was there, nor the undistinguished black Honda which had brought the woman Jessica was arguing with. The woman who wasn't a guest.

"You have a criminal living across the street?" Rosie asked.

I shook my head. "As far as I know, I've a pleasant, strikingly pretty woman named Jessica who is quite pregnant, and who is extremely careful not to reveal anything about herself. There's no husband or partner in the picture, and I sense some tension about that. Otherwise, I know nothing. I just met her for the first time yesterday. This morning we went shopping for baby gear. We had fun, but she wasn't very talkative. Forthcoming, I mean. She's got a wicked sense of humor."

"Well, something's up," Rosie said. "Neither Fed Ex nor UPS arrive in vehicles like those. Looks like law enforcement to me."

We stayed in the window, watching. I had to force myself not to rush over there and demand to know what was happening. I have a bad habit of sticking my oar into things, especially where someone seems vulnerable. And there's no doubt in my mind that a very pregnant woman is vulnerable to an aggressive pair of guys in a black SUV even when she isn't trying to meet the challenge of making a tired cottage into a home. Of course, for all I knew, she might be a bank robber or a serial killer. Or they were her friends, stopping in to see how she was doing. But I didn't think so. Their behavior was neither casual nor friendly. I've been fooled, it's true, but I'm generally a good judge of character and situations.

They must not have found what they were looking for, because after a bit, they both came back down the driveway, the man in the lead in a very bad mood. Even at this distance, I could tell that. Maybe from the way he kicked the tire and yelled at the other man? I'm such a fine detective. He was tall and stiff, with graying hair, a brusque way of moving, and a definite propensity for bossing people around.

"That is not a nice man," Rosie said.

"You think?"

"I know," she said softly. "And now, like you, I am worried about your neighbor."

FOUR

I wish that I could report we then sat on the back deck, drank wine, ate my good cheese, and enjoyed the peaceful evening before digging into Rosie's great lasagna and a salad from my very own lettuce. But that's not what happened. Instead, as Rosie and I were turning away from the window, the angry man and his buddy got into the SUV, drove a couple hundred yards, and turned into our driveway.

I was not eager to make his acquaintance.

Rosie and I went downstairs, and before whoever he was could get out of the car and bang on our door—I was sure he was a banger—we went through the kitchen and out the side door closest to the barn. We found Andre and Dom still immersed in inspecting the workshop, Andre describing how it would look when finished, and Dom nodding.

They fell silent as we entered, two long-time cops immediately aware that something was up. I gave a quick explanation of what we'd seen and my two meetings with Jessica. "And now the lead guy is parked in our driveway and you two can deal with him. I have endured a lifetime of angry, self-important men."

"And we haven't?" Dom asked, raising one eyebrow.

28

"It's what you get paid for."

"So do you," said my loving husband. "Self-important men and women. Let's go see what they want."

He's ever so much nicer than I am under these circumstances. All that cool, cop-like self-control. I tend to get what the Brits might call "shirty."

So out we went, Andre and Dom in the lead, two big, no-nonsense men, followed by their timid little women. Ha. People tend to underestimate me, and when she was stuck in her wheelchair, labeled an invalid for life, Rosie got more than her share of condescension. People are making a mistake if they underestimate her. She's a gorgeous, gracious, quiet powerhouse.

The two men were standing on the porch that faced the street where the official doorway was. This being the country, we used the side door that opened into the kitchen. Obviously, these fellows didn't know that. The one I'd dubbed "Angry Man" was banging our lobster knocker much too roughly on our newly painted front door. I'd half-expected to see "FBI" on the backs of their navy windbreakers, but there was no identifying information. But still, they wore navy windbreakers on a warm summer afternoon. Silly fellows.

They were surprised when we appeared behind them, turning rapidly. The second man, tall and rangy and wearing a ridiculously fancy pair of cowboy boots, actually slipped a hand inside his coat, where I assume he kept a gun.

"Can I help you?" Andre asked.

Mildly. Calmly. Like any puzzled homeowner finding two men who clearly didn't belong in this nice Maine town on their doorstep. While Andre dealt with them, I turned and looked at the license plate on the SUV. Massachusetts. From the way they acted, I'd expected a government plate. Who the heck were they, and why did they act like they had rights here?

Without introducing himself, the man said, "We'd like to ask you some questions about your neighbor, Jessica Whitlow." He sure acted like some kind of government agent. TV might not be wrong in often depicting them as having no manners.

"We don't know Jessica Whitlow," Andre said. And that was all he said.

"Lives over there," the unnamed man said, pointing toward the cottage.

Andre said, "Oh?" so calmly.

The unnamed man clenched his fists. "Come on, you must have seen her. This is a small town. Blonde. About five-seven. Very athletic. She's a runner."

The woman I'd met, who introduced herself as Jesssica, was maybe five three, and as far from blonde as hair can get. What the heck was going on?

"Nope. Sorry. Can't help you," Andre said. "That cottage is pretty well screened from the road, and in the summer, we do most of our living out back. I thought that place was empty. Why are you looking for her?"

He knew the guy wasn't going to answer, but he waited, all innocent and curious.

"Government business," the guy said, though he still hadn't produced a government ID.

"Has she committed a crime?" Me this time, the timid little woman. "Do you mean we may have a criminal living right across the street?"

"Sorry, ma'am. I'm not at liberty—"

I turned away to hide my eye roll. Of course, he was at liberty. He was free to drive about and stand on other people's porches and bang on their doors. Free to try to use his cold-eyed stare to intimidate ordinary citizens. Except, of course, that Andre and Dom were hardly ordinary. For that matter, neither was I. Nor Rosie.

"Well, that's it then," Andre said. "Sorry we can't help you."

"How long have you lived here?" the man asked.

No one answered.

Like someone slowly getting a message written in capital letters on a blackboard, the man nodded, then searched in his bullying vocabulary for some gentler words. "It's important that we find her," he said. "She's a critical witness in a—" Oops. Now he'd told us something he hadn't meant to.

Quickly, he changed back to bullying, focusing on me. He said, "Are you sure you haven't seen her?" like I was a liar. Did I really look like the weakest member of this team?

I donned my sweetest avatar and said, all cheerful and chipper, "Well, you see, I've been so busy getting the house ready for the baby." Patting the basketball. "I'm not sure I'd notice if Godzilla lumbered down the street." Pause. "Except to be concerned about MOC's safety."

Andre gave me his "put a sock in it, Thea," look. He didn't want me to provoke the guy, so I switched gears. "I've got dinner in the oven and I don't want it to burn," I said. "Sorry we can't help you. Good luck finding your witness."

I tried to step around them to go inside, but they weren't moving. Jerks. Stay calm and stress-free, I reminded myself. What mommy feels, baby feels. I shrugged, went down the steps, and headed for the side door. The rest of my team came with me. I wondered if they would follow, if we'd have to go through this dance again. But after consulting like their team was deciding on the next play, they walked briskly to the SUV and drove away. Probably to harass another innocent citizen. I knew why Andre and Dom hadn't asked for ID. They wanted to keep this low key. Just let the men leave.

"Charming fellow," Rosie said. "Dom, who do you think they are? And why would they behave like that, when it is so unlikely to produce any kind of cooperation?"

Dom gave her his warm smile. "Your government at work," he said. "Or so they'd like us to think."

"They didn't have government plates," I said.

Dom gave me an avuncular smile. He liked that I was smart and observant.

I wasn't comforted, though. I headed into the house feeling far too shaken for such a brief encounter. Being pregnant can be a hormonal nightmare. I simultaneously wanted to gulp a large glass of wine and curl up in a ball and weep. My emotional volatility didn't bode well for managing my client school's current emergency, but I couldn't not work just because I was pregnant. I took a deep breath and joined Rosie in the kitchen, where she was putting our dinner in the oven—lasagna and a foil-wrapped loaf of garlic bread. I was so grateful I almost cried. It can be so nice to be fed by someone you love.

"Wine and cheese outside?" I said, waving toward the sliders that led out to our big back deck.

"Wonderful," Dom said, scooping up the platter from the kitchen island. He hesitated. "Are you okay?"

Dom has asked me that dozens of times, often when I am very much not okay. It's his way of saying, "It's okay to have your feelings," and "Do you want to talk about it?"

"I'm pregnant," I said, which lately was my answer to everything. Not one I liked very much. I prefer being fierce and terrible.

Andre, who was behind me, wrapped his arms around me and pulled me against him and spread his hand protectively over MOC. "Who knew how complicated this would be?"

I leaned against him and inhaled his special scent. His chest felt like a warm wall. "I guess I'm not very good at this," I said. "All my moods feel exaggerated."

"Something they don't warn us about," Rosie agreed. "Hard when you're used to being in control and in charge. But the end result is a good one."

"It's just so darned public. Perfect strangers feel free to pat the basketball."

"Basketball?" Dom burst out laughing, and Andre led me out to the deck.

When we were all settled in our chairs, gazing out over the backyard and listening to the night sounds, Andre said, "Tell me about Jessica."

"Here's the little I know. She rang the doorbell when I was getting ready to finish painting MOC's room. She introduced herself as Jessica, no last name, and said she was my new neighbor across the street and that Jeannine down at the library told her we should meet. Maybe because we're both pregnant. I don't know." I shrugged. There was so little to our meeting beyond a sense that she wasn't being forthcoming.

"Is she medium tall and blonde and looks like a runner?"

"No. She's short, maybe 5' 3", and she's gorgeous. She has raven black hair and startling blue eyes and dresses in wild hippie colors. She's got secrets, for sure. I think she's hiding from something. Not from anything she's said, but from what she isn't saying. But yesterday I invited her to go shopping today for baby things, and while she didn't reveal much about herself, we had a really good time."

I considered what else I knew. "When we got back, the woman she describes as helping her get settled helped us unload the crib from the car. Jessica didn't introduce her, and she didn't share her name when I shared mine. I don't think Jessica likes her much."

Dom and Andre exchanged looks, while Rosie said, "This is very strange."

I thought so, too.

"I saw Jessica there later, in her driveway, arguing with the same woman. A woman fitting the description of the one those men were looking for—she was tallish, blonde, and thin. Then I saw her, my dark-haired, pregnant neighbor, again, when I stopped to drop off some flowers. She was wearing black jeans and a black tee-shirt and putting a big plastic trash bag into a Volvo with Virginia plates."

"That's all?" Andre and Dom said it together, and we all laughed.

"Well, mostly we talked about our babies. Like pregnant women do. She said she was having a girl and that the baby's father wanted her named Amaryllis. Amy for short."

"What else did she say about the baby's father?" Andre asked.

I shrugged.

"Princess," Dom said, "You're a good reader of people. What else did you notice?"

"This is unfair, you know. You guys ganging up on me. I am not a witness in a criminal case. I am a poor whale of a woman who was just being kind to a pregnant stranger."

"And?" Dom said.

There's no ducking things when your husband and one of your dearest friends are both detectives. Both men have laser focus and are used to not letting people off the hook. "And I think you guys are mean. I don't know anything else."

"Right," Andre said. "Because you're so unobservant."

"It's a gorgeous summer night. Can't we just sit out here and enjoy it?"

"Soon," Andre said.

"When the interrogation is over," Dom said.

"Interview," I corrected.

Rosie sighed. "Give them what they want, Thea, or we'll never have any peace."

Sadly, that was true. Half the time, they don't even know they're doing it, it's so ingrained. Poor MOC is going to have a miserable time being a teenager.

"She said that the baby's father was no longer in the picture. I got the sense that there was a story there. That he was dead, or somehow unavailable. Overall, my sense was that she was being very cautious about revealing anything about herself. That she even wondered if her comment about the baby's name was a mistake. And she was jumpy. She was anxious when Andre's dad drove up the driveway, and again when a tool that Ronnie was using made a big clang. She did say she worked for a government agency, she planned to work remotely, and was frustrated by how long it was taking to get cable installed. Then she appeared to be sorry she'd revealed so much, and rushed away. When I watched her walk home, she kept looking around, like she was afraid of something. Or someone."

I shrugged. "It looked to me like she's hiding out here from someone who is looking for her. And that maybe it involves her husband. But a lot of that is conjecture."

"But unless that guy was lying, or saying it to test us and see if we'd correct him, the person they're looking for isn't the woman you met," Andre said.

I shrugged. "Just so long as he doesn't come back."

"We hope," Andre said.

"Oh, and when I saw her in the yard when I was coming back from Agway, when I stopped and gave her a pot of calendulas to brighten things up, she was trying to be optimistic, but it looks like that place is a dump. I think that's what she and the other woman were arguing about."

Rosie smiled. "That was nice. The flowers, I mean."

Dom picked up the cheese plate and passed it to me. "Have some yummy cheese," he said.

And the subject of the mysterious Jessica, or two mysterious Jessicas, or two women, one of whom was named Jessica and might be a witness of some sort, was abandoned in favor of good company and good food. I was a little anxious that our unwanted visitors would return, but they didn't, and we had a lovely evening.

It was an added pleasure that I got to have two such good friends to inaugurate our guestroom, and Rosie found it charming. This house was bringing out a domestic side I hadn't known I possessed. I liked finding nice things that fit its country charm. When I had time, which was rarely. Good thing there wasn't an antique store next to Agway.

As Andre and I were settling into bed—a task that took some doing, since it was hard to find a position that MOC liked—I said, "What do I do if those men come back?"

He curled around me, making us spoons, patted MOC lightly, and said, "Smile and act utterly bewildered. And don't let him in the house, no matter how pushy he gets. If he...or they don't leave, call us."

"That's your best advice?" I really was anxious about them returning.

All I got in return was the quiet sound of his breathing. Andre was asleep.

FIVE

We had a peaceful and lovely breakfast out on the deck the next morning, a soft, warm, and sunny morning with chirping birds and the sweet smell of flowers and grass. From her Adirondack chair, Rosie took it all in with a smile. "Dom, I think I'm going to stay right here and not go back to Belmont with you. It gets so hot and sticky in the summers now."

Not likely, given how devoted to each other they were, but I would have been very happy to have Rosie here for as long as she wanted. I enjoy having a substitute mom who doesn't judge me.

"It's nice here," Dom agreed. "You can stay if you want. I can pick you up next week. But bear in mind that Thea isn't going to be here for you to mother. You know how she is. She'll be heading off to shoot troubles at some school somewhere, and you'll be stuck here without a car in the middle of nowhere, with mysterious strangers who might be government agents at the door and deer in the vegetables."

Like he'd summoned them from the forest, my rapacious doe and her fawn were even now trotting across the lawn toward the garden. Oblivious to our presence or to anything that might come between them and tender lettuce.

"No!" I yelled, charging down off the deck and across the lawn. "Absolutely not! I did not grow these for you." I thought wild animals were supposed to be deterred by human presence, but this deer just paused and tipped her head, as though she was saying, "Hey, lady. You know we mamas have to feed our babies. What's your problem?" Then, having done her best to make me feel guilty, she turned and trotted gracefully away.

"You sure told her," Andre said, when I climbed back to the deck.

"Thea the great and terrible doesn't seem to be working today," I said.

My beloved husband just grinned and said, "Nope."

"What am I going to do?"

"Dad's going to get some fencing, and he and Ronnie will put it up today."

Andre. My hero. The man who brings me chocolate cake and shares my bed picnics. Now he was rescuing me from rapacious wildlife. I leaned back in my chair, resting my coffee cup on the basketball, and looked up at the summer sky. Deep blue with small, puffy clouds. MOC kicked the cup and my coffee spilled.

"Was that?" Andre asked.

"The acrobat," I said. "And this is supposed to be the quiet time."

"Do you want me to come when the baby is born?" Rosie asked.

"Both of us," Dom added. "I don't want to be left out."

Would my mother's nose be out of joint? My father's? I really didn't know. Mom was very caught up with Michael and Sonia's baby. She'd expressed an interest in mine, but she regards Maine as the Northwest Territory. She thinks we live in a log cabin surrounded by bears.

"Sounds lovely," I said. "Can we play it by ear for now?"

"Of course."

Andre was looking at his watch. So far today, no homicides or violent sexual assaults had called him away, but he was a slave of the phone. We both were. And of our jobs. There was always something that needed his or my attention. He was only quelling his impatience to get back to this week's crimes because we had company.

Dom, a professional reader of people, stood, stretched, and said, "We'll be off soon. I'm taking Rosie to that botanical garden near Boothbay and then for lobster rolls and onion rings. But you two better stay in touch. No having babies without us."

"Besides," Rosie said, "we want to know if there are further developments in the mystery of the two Jessicas."

It sounded like the title of a book. "We will," I said. "Though I hope the mystery doesn't involve any further visits from those rude men. Even though she radiates independence, I worry about Jessica."

"If I had lovely men like those looking for me, I think I'd find a way to disappear," Rosie said.

"Sadly, I think that's what she was trying to do here."

There was a bit of flurry and bustle, some sad goodbyes, and then Dom and Rosie departed, followed shortly after by Andre. I was left alone with a full refrigerator, a draft client survey to give advice about, and a visit to the doctor. After that, I'd be checking in with Sarah and adding to my to-do list. I had a call scheduled at 4:00 with LaDonna to fill her in a little more about the situation at Eastern Shore Academy. I also had a long-time client who wanted me at their trustees' meeting, so I had to consult with Sarah about schedules, along with a report to write, and a conference call tonight about branding.

Ah, the leisurely life. Tell people you're a consultant and they immediately look bored, what Andre calls the "MEGO" effect, for My Eyes Glaze Over, but my life is far from boring. I've been trying to imagine how to make it more boring, so I can be a serene mother to MOC. Andre thinks that's impossible.

I took a quick shower, pulled on a sleeveless linen tunic and black capris, and headed out to see my doctor. These visits felt pretty pro-forma, but I wasn't taking any chances with MOC.

After spilling my coffee, MOC had settled down, and we were enjoying some quiet time together as I headed out to my Jeep. I climbed in and started backing down the driveway. Halfway down, my egress was blocked by a black SUV.

I'd been in such a good mood, too. Now, the jerk who was climbing out the driver's side, the same one who'd annoyed us last night, was going to make me late. I kept backing up until I was just off his bumper. Backing up used to be a challenge for me, but I've had lessons from the best. I rolled down my window and waited.

Once again, without the courtesy of a good morning or sharing his name, the rude guy leaned into my space and said, "We need to talk."

Thin lips, receding fair hair, cold gray eyes. Today he was alone.

"You have some ID?" I said.

He whipped out a leather folder and flashed a badge too fast for me to read it. For all I knew, it had come from Ebay or the five and dime. Heck, I could go around flashing one of Andre's badges. Maybe I'd get better results from some of my clients.

"Let's talk," he said.

"Not right now," I said. "I am a very pregnant woman on her way to a doctor's visit, and it's not okay for you to make me late."

He just stared at me, expressionless, and said, "This is important."

"So is making sure that this baby is okay and on schedule."

I made a show of checking the time. "I expect to be back in an hour and a half, if she's not running late. Maybe you could come back then?" I wasn't making a date. I was just in a hurry to get him off my back.

"I'm here now," he said.

I was using the driveway because I was parked in the driveway, but there was a gravel track that led out past the barn and then curved out to the road. Seeing that I was not going to make any headway with a man who had such poor interpersonal skills, I put my Jeep in gear, went up the driveway, and headed past the barn. It looked like a road to nowhere. I didn't know if he'd follow me, but I had a head start, and once I was on the main road, I knew the territory, and he didn't. By the time he figured out that I wasn't just going back to the house to entertain his questions, I was beyond the barn, around the curve, and turning onto the road. I took the shortcut past the church and the school, and I was on my way, grateful that Andre has given me lessons in driving like a cop.

If the guy wanted to cool his heels in my driveway for a while, that was fine with me. I don't like people who interfere with my schedule, but sometimes setting them straight takes too long.

I never went to these appointments without my briefcase. I love my OB, but she always runs late. I've learned to treat her waiting room as an extension of my office, though I am considerate enough to step out to make my phone calls. The anxious moms-to-be didn't need to hear about some of the things I deal with, like drug-dealing students, an unexpected birth in a school bathroom, a colleague strangled with her stocking, or a student who mysteriously drowned in a frozen campus pond. Today I confined myself to paperwork, except for a brief call from my partner, Suzanne, with the ominous "We have a problem," that we agreed could be dealt with later in the day.

We always had a problem, which meant that sooner rather than later, I was going to have to start looking for a nanny who could take care of MOC when I was taking care of other people's problems. These days, working women would be better off if the stork brought nannies instead of babies. Most of us know where babies come from. Good nannies are more of a mystery.

I did a quick edit on a proposal, making enough changes so that Sarah would have something to complain about. I sent an email with some suggestions for our newest employee, Marlene, about a survey she was designing. I said yes, Andre and I would definitely attend Bobby and Quinn's anniversary party. Bobby was a fabulous employee and a good friend. His husband Quinn was a chef, which meant the food would be great. The only hitch was that Quinn doesn't like Bobby working at EDGE. He thinks we work Bobby too hard, and nothing, including Bobby's protests that he loves the work, seems to change Quinn's mind. I was glad to celebrate Bobby's happiness. Less glad about an event where I'd be walking on eggs instead of unconditionally joyous.

Eventually, the nurse came to collect me, and Dr. Robinson

surveyed my vitals and began her litany of questions. Things were generally fine, but my blood pressure was elevated. Was I being careful about avoiding stress and conflict? She knows me pretty well. Knows that stress and conflict are part of my job. When you're Jane Wayne, the girl in the white hat who rides into town when there's trouble brewing, conflict comes with the territory. I'd been trying to avoid it as much as possible. The guys in the black SUV were not helping.

"I was doing very well until yesterday," I said.

"And will you do very well today?" she asked.

"That depends," wasn't what she wanted to hear. I sighed. "I'll try."

"Your baby would like you to try harder," she said. She imparted a few pieces of advice about resting and letting people help me and trying to scale back on work if I could. We both knew it was hard advice to take.

"I have to say this, Thea," she said. "My job is to help you have a successful pregnancy and a healthy baby. Not encourage you to get out there and fight bad guys and wrong-doing. None of us can change our natures. I understand that. But just try to take a deep breath and slow down when you can." She gave a quick grin. "I don't want to have to call the police on you."

Dr. Robinson has a crush on Andre. It's hard not to. He's a pretty great guy and absolute eye candy. Of course, she's never seen him when he's in full tough-guy mode. Then he becomes a fearsome creature.

"Please don't," I said. "He has enough to worry about trying to finish the house so MOC will have a safe place to live."

"You're still calling this baby Mock?"

I nodded.

"Kid's gonna be Mock forever, girl or boy." Of course, she knew the sex of this baby. She was doing an excellent job of not spilling the beans. She stood and held out her hand. "I'll see you in two weeks. No. Wait. Next week."

I headed out into the warm summer day with a to-do list hanging like a sword over my head. I decided to stop at the local farm stand for some berries before calling Suzanne about the new problem. Then, worried that I'd find a blood-pressure-raising black SUV in my driveway, I stopped at Reny's—Maine's bargain treasure house—to see if there was anything likely to fit the basketball. It was one of the good days. I scored two great summer dresses, one in aubergine and one with small blue flowers, and two flowing tunic tops, one in deep indigo and the other white. Everything had pockets.

One strategy for lowering my blood pressure was to end the daily battle with my closet. Flushed with success, I headed home, instructing Siri to call Suzanne on the way.

"How's the mom-to-be?" Suzanne asked.

"I'm supposed to avoid stress and conflict."

"Then I'd better hang up right now," she said, "because it's Denzel again."

Denzel Ellis-Jackson was the headmaster of the King School, a private school with a mission of giving underprivileged boys a chance for a better future. Devoted to his school's purpose, and a charismatic fellow who was a brilliant fundraiser, Denzel unfortunately had too much of an eye for the ladies. A few years back, we'd saved his bacon when he was accused of an assault on a woman. Innocent that time, but he walked a fine line.

"Something old or something new?" I asked.

"New. An altercation with a student. Denzel says he was set up. That it was planned. And, of course, captured on a student's phones."

"Physical?"

Suzanne sighed. "I'm afraid so. Denzel says he was attacked and had to push back, but that won't carry much weight. He's the grownup."

A big, strong, athletic grownup. But then, plenty of his students were big, strong males as well. "Has he been arrested?"

"Not yet. Police are still investigating, whatever that means. But the parents have a lawyer and are threatening to sue."

"And what does the King School's lawyer say?"

The King School had Emmet Hampton, one of the best lawyers in Boston, on the board.

"He says for Denzel to keep quiet and let him handle it."

"Which, as we both know, is not Denzel's style. How's it working so far?"

"So far, so good, but Yanita Emery says he's like a caged beast, and it's only a matter of time before he does something to damage his case."

"I don't suppose they could just lock him up somewhere?"

"I think Denzel locked up is what they're trying to avoid."

"Hold on," I said, steering around a tractor hauling a giant load of hay. "Do we have the name of the boy, or boys, involved?"

"We do."

"Let's get Bobby to do a search on Facebook, Instagram, and What's App. Maybe TikTok. Any place he thinks the kids may be talking or posting videos. YouTube, maybe? Too often, bad for them, good for us, these kids have no idea that people other than their friends can see their social media posts."

"I'll get right on it," she agreed. "Why didn't I think of that?"

"Because we're dinosaurs?" I said. "Because we were taught by our mothers to live cautiously, and it's hard to believe we live in a world where selfies, sexting, and explicit pictures are part of the normal social landscape."

"Right."

"Bobby is good at this, and if he doesn't know where or how to look, he has a friend who is a genius at this."

"I'm feeling better," she said. "So you're off to Baltimore tomorrow?"

"That's what the calendar says."

"You don't sound psyched."

"Would you? It's summer in Maine, and I am very happy puttering around the house."

"Uh oh!"

"What is that supposed to mean?"

"That my workaholic partner is beginning to nest. Which is not

43

a bad thing, for you and Andre and MOC, but may be less good news for EDGE."

"EDGE is worried that I'll lose my edge?"

She laughed. "Something like that."

"You've had two babies and haven't lost your edge," I reminded her. And had a thought.

"You might ask Lindsay if she has some ideas," I said, flipping back to our Denzel problem. "She's closer to her prep school days than we are."

"Hold on," Suzanne said. "I live at a prep school. I observe prep school life every darned day."

"As an authority figure. Lindsay has lived it as a student."

Lindsay Livermore was our newest hire. Actually, only a summer intern, since she was still in college, going into her senior year, but she was a go-getter, and we were eager to hire her when she graduated. It was great to have someone so young and energetic on staff. Not that we were old, but Lindsay was plugged into youth culture in a way that was very helpful to some of our challenging problems. This conversation reminded me that I ought to pick her brain about our cheating issue before I headed off to Maryland. She might have some valuable insights.

What I already knew was that this was a little different from most of the hacks schools dealt with. They tended to be of two sorts —computer-savvy students who hacked the school's computers and poked around just to show they could do it, and students who hacked in to change their grades. Eastern Shore's hacker, or hackers, had cheated not only on their own behalf, but had helped other students cheat as well. It undermined the whole purpose of the program, which was to give promising students who'd had less than optimal educations a head-start on the challenges they'd face. Students who were fed the test questions weren't getting the educational benefits they were in the summer program to get.

But Suzanne was saying something. I brought my attention back to our conversation. "If we're lucky, she'll join us when she graduates."

"I hope we do get lucky," I said. "How's everyone else doing?"

"You should know. We only sent you home a few days ago."

"Sent me home makes me feel like I'm still in grade school, Suzanne."

"Nope. Just pregnant. You can come back any time. Just don't be so fretful. I think Bobby was expecting he'd have to deliver your baby right there in the office."

She flipped seamlessly back to staff issues and our two recent hires. "So, Jason Barbour looks like he'll be a keeper. He's already taking a lot off Bobby's shoulders, which means we're seeing a lot more of Bobby's smiles. And Marlene seems like she'll enjoy being a backroom person, working on our surveys and compiling data for our reports, which you and I both hate. I'm a little concerned that she's not a self-starter, but it's early days yet."

"Can we really support all these people?"

She sighed. "I hope so."

I swore at a bad driver and Suzanne said, "Are you still in the car?"

"Taking my time going home. This morning there was a self-important jerk in a big black SUV parked in my driveway who thought my day's work was to talk to him. I got away, but I'm afraid I may still find him there when I get back."

"You're like a magnet," she said.

"A magnet? You think I attract these jerks? He wanted to ask questions about a neighbor I've only just met. I've already told him I don't know anything. He refuses to believe it."

"Never happens to me," she said.

"That's why I have the hat and the gun and the horse and get to ride into town and sort out the bad guys," I said.

"Don't even joke about it. You have sorted out enough bad guys for ten Jane Waynes. So we're okay? I'll talk to Bobby about social media and Denzel's problem and you'll talk to Lindsay about hacking?"

I thought Suzanne was going to talk to Lindsay, but I could kill two birds with one stone, so I said, "Sure. I'll put Lindsay on my list. About hacking and our Denzel problem. You can give her the boys names."

I looked at the dashboard clock. "I'd better sign off and speed up. I've got that conference call at four."

"And I have two small children and a nanny who has to leave early."

I disconnected and put my foot down. I wanted some quiet time at home to prep for the call. Of course, when I turned into my yard, the infuriating black SUV was still there, or there again, and I could tell by the way he slammed his door and stomped toward me that the nameless rude guy from last night was not in a pleasant mood. I decided to leave my purchases and the berries in the car. None of his business that I'd run errands on my way back.

"You said an hour and a half," he said accusingly.

I shrugged. I did not owe this man anything. "I hoped it would be."

"Well, you're here now. Let's talk."

"I've already told you. I don't know this person you're looking for. Who are you, anyway?"

He'd followed me up onto the porch, hovering so close he barely gave me room to put my key in the lock. "I'd like you to leave," I said. "I'm sorry if I gave you the impression I was willing to talk. I'm not." I opened the door.

Instead of leaving, he pushed his way inside and shut the door behind us. As he turned to close the door, I spotted a white paper on the floor that hadn't been there before. Instinctively, I used my foot to slip it under the console, hoping he hadn't seen it.

As I stood there alone in my house with an aggressive stranger, I realized that I had failed to follow Andre's advice. The guy was inside my house, and I still had no idea who he was or whether I was safe.

SIX

I headed for the kitchen. He could follow or not. I really didn't care. In my guise as the girl in the white hat who rides into town and takes on bad guys, I had had enough of rude and angry men who thought they were entitled to push me around. He might think he was special, or had a special mission, or was ordained by God or the government to carry out his task, but frankly, Scarlett, I didn't give a damn.

I kicked off my sandals and got a glass of water. I would have offered him one, but then he might think he was invited to stay. He shook his head with a frown and said, "Quit stalling."

I said, "Excuse me? I am in my own house. In my kitchen. You are an intrusive stranger who has, thus far, refused to identify himself or otherwise behave in a civilized manner. You do not get to tell me what to do."

Then I added, "Do you have any credentials to justify this intrusion, or are you just some rude guy who has bullied his way into my kitchen? Do I need to call the police?" I hadn't had a good look at the badge he flashed this morning, so I added, "Let me see that badge again."

He made no move to comply.

Some guys. They get so used to intimidating people into cooperating they forget that they can't just walk all over us. I might be barefoot and pregnant and living in an unfinished old house in a small Maine town, but I hadn't just tumbled off the cabbage truck. I'd dealt with some serious bad guys.

He just stared at me, like my words were so unfamiliar he couldn't process them. Phooey. Maybe I'd made a mistake and I *had* let a bad guy into my house. Except I hadn't let him, he shoved his way in. I wasn't a dumb bunny, and I wasn't usually careless. Sometimes I forget that I'm both Thea the Great and Terrible and MOC's mom. MOC's mom doesn't take so many chances.

I glanced quickly out the window to see if Andre's dad or Ronnie was here working, but there was no truck, and no one was out there making the garden safe from deer. No one to keep me safe from strangers. This was making me very nervous, and being nervous was against doctor's orders.

"I'd like you to leave now," I said again. "I have nothing more to say to you. You are not welcome in this house."

He made no move to leave. Gave no sign that he'd heard me. So I repeated myself. "I am asking you to leave."

He shook his head. "We're not done."

"I'm done."

So, okay. I'd been an idiot to let him in in the first place, but he'd pushed his way in, and I wasn't getting into a shoving match. Not with MOC on board.

One reason I prefer clothes with pockets is that there are a few things I have to have with me at all times. My phone. My panic button. My pepper spray. Andre, in a moment of slightly ghoulish humor, recently got me a canister of pepper spray that is girly pink and glittery. I am not afraid to use it, either, something bad guys can be surprised by. I checked my pockets. Everything in place. I pulled out my phone.

I could have just dialed 9-1-1, but I called Andre, who, because of my whale-like status, answered on the first ring. He can't always do it, but when he can, he does. He always sounds anxious when he comes on the line.

"Thea. Is everything okay? What did the doctor say?"

"That I'm fine except my blood pressure is elevated and she wants me to avoid stress. But that man is here again. The one who was here last night. He pushed his way into the house, and he refuses to identify himself or show me his credentials. I've asked him to leave and he won't. I need a police officer here, and I need him or her right now."

"I'm ten minutes away. Heading home now. I'll call the sheriff's department and see if they have someone closer."

"Thank you."

I put the phone back in my pocket. The man was staring at me like I'd lost my mind. Still, instead of producing any ID, he said, "You fucking called the police?" Loud and incredulous, like I'd done something astonishing. Maybe most of the people he bullied were more compliant?

"I did."

"What the fuck is wrong with you?"

"Oh. Thanks for asking. As you may have just overheard, according to my OB, I'm a pregnant lady with elevated blood pressure who is supposed to avoid stress and anxiety. Strange men who push their way into my house produce stress and anxiety. People who act like they have some authority to question me but refuse to provide identification exacerbate that stress and anxiety, and that badge flash this morning does not constitute identification. That shouldn't surprise you. Nor should the fact that once you've been asked to leave and you refuse, legally you become a trespasser."

I know. I shouldn't wave red flags in front of bulls. But it's a flaw in my nature. When people, especially self-important men who treat me like a simpleton, start pushing me around, I do not react well.

I waved a hand toward the back deck. "I'm going to go and sit outside. I'm supposed to rest and put my feet up. You have to go." I picked my briefcase up off a kitchen chair, walked out the back door, and settled myself in an Adirondack chair. He could stay. He could go. I didn't care. Well, of course I'd rather have him gone, but I've met some genuinely scary men and my read was that he wasn't a physical threat so much as someone used to getting his way through intimidation.

In any case, I had work to do. Putting my feet up didn't mean turning my head off. My watch said I had an hour before my call with LaDonna, making this a good time to call Lindsay.

"I can't believe this," he said, following me out and pulling up a chair. Pulling it so close I could feel the heat coming off his jittery legs. "I just want to ask you a few damned questions about your neighbor."

"You already did. I said I didn't know anyone named Jessica Whitlow. Asked and answered. Now get off my property."

There was a nice afternoon breeze coming up from the lake and he was blocking it. Not a good move. Pregnancy makes me hot, and being too hot does nothing for my mood or my blood pressure. I leaned back in my chair and closed my eyes. I try to be brave about it, but going to the doctor makes me very anxious. Not only because my extensive experience with docs and hospitals has been pretty negative, but because I'd already lost one pregnancy. If MOC were born now, the kid would probably be okay, but I wanted to give the little acrobat every chance for a great start in life.

MOC knows when I'm thinking about its antics, and gave me a couple of reassuring kicks. I gave the kid a pat. "Quiet time," I said.

"Are we all set now? You ready to talk to me?" he said, as though he hadn't been asked to leave and hadn't heard me call the police.

"Do you not understand English?" I said. "There is no 'we' about this. I have nothing to say to you, and you've been asked to leave."

I opened my eyes and studied his face, wondering if I should be more scared. If I'd misread him and he was dangerous as well as a bully. He definitely looked pissed off and determined. Beyond that, I was getting nothing. I decided that I would do nothing more to provoke him. I would rest, and be taciturn until help arrived.

"Goddammit!" he said, raising his voice and leaning into my space. "All I want is…"

With a roar of sirens and flashing blue lights, a state police cruiser flew up the driveway and rocked to a stop in front of the barn. Norah Kavanaugh got out, spotted us on the porch, and approached. Norah is tall, like me. Slim. Smart. And tough as nails. I was awfully glad to see her. "Kavanaugh, state police," she said to the guy. "Stand up and come down off that deck. Keep your hands where I can see them."

Ignoring her, the man said to me, "You are fucking unbelievable!"

I chose to take it as a compliment. I stood, stepped past him, and went back into the kitchen, locking the door behind me.

I watched through the window as she got him off the porch and down in the driveway. Through the open window, I heard her asking for ID as Andre came up the driveway and joined her.

The man stared at him in disbelief. Bullies are often surprised to find themselves outgunned. "You, too?" he said. "How many cops are there in this podunk backwater town?"

This time, though, faced with two hard-faced cops, he reached into his pocket and pulled out some ID. He might have said "Government business" earlier, but the words that reached my listening ears were "private investigator" and "Boston."

I really wanted to go outside where I could hear their conversation more clearly, but I'd called the cops because I was a woman who felt threatened. Therefore I had to remain inside where the threat was minimized and let the cops handle it. Besides, if he did present a threat, I couldn't take chances with MOC. I'd already been unable to stop him from pushing his way inside. I shivered at how careless I'd been, letting him get so close I couldn't safely stop him. It stems from being pretty sure I can take care of myself. Taking care of MOC really changed the game. Far from being "Thea the great and terrible," which I've kind of liked, I am now "Thea who doesn't take risks." It's a very different and challenging role for me.

My phone beeped to give me the reminder about my conference call. My time to prep for the call was running out. No more lingering at the kitchen window, trying to overhear their conversation. I went outside, grabbed my briefcase, hurried back inside, and spread out my notes on the kitchen table. Lounging on the back deck doing a leisurely prep was no longer an option. I might like to think that I am enjoying a peaceful Maine summer, but that peace is still interspersed with a lot of work. It's a good thing I like my work.

I'd gotten as far as writing "Call Lindsay," on my legal pad when the phone rang. Sarah, calling with the afternoon update.

"Hey," she said when I answered, "hope you're enjoying a quiet afternoon. It's like someone released a box of crickets around here."

"Blissfully quiet except for a mysterious intruder and two cops in my driveway."

"Oh, no. Is everything okay?"

"I think so. One of the cops is Andre, and the intruder looks suitably intimidated. So what's going on?"

"What's not? Three schools that have ignored our proposals for months want us to write crisis plans before the school year starts. Jameson Jones wants your advice. Jason Barbour, who seemed so promising, disappeared at lunchtime without a word and hasn't reappeared, and Marlene is weeping in the ladies' room. Lisa is out this afternoon and Bobby is looking frazzled. Suzanne has gone home. Magda is muttering in Hungarian, and I'm ready for some noise-canceling headphones."

"Sounds like a regular day, except for Jason's disappearance. Can you give me his phone number?" It had been a struggle to find good people to hire. The last thing we needed was employees who didn't understand the concept of work.

"A regular day at the circus," she said, giving me the phone number. "And you won't be in tomorrow to sort us out. I've emailed the info for Baltimore. Everything should be all set there."

I sighed. What happens when you're a troubleshooter who is sick of shooting troubles? "But wait," I said, "Do you know what Marlene is weeping about?"

"I guess you sent her some thoughts about the survey?"

"I did."

"Well, she thinks you hate her. Or that she's incompetent. Or she can't understand why you are so critical. I couldn't quite get a straight story."

Ah, the risks of expanding the business. "Not your problem. Let

Suzanne know when she comes in tomorrow. She'll handle it."
Better than I. Suzanne has kid gloves. I tend to weigh in with more
blunt objects. "I'll try to track down Jason."

I made more notes, including "Call Suzanne about Marlene and
Jason." Sarah and I made plans to talk tomorrow in the afternoon if
I could find the time while I was in Baltimore, and ended the call.
Even less time to prep for LaDonna, but that mysterious sheet of
paper I'd kicked under the console was demanding my attention.

I went back to the hall, got down on all fours—an act that is no
longer as simple as it once was—and pulled out the paper.

Scrawled in hasty writing it read:

```
Thea. Don't tell anyone you met me. Don't say
anything about me. No matter who asks and what
credentials they present. Please don't. Also, I
left a package under some wood out behind your
barn. Can you put it somewhere safe and don't let
anyone find it? Don't look inside, either, unless
something happens to me, or you might be in
danger. Sorry to do this to you. Things are too
crazy. I think I've been found and I don't know
what to do right now. I just want my baby to be
safe.
Jessica
```

SEVEN

I carried the note back to the kitchen and checked on the situation in the yard. The black SUV was gone, and Andre and Norah were leaning against her car, talking. Maybe they were discussing a strategy. Maybe just gossiping. My intruder hadn't been arrested. I wondered what they'd said or done that would deter him from coming back. I definitely never wanted to see him again.

Much as I needed to know the story, I left them to whatever it was and turned my attention to the materials on the table. I was impatient for Andre to come inside so I could show him Jessica's note and get his reaction, but it would be four soon, time for my call. I realized I didn't have much to share with LaDonna. All I could do was give her some background on the situation—who these students were and why the matter was delicate. She'd be okay, though. Most of the important questions were ones she needed to ask Dr. Kingsley, the instructor whose tests had been stolen, and the school's IT director. Also likely the students who'd gotten the test questions. I hoped the school's administration had arranged for her to have access to the relevant people and computers.

The call went exactly as I expected. I told her what I knew to help put her in the picture, and she said she was looking forward to joining me in tackling Eastern Shore's problem. I gave her Dr. Kingsley's contact information so she could verify her access to the necessary personnel and computers. I love working with competent experts. Over the years, I've developed a number of them who can be called in for crisis situations, and I find that once schools take a big gulp and accept that good help is expensive, they are always grateful. Besides, LaDonna is great company. She looks so young and inexperienced, and she's lightning smart, fast on her feet, and loves to knock down egos and disbelief with a completely straight face. People can't pat me on the head because I'm too tall. While they could pat LaDonna, it's a bad idea. People never make the mistake of treating her like a kid twice. Trust me. It's fun to watch.

It was almost time to start dinner, but I wanted to check in with Lindsay before she left for the day. She was pleased to be asked about social media and how we might use it to investigate Denzel's situation, so I told her to get the names of the involved students from Bobby and dig in. Then, a little nervous that I might be piling on too much, I asked her if she had some thoughts on Eastern Shore's cheating and hacking situation. I didn't get a sigh or any reluctance suggesting she was feeling burdened by too many requests.

"I hate to say it, but cheating is becoming almost a standard practice, Thea," she said. "Students in the pressure cooker to get good grades and get into a good college tend to regard it as just another necessary thing to do. An end justifies the means sort of thing."

"That's depressing."

"I know. At my school, there was an honor code. They were very clear about the importance of honesty and the consequences of cheating and explicit about the actions that constituted cheating. That helped a lot. Especially after a couple of students got expelled. Unfortunate that had to happen, but it made the point more effectively than any lecture or some paragraphs in a student handbook ever could."

Her comment reminded me to ask Eastern Shore whether they had an honor code, and what kind of orientation their summer students were given about the rules. Because I suffer from pregnancy brain, I wrote those questions down.

"What about hacking into the school's computers or individual teachers' computers? Were there rules about that?"

Lindsay laughed. "We were supposed to know that was wrong. Just to make the point very clear, they included the state laws in our handbook. Since typically many students or their parents don't bother to read the handbook, there was actually a quiz we all had to take to check that we'd read it. Some kids got mad about that. The usual 'Don't they trust us?' and 'Do they think we're stupid' responses. I thought it was smart."

I repressed the temptation to ask if she'd skip her senior year and come right to work. She wouldn't be with us forever and would need her degree. As though she'd read my mind, she said, "You know I'm graduating a semester early, in January, just, you know, in case you're looking to do another hire. It is so much fun to work here."

Fun? I thought about some of the adventures, and misadventures, I'd had on campuses and decided not to mention them. Suzanne likes to point out that these things don't happen to other people. Just me. I rather thought Lindsay would like some of my adventures, hair-raising though they might be. She was delightfully professional, but I sensed an edginess, and courage, that could be very effective in handling a campus crisis.

"That's great news," I said. "Let me talk to Suzanne."

"Oh. Before you go," she said. "It's about Jason. Something I think you should know. He made a pass at me, if you can call patting my butt a pass. I told him that since he was an employee and I was only an intern, it constituted sexual harassment, and I would report it to Suzanne if anything happened again. I guess he's not far from his frat boy days. The idea that there are boundaries to his misbehavior really surprised him."

There was a pause, then she said, "I'm sorry if this screws things up for you. I know you want to expand and he's supposed to be helping with that. But I decided it was better to get it out on the table right away, before he made patting women's butts a habit..."

She lowered her voice, "…if it isn't already. He can't be doing that at a client school."

"Or anywhere else," I agreed. "Is that why he left in the middle of the day? Because you called him on his inappropriate behavior?"

"I don't know," she said, "maybe he's such a wimp he needed to go console himself with a beer. How pathetic is that?"

Damn. On paper and in his interview, he'd looked good. Suzanne and I would have to talk to him. I hoped the situation could be salvaged.

I left Lindsay to her tasks and opened the fridge to figure out what we'd have for dinner. Rosie must have worried that Andre and I were starving up here in rural Maine. The shelves were packed with food, all of it neatly labeled. There was more in the freezer. People from away, as they're called up here, think of most of Maine as a vast rural backwater. Andre and I were twenty-five minutes from Portland, with its international jetport and many great restaurants. We could quickly be at a Trader Joe's or a Whole Foods, and the local farmers' markets were amazing.

Whenever I find myself eager to correct them, though, I think about how hard it already is to find a parking space in some of my favorite places, and refrain. I've become a 'want to pull up the drawbridge now that I'm here' type. Maybe I'll feel differently after my first winter in a small town.

Better soon than later, I figured, and dialed Jason's number. I got a slightly slurred, "Hello?" followed by a loud "Oh no!" and then silence.

"Jason? It's Thea Kozak. You left work in the middle of the day today. Do we have a problem?"

By way of confirmation, he hung up on me.

I called Suzanne and reported on what Lindsay had told me about Jason and his disappearance, and about Marlene's crying jag, and left dealing with them in her capable hands.

Still no sign that Andre was coming in, so I went to my office and printed out my directions and boarding pass for tomorrow and went upstairs to pack. From the upstairs window, I could see the rear of a black car parked in Jessica's driveway. Her note suggested she was gone, safely away, but I wondered where she could go. How she'd find another place, when the one she'd landed in was so marginal, and whether whoever the people looking for her were, they would find her again. I was very curious about the package she'd referred to, but I certainly wasn't looking for that while the bully was still in the neighborhood. I could imagine myself trundling back from behind the barn, package in hand, just as the guy, or guys, decided to make another visit despite being warned off by Norah and Andre. No. I would leave the logistics of that operation to a professional.

On the way to my car to retrieve my new clothes and the berries, I stopped to say a proper hello to Norah. Earlier, as she was removing my intruder from the deck, we'd only exchanged nods.

"Hey, Thea," she said with an admiring grin at the basketball. "So glad to see you like this."

"Ha!" I said. "May it happen to you one day."

Her grin got bigger, and she held out her left hand, which sported a beautiful marquise-cut diamond. "October 2nd," she said. "A lakeside wedding. It better not rain."

"Tommy Munro is a lucky guy," I said.

Pleasantries attended to, I asked the essential question. "So who was that guy?"

"That is the question," Andre agreed. "Yesterday he said he was on government business, looking for an important witness. Today he says he's a PI from Boston and won't say why he's looking for someone named Jessica Whitlow."

"Did he show you some ID, at least?"

"Sure," Norah said. "Massachusetts P.I. license. We'll check it out, but there's something very wrong about the guy."

"I hope you told him to stay away from here?"

"You bet," Andre said. "Quite forcefully."

"But he didn't look adequately intimidated," she said.

"I guess not. Looks like he's back in Jessica's driveway again," I said. The thought of him right next door made my skin crawl.

I wanted to show Andre the note, and I figured Norah was in this, so she might as well see it, too. "I've got something to show you," I said. "It was on the floor when I came in. A note from Jessica. I slipped it under the console so that bully wouldn't see it. What's his name, anyway?"

"Davenport," Andre said. "Nathaniel Davenport."

"Probably not his real name," Norah added. She checked her watch, said she was off the clock, and yes, she would love a beer and anything else we might have to eat.

"Stay for supper," Andre and I said together.

"Call Tommy, see if he can join us," Andre added.

Norah did, and reported that he would be along in about half an hour.

I met Norah Kavanaugh during the horrible week when I was supposed to marry Andre and ended up working in a miserable restaurant in a Maine town dominated by a local militia, instead. They'd taken Andre hostage and I was trying to be a fly on the wall to gather information that might secure his release. I was probably being a damned fool to get involved. Andre's boss was certain that I was. And Norah Kavanaugh was my contact to pass information back to the Maine state police.

It was a week I'd like to forget, and one of the horrible events was when Norah got in a gunfight with a young militia hothead. Both of them got shot. Norah survived. She's one of the still too rare women in the MSP, and that means she's had to be tougher than most of the guys. She's got red hair and a temper to match, and now she was going to marry Tommy Munro, another MSP officer, and one of the few people I know who makes Andre look small.

In the kitchen, Andre got them both beers, and they bent over the note, reading it several times before Andre turned to me. "You get the package yet?"

I shook my head. "Not while that black car is in the neighborhood."

"He's still here?"

"Well, there's some black car over there in the driveway of the cottage, and from what I can see, it looks more like an SUV than the little black Honda the blonde woman helping Jessica get settled drives."

"I guess he took 'stay away from here' pretty literally," Norah said.

"Let's check it out," Andre said, and the two of them headed out to find the package.

It felt funny to be the little woman, huddling inside while brave, tough cops went on a mission. But I've done my share of brave things, and I have the scars—on my body and on my soul—to prove it. It was challenging to be more careful, to be mindful that I was not in this alone, but I could embrace that challenge. I was, as Suzanne had put it, nesting.

I was fixing a tray of cheese, crackers, and other delicious nibbles—one form of nesting, for sure—when the thought hit me: what if this was some kind of trap? I had no idea what Jessica's handwriting looked like. Nor any reason to believe she'd trust me with something of great importance. Why would she? We'd met a few times, shopped, and talked about babies. I rushed outside, crossed the lawn, and went around the side of the barn just as Andre straightened, holding a small cardboard box.

EIGHT

Andre carried the box inside and set it on the kitchen island. Then he stepped back and looked at me. "What do you think? Should we open it?"

"Jessica says we shouldn't."

He nodded. "But?"

"But if she really is in danger, I don't see how we can help her if we don't have any information. I don't get why she left it for me, though."

"Maybe you're all she has?"

That was kind of heartbreaking.

He looked at Norah. He wasn't hesitating because he was worried about opening the box, but because the note and box had come to me, so he wanted my buy-in. And Norah's.

"Open it," she said. Then, in what I hoped was an excess of caution, she said, "Thea, why don't you go in the other room?"

I hesitated. I have a visceral reaction when cops, when anyone, tries to treat me like a mushroom. I decided that she knew I was as brave as a knight facing a dragon and this was deference to MOC. Also so that if the box blew up, there would be someone left to call for help. I stepped out into the hall and waited.

There was silence, a silence so total that I could hear the birds beginning their evening songs, before he said, "It's okay. You can come back now."

Norah had moved the tray of snacks over to the island, and was nibbling on cheese and salami as she watched him take a leather item from the box. An ID wallet. Norah and I leaned in as he opened it. A U.S. Marshals Service ID for a Jessica Whitlow.

I stared at the photograph. ID photos are notoriously awful, but they usually bear some resemblance to the people who carry them. It was definitely not a picture of the gorgeous dark-haired woman who'd knocked on my door. This was a picture of the woman our rude visitor said he was looking for, the one I'd seen my neighbor who called herself Jessica arguing with. The tough, slender, athletic-looking woman who hadn't given her name when I introduced myself.

"I don't get it," I said. "That's not the woman from across the street. I mean, the woman who introduced herself as Jessica. This is the woman who is supposedly helping her settle in. The one who helped us get the crib off the car. My Jessica—whatever her name is —didn't seem to like this woman very much."

I told them about what appeared to be an argument that I'd seen through the window. About the comments my Jessica had made when we went shopping. Her frustration at being settled in such an unsuitable place. It wasn't much. I said, "Let's see what else is in the box."

Under the ID wallet was a small packet of plastic items held together with a thick elastic. There was a driver's license, a credit card, an ATM card, and a few other cards. The name on each of them was Charity Kinsman. Only the license had a photo, and that photo was definitely of the striking pregnant woman who had come to my door and identified herself as Jessica. The address was Austin, Texas. She was twenty-seven.

I stabbed the license photo. "This is the woman I had tea with. Went shopping with. Charity. The one I saw putting a trash bag into a gray Volvo with Virginia plates. There was another car, a black Honda, that I assumed belonged to the blonde woman."

Andre and Norah exchanged looks. "Witness protection?" she said.

"But then why would Charity Kinsman keep this stuff around? Why would she have Jessica Whitlow's ID? Why would the Marshals Service be stashing this woman in Maine? And if she is here under some form of protection, why was that private investigator, Nathaniel Davenport, able to find her?" Andre said. "Why was he looking for her?"

I thought there were too many whys and not enough answers.

"Too bad Nathaniel Davenport isn't in the business of answering questions," I said. "He might know. Though I expect it is pretty important that he not find Charity. Or Jessica." Suddenly I had to sit down. "From what I saw, she's more pregnant than I am. She shouldn't have to be on the run and hiding from someone."

It bothered me, imagining her holed up someplace even worse than that cottage. I hadn't seen the inside, but she'd admitted it was awful and depressed her. She was pregnant. Away from the baby's father. Just wanting her Amy to be safe. What if she went into labor? Was there anyone with her? Had the real Jessica, Jessica Whitlow, left with her? Or did she have someone she could call if she needed help? Maybe that's why she'd knocked on my door. She was looking for another pregnant woman who could advise her about things in her new town. But if that was so, why had she suddenly fled without asking me any questions?

Once it got going, my imagination took off like a runaway horse. What if Whitlow had stashed her here and then gone off to do some other government business? What if Charity was here alone, trying to settle into someplace safe while waiting for her baby, and then Davenport and the other man showed up? Who was the other man? Those cowboy boots didn't look like something a Boston PI would wear. Why was Charity Kinsman calling herself Jessica?

Too many questions and no way to get any answers. All I knew about the Marshals Service was from TV, so it probably wasn't very accurate.

While Andre and Norah were engaged in their own speculations, speaking some kind of cop shorthand, I put a pan of Rosie's lasagna in the oven and went out to the garden to get some lettuce and see if there was another ripe tomato and maybe a cucumber. I found both, and came back into the kitchen feeling like a very successful farmer. Tommy Munro had arrived while I was harvesting, and now he was having a beer, examining the contents of the box, and being brought up to date on the story.

We took the tray of munchies out to the deck, arranged our Adirondack chairs in a circle, and spent a pleasant hour getting caught up on state police gossip while ignoring the mystery of a pregnant woman and a miserable bully in a black SUV who might be looking for a U.S. Marshal. It was delightful, followed by an equally delightful dinner in our dining room. Norah and I set the table, putting blue placemats on the warm cherry table, and we settled in to eat salad, hot bread, and Rosie Florio's lasagna.

Far too often, when I am in the company of Andre's colleagues, or even Andre himself, meals are interrupted by peremptory summonses from their cell phones. Tonight their phones were blissfully quiet. I was the one who was called away, having totally forgotten I had a conference call about branding with a client school.

I may find the term "branding" repulsive, but in the competitive world of private schools, protecting a school's individual niche and the things that are its particular selling points is important. The call went smoothly. It was so pleasant sitting in my little study with the murmur of conversation coming from another part of the house that when the call ended, I lingered a moment, taking pleasure in my lovely, if unfinished, house and the bucolic view out our back yard to the woods. At long last, we did have a place to call "home."

Before I returned to the dining room, I went to the front of the house and looked across the street toward the little cottage. The black SUV was still there. Its presence bothered me. Not only because it was still there, but because I could swear I saw something dark on the ground beside it. Jacket, briefcase, trash bag? From here, I couldn't tell.

I went out on the porch for a better view, but in the slanted evening light, I simply couldn't see anything clearly. Seen from this angle, it looked like nothing more than a shadow. I didn't want to interrupt the friendly conversation for something that was likely a trick of my imagination or of the light, but after dinner, maybe we would stroll over there and take a closer look. I was torn about doing so, though, since following my hunches has a tendency to result in bodies or other bad stuff.

Except for our occasional indulgence in rich, gooey chocolate cake, Andre and I don't often eat dessert. I have a sweet tooth, but I'm trying to do more healthy eating in the interest of little fingers, toes, and brains and so I'll have the energy to get through my days. Andre is happy to keep me company, although he has muttered some very negative things about kale. Kale rarely appears on our menu except as tenderly massaged kale in a salad. Tonight, though, would be an exception. Not to kale—why ruin a lovely evening?— but to the absence of dessert. The subversive and wonderful Rosie Florio had brought tiramisu. That delicious, creamy dessert must have a thousand calories per bite, so if I could get Norah and Tommy to eat some, they would save me from myself.

I have no idea how much a guy as big as Munro has to eat in day—probably a small ox, a dozen eggs, and a bushel of potatoes— all I could go on was the evidence of tonight. We'd started with a full pan of lasagna, the size that could easily feed eight. Now there was a single, lonely square left. The bread was gone. There were a few shreds of lettuce clinging to the salad bowl. When I suggested dessert, Tommy's face lit up, and when I brought the pan of tiramisu to the table, there was an actual chorus of sighs. I'd have to share that with Rosie. She loves feeding people.

Once again, a pan of the heavenly stuff could have served eight. When we were done, there were only crumbs left. I decided I was going to have to get Rosie's recipe. I could imagine that if I brought this in to work, I'd go right to the top of everyone's favorite person lists. Food is the best kind of a bribe.

Thinking of work immediately made me anxious about the situation with our two new hires. I reminded myself that Suzanne was an exceptionally competent manager who could handle personnel glitches. I leaned back in my chair and smiled. Tiramisu was probably a mistake. MOC liked sugar way too much, meaning that the nightly acrobatics would likely start early and be very energetic. Worth it, though. It had been such a delicious meal, and we rarely had an opportunity to spend time with our friends.

Norah patted her stomach—a strong, gym-tight stomach—and said, "I've got to take it easy if I'm going to fit into my wedding dress."

Tommy smiled a proprietary smile and said nothing.

Our companionable meal having ended without any of them receiving a phone call, I was reluctant to suggest a post-dinner perambulation to the cottage. I didn't want to spoil a perfect evening. Turned out, I didn't have to. Andre looked out, saw that the SUV was still there, and suggested they check it out. They, of course, meant the cops. But I am far from a shrinking violet, and figured MOC and I would be safe in the company of three of Maine's finest. In the interest of preserving the peace, they let me come along.

I thought humoring me—and a walk in the long summer evening—was a smart move until the four of us came around the edge of that big row of hemlocks. Then the pleasant summer evening crashed and burned.

Nathaniel Davenport was sprawled on the ground beside his car, his head surrounded by a pool of blood. A large stone lay nearby. The state of his head made it clear that this was Davenport's last case.

It was an "aha, the plot thickens" moment, but I had wanted the plot to thin, attenuate, die out. I had very much wanted the black SUV and that bully Davenport to depart, and the exotic Jessica, or Charity, to reappear. I have met few people in my life that I would wish to depart in a body bag. So much for the phones not ringing. We seemed to be able to find homicide practically on the doorstep.

The sight of three cops suddenly pulling out three phones and getting down to business might have been interesting, except that someone had died. Andre had established that by examining Davenport and checking his pulse. The black Honda was still there. The Volvo was gone. While they were attending to the process of summoning the necessary personnel to a crime scene, I worried that the attack on Davenport might mean something had happened to Jessica or Charity and there were more bodies inside the cottage.

No one noticed when I headed off in that direction. When I found the door standing open, the cheerful pot of calendulas kicked into the grass, I walked in, calling, "Jessica. Jessica. Are you here?"

No one answered.

I tried calling Charity. Still no answer.

My Jessica, or the woman who seemed to be named Charity Kinsman, wasn't anywhere on the first floor, though pulled-out drawers and things spilled on the floor suggested either a hasty departure or that someone had been searching the place. The rooms were so dark and gloomy and poorly furnished, I wondered how Charity had planned to fix it up in time to welcome an infant to the place. There was effort in some bright quilts and pillows piled on the floor, ready to cover the furniture.

No one in the living room, so I stepped into the kitchen. It had a small gas stove, a few open shelves for food and dishes, an empty space where a refrigerator would go, and a rust-stained white sink. There was a meager stack of cobalt plates and bowls and a few battered pots and pans. How could she be so vibrant and positive, living with this? Had it all been an act?

No. The colors of those quilts and pillows were completely her, and her comments about the baby, about Amy, were those of any excited, anxious mother-to-be. I stood in that threadbare kitchen, trying to remember what she'd said about the baby's father. He wasn't in the picture. But there had been that hesitation, that careful choosing of the words. She'd definitely wanted him in the picture. The way she'd described him choosing their baby's name told me that.

I had no basis for it, but I could conjure up a man, an American, held hostage somewhere, or hiding somewhere, and someone else who wanted to find and use Charity for leverage. Charity and the baby.

If that was the case, why had she thought she'd be safe here, and how had Davenport found her? How had he found her, who had killed him, and where had poor Charity gone? Or was she upstairs, injured or worse? Had Charity killed him and then fled? But she'd left me the note indicating she was leaving while Davenport was still alive. I was relieved to turn Davenport and his death over to the professionals, but I couldn't also turn over my worry about Charity.

Suzanne calls them my "waifs," the people I find in my travels whom I believe I have to help. I was supposed to be leaving all that behind now. Living a far more careful life and working on thinking ahead to my new job as MOC's mother. But here I was, standing in a grubby kitchen, speculating about a woman I'd only met twice. Three times, if you counted the brief moment when I handed over those flowers. Time to finish my search and get out of here, back to my own pretty kitchen. Back to my new safe and careful life.

The bathroom had an iron-streaked cream-colored plastic stall shower with a wildly colored curtain that smelled new, a toilet, and a mirror with half the silver gone, so it gave a distorted reflection. There was a hole in the worn linoleum floor. The shower was barely big enough to fit a pregnant woman, but there was shampoo and conditioner and soap, towels on the rack, and a thick melon-colored terry robe hung on the back of the door.

Mentally, I contrasted the vibrant and vivacious woman who had knocked on my door with this sad place, which she had pretty accurately called a hovel.

Hoping all I would find up there was dust and empty rooms, I climbed the narrow, uncarpeted stairs with trepidation. Upstairs, I checked out the room with a double bed that must have been hers. Here, some effort had been made. There were clean white curtains on the windows, the windows had been washed, and there was a pretty patchwork quilt on the bed. The floor was bare, but clean. The bedside tables were empty except for one flimsy lamp, a clock, a box of tissues, and a paperback novel. The dresser drawers were pulled out and looked empty.

I knelt down and peered under the bed. No dust. No anything else, either. I was straightening up in my slow and awkward way when I spotted something that had fallen down behind the bedside table. I moved the table away from the wall and picked it up. It was a framed photo of a man in what looked to me like full combat gear. An expert would know. I was just someone who occasionally watched TV. Even though it was nosy and interfering and I might be smudging important fingerprints, I sat on the edge of the bed and worked it out of the frame. Nothing on the back of the photo except the scrawled words, "Charity. Keep me in your heart. D."

Not something she intentionally left behind, I was sure. I put it back in the frame. Carrying it with me, I headed for the room across the hall.

In the small second bedroom, the one that would likely have been the baby's room, I found a still life. At the end of the twin bed, there was a small cardboard box of baby things, mostly pink. In the corner by the window, the crib we'd bought was half-constructed. Tools still lay on the floor next to the instructions to assemble it. I stopped, struck by the sadness of that, and by the sense of an urgent departure it conveyed. One minute she's building a crib, the next she's grabbing her things and running.

Or was I making up a story to fit what I was seeing? I remembered in our brief conversation that she'd said she was struggling to put the crib together, and I'd offered to send Andre's dad to help her.

There were new curtains here in a pink floral print, echoing the bits of pink in the cardboard box. A room for baby Amy. There was no sign of the bags of things we'd bought, nor the giant package of disposable diapers. Might they have been in the black plastic bag I'd seen her putting in the Volvo?

Also, no sign that the real Jessica Whitlow was staying here, despite the car downstairs.

I was ready to be gone. This was just so sad. There was no rocking chair. No bedside table or lamp beside this twin bed, only the bed and a small cheap dresser. On top of the dresser was a can of paint and a brush. I was sure, if I looked, the paint would be pink.

Just to be thorough, I slipped past the tilted, one-sided crib and the large cardboard box it had come in to check the far side of the bed. I was very sorry that I had.

There was a woman's body wedged between the bed and the wall.

NINE

I trudged back down the stairs, clinging to the railing. Shock had turned my legs into unreliable noodles. I ordered them to keep working. I was Thea the Great and Terrible, after all. The reminder didn't help. I couldn't catch my breath and barely made it back to the public safety trio, all still on their phones, before I burst into tears. Hormones, I reminded myself. I hadn't really lost my edge just because there were two homicide victims only steps from my front door, had I?

Andre lowered his phone. "What's the matter?" he said. "What's happened? Are you okay?"

"I'm fine," I said, which was obviously a lie. "But a woman who may be Jessica Whitlow, the real Jessica, blonde Jessica, is in one of the bedrooms upstairs. And she's…her body is…"

I stopped. I wasn't sure she was dead. I'd just assumed it. The professionals could check. "I think she's dead."

Then, even though it was totally irrational, I said, "Why did this have to happen here, when we've just found our perfect house. Dammit! I am not going to let a second house be ruined."

The last time I'd found our dream house, I'd also found our realtor, Ginger Stevens, dying in the beautiful living room. It had tainted that house forever and plunged me unwillingly into investigating her death.

Andre put his arms around me and pulled me close. "This is not going to ruin our house, Thea. This has nothing to do with our house."

Right. I really wanted to believe that. It was a lot better than thinking it was my fate to find bodies wherever I went. The Jessica Fletcher of my generation. Hadn't she lived in some fictitious Maine town?

"Where is the...where is she?" he asked.

I swallowed. "On the second floor, in the smaller bedroom. The one with the half-built crib. She's wedged between the bed and the outside wall."

"You recognize her?"

"She looks like the picture in that Marshals Service badge. Jessica Whitlow. Like the woman I saw arguing with Jessica... uh...Charity."

"I'll check it out," he said. "There's no sense in keeping you here. We're going to be tied up for a while. Why don't you go home? I'll come along as soon as I can. But you know——"

"How crime scenes can be? Of course I do. I'll just bustle around and do the dishes and fluff up the nest."

I wanted to scream and break things. Have a good cry and hit the bottle. I would do none of those things. Well, I could cry. Sadly, any alcoholic drink has been sidelined until after MOC's debut. And lacking a staff of devoted servants, if I broke something, I'd just have to clean it up myself.

He put a finger under my chin and gently lifted my head. "I'm sorry about this, Thea. Will you be okay?"

Even if I wasn't going to be okay, he wasn't going to abandon a dead body practically on his front lawn to take care of a scared little woman. Two dead bodies. Anyway, I wasn't scared. Not in the shaken up, out of control, hysterical way someone else might be. This wasn't my first rodeo. I might hate that that was true, but it was my reality. Being Jane Wayne had brought some ugly stuff my way, and being in a relationship with a cop had brought some more. I might be trying to paper my external life with lettuce and calendulas and a baby's room done in cool green paint, but the inside of my head contained more than an ordinary civilian's share of ugly images.

I do have a tendency, in my avatar as Thea the Human Tow Truck, to collect people in dire circumstances or badly in need of help. But just because I was a tough guy and could handle adversity, it wasn't fair for the universe to drop it right on my doorstep. Still, I stepped back from him and said, "You know me. I'll be okay."

"I know you," he agreed. "And I wish you didn't have to be okay about something like this." Then, because he can be romantic, even at a crime scene, he kissed me. One of those "Damn, I'd much rather get a room than deal with this" kisses. The one that said we're still alive and we're okay. The one that said be there because I need you.

I realized I was still holding the photo I'd found. I held it out to him. "I found this in the bedroom. The one with the double bed. It had fallen down behind the nightstand. I think this is part of the story of who Charity Kinsman is, and why she's here."

He took it from me and looked at the picture. No doubt it was telling him lots of things it wouldn't tell me. Then he nodded. "Thanks. This is helpful." He didn't exactly swat me on the bottom and tell me to go home, but that was in the air between us. He needed me gone so he wouldn't be torn between loyalties.

I left the professionals doing their professional thing and went back up the driveway to the house. He got on the phone again while Norah and Tommy headed for the house.

Inside my own house, I told Alexa to play some dance music and started cleaning up. Soon the dishwasher was whooshing softly to itself, and I was back in my office, checking my mail and reviewing my materials for the morning. Among the many emails that needed a response was one from Bobby. Following the subject line "Dynamite," he reported finding some interesting things posted online from the boys involved in, or who were witnesses to, the altercation with Denzel Ellis-Jackson.

Since youthful postings, particularly ones that reflect negatively

73

on the posters, have a tendency to vanish, Bobby had taken screen-shots. He'd posted some of the most relevant ones and they were, as he'd said, dynamite. Prior to the event, three boys had made an amateur rap video of themselves chanting a song in which the words "Gon' get that Denzel, gon' a bring him low, gonna trick him inta, fight will go to show, he ain't the man who the boss of us. Gon' tape that fight, gon' make a fuss. Gon' see that bas', out right on his ass."

There was a lot more. But as evidence of premeditation, it was solid. Seriously, if you're going to set someone up, don't post your intentions in a YouTube video *before* the event.

There was more. Plenty more. Bobby was a genius. And Emmet Hampton was going to be very pleased.

I sent an email thanking Bobby, and then forwarded his email with attachments to Emmett. One thing, at least, was going right today.

An email from Bobby popped right back saying he'd had some help from Lindsay, were we please going to hire her, and he said that she was also working on stuff for the Eastern Shore Academy meeting and if she found anything she'd be forwarding it directly to me. I felt a twinge of guilt that I was here in my cozy house while they, or at least Lindsay, were still at the office, then reminded myself I had put in plenty of late hours over the years. That was how jobs were when they were worth giving them your all.

It was nearly dark by now, and bright lights and a commotion of vehicles across the street told me that the crime scene investigation was well underway. I didn't expect to see Andre—who'd kissed me with so much promise—for many hours. To keep myself busy, I went upstairs, took the tags off one of my new dresses and the tunics, and put them in my suitcase. I might wish that I could pop down to Maryland, put their world right, and be back by the end of the day, but experience has taught me that life rarely moves so effi-ciently.

I closed the suitcase and set it by the door. Then, though I was tired and my flight in the morning meant getting up at a ridiculously early hour, I went back down to my computer and started playing around with the two names I had—Jessica Whitlow and Charity Kinsman. I wondered if my searches would bring me anything. Also, I wondered who the mysterious, and very tough-looking D was. Charity's husband? The father of her child? What was up with him that he couldn't be here with her, and she had to hide?

The internet is a wonderful and scary place to search. I found Charity as a high school athlete. Charity graduating from high school. Charity getting an award as an outstanding political science major, and Charity in uniform as a member of the National Guard. I even found her engagement announcement, which gave me the name I was looking for: David Peckham. But when I did a search for David Peckham, I drew a total blank. It was kind of spooky, as though Peckham had gotten engaged to Charity and then vanished from the face of the earth. For that matter, while there were many events involving Charity up to the time of her engagement, after that there was no further mention of her, either.

If her information was scrubbed, why hadn't that early information been deleted as well? The answers were beyond my pay grade. It was just another mystery.

It was while I was staring at my screen, puzzling over this, a possible answer hit me like a load of bricks. Charity's husband had a job where he was engaged in something secret. She had become invisible to help protect that secret, and what? Gone into hiding so she couldn't be used against him? It was wild conjecture, but if it was true, now a dumb broad sitting at a computer in Maine was conducting searches that could put them both at further risk. Or put herself, that is, myself, at risk. Because why would I be doing this search if I didn't know something?

Oh crap. My curiosity might not kill me, but what if it produced someone from the government on my doorstep? Or a bad guy? I'd already had a person on my doorstep looking for Jessica. Was that person really looking for Charity? Had I just made an enormous blunder? Would my foolish curiosity now bring more of them?

What had she said in her note? Don't look inside the box or it might put me in danger? And like Pandora, I had let my unbridled and unreflective curiosity lead me down a potentially dangerous path.

I wanted to talk to Andre about it, but he was unavailable.

I paced the hall, wondering where I could put the materials from that box that no one was likely to look. Once, years ago, when I was doing my first and last undercover stint in a town full of dangerous militia, I'd hidden my gun under a sink, behind a veil of spider webs, in a box of sanitary pads. I figured it was the place a tough guy was least likely to search. But I didn't have spiders or pads under my sinks. So where?

Off my back deck, I had a small area with my gardening supplies, a potting bench, and bags of compost, manure, and planting soil. I left out Jessica Whitlow's ID, which I knew they'd need. Then I wrapped the other stuff in foil, double-bagged it in sealable plastic bags, and buried it in the bag of manure. Amateur night, for sure, and of course I would tell Andre. But it was the best hiding place I could think of. Probably silly. Andre would likely want Charity's items as part of his investigation, too, and be annoyed and digging it out of the manure before the sun rose. But she'd asked me to keep it safe.

Then, my evening as an incompetent spy and idiot having worn me out, I went through the nightly rituals, and MOC and I went to bed. People often say that as soon as their heads hit the pillow they are asleep. Not me. I only slept well when I was with Andre, and he wasn't here. There was another sleep-killing thing in effect these days as well. Lying down and putting my head on a pillow was the signal for MOC's acrobatic act to begin. I lay in the quiet darkness, hand on the basketball, feeling the blanket hop and jump like there was a frog under the covers. The performance is usually about twenty minutes long. Tonight, when I really needed sleep, it went on far longer.

I had finally fallen asleep when I heard Andre come in. He undressed quietly in the dark and slid into bed. I dragged myself back from the arms of his rival, Morpheus, and said, "I made a big mistake tonight."

His "Uh oh," was weary. And wary. I told him about my

internet search and what I'd found, and where I'd hidden the contents of the box and the photo.

"You'll probably have some other government acronym breathing down your neck, looking for them."

"By morning, I expect."

"Am I a total idiot?"

"Not total."

Well, he was being reassuring, wasn't he? But I'd asked.

"Don't worry about it," he said. "Things will be okay. Go to sleep."

"MOC was thrashing for almost an hour," I said. " Boy, are we in for it."

He pulled me against him and spread his hands over the basketball. "Hey, kiddo," he whispered. "It's your dad. You wanna take it easy on your poor mom?"

In response, MOC kicked him.

"Listen," he whispered. "Be aware that you just assaulted a cop."

I laughed, MOC settled down, and we all fell asleep. I, at least, was hoping that no one came pounding on our door before I could get safely out of town. As people often say, I was going to let the cops handle it.

TEN

T he sun was already up and promising a perfect summer day as
I drove to the airport. I would have had a worse case of "I
don't wanna" if it weren't for crime scene tape and flashing blue
lights across the street. Andre was up and out the door before I left.
Being a gentleman, though, he did carry out my suitcase. For once, I
was glad to see our house in the rearview mirror.

As long as I stayed off the main roads, the journey was quiet.
Few tourists were abroad this early, and the people who were out
were attentive and business-like. I had a paranoid moment when a
small silver Subaru kept appearing in my rearview mirror, but silver
Subarus are so common in Maine I decided I was being silly. I
found a parking space easily at the airport and had an unusually
smooth journey through TSA to the gate.

Because I am not a trusting soul, I checked in at the desk that I
did, indeed, have an aisle seat with extra legroom. The man behind
me, one of those impatient business guys, stood so close I could
smell the nose-prickling scent of Dial soap.

I found a seat in the waiting area and pulled out my notes,
refreshing myself about the details of Eastern Shore Academy's
problem, and filing the names of the major players in my memory

for when I got there. People like to be remembered, and Dr. Kingsley, Leora Simms, director of the summer program, and Luke Bascomb, their IT person, would be my primary contacts today.

I was shifting to a review of honor codes—I had quite a file of them—when I felt a tapping on my knee. When I looked down, a small girl in a swirly pink dress, with her golden curls in two goofy ponytails, was trying to get my attention. When I looked up, she held out a book. "Will you read to me?"

The book was "Caps for Sale," which I remembered from my own childhood. I didn't think anyone read it anymore. I looked around for an adult to consult for permission, but no one seemed to be attached to the child, at least no one who wasn't buried in a phone or iPad.

"Sure," I said, shifting my briefcase onto the floor. She handed me the book and climbed into the chair beside me.

We got through the whole book without anyone interrupting us. When we finished, she said, "Read another?"

I looked at the monitor. We had fifteen minutes before boarding began. "Okay," I said. She wiggled down, crossed to a colorful pink plaid bag on the floor beside a man deeply immersed in his screen, and got out another book. She brought it to me, wriggled back onto her seat, and said, "Read Corduroy."

We finished it just as boarding began. I sent her back to the oblivious man and gathered my things. I like aisle seats, and being tall, I always get extra legroom, which means I can get on earlier and have a shot at space in the overhead bin. Stowing my suitcase is easier because I'm tall, but harder because somehow the basketball gets in the way. I managed, and dropped into my seat feeling like I'd already done a day's work just driving to the airport and getting on the plane. Maybe eating breakfast would have helped, but I can't face food early in the morning unless I've been up all night.

I hoped, as one always does, that the middle seat would be empty, a hope that was shattered when a tall, fierce-faced man in a dark suit arrived to claim the seat. It was Mr. Dial Soap. He didn't look like a middle seat passenger, the flight wasn't full, and my finely tuned alarm sensors started going off. They rang louder when the doors closed and the plane pushed back with no one in the window seat.

I got out the papers I'd set aside while reading books to my small friend and immersed myself in honor codes. We were maybe twenty minutes into the flight before he spoke. Just two words that signaled he was ready to talk. He said, "Honor codes?"

I said, "Work."

"What kind of work do you do?"

Either he was one of those guys who chat to make the time pass, which I doubted, or this was just the lead up to what he really wanted to discuss. I doubted that a trip to the lavatory would discourage him, but I went anyway. Being pregnant has made me far more attuned to the location of the facilities. I took my purse with me, but left my briefcase behind. If he wanted to read more about honor codes, he could go to town.

Airplane lavatories were getting smaller even as I was getting bigger. I wondered what really large people did. I could barely turn around, and it was a challenge to wash my hands without soaking the front of my dress. Luckily, the dress was black.

As I slid back into my seat, I could tell that my briefcase had been moved. Nothing in there of any interest to him, unless he could access my laptop, and that required my password. Before I left for the airport, I'd quickly checked my email, and downloaded a draft of the questionnaire Marlene was working on. This flight was the ideal time to review it, so I pulled out the laptop and scrolled to the draft. Sarah's report of Marlene crying in the bathroom because of some simple suggestions did not make me optimistic. I took a breath and started scanning it. It was bad. I was immediately reminded of another employee we'd had who couldn't take criticism. The employee from hell who reacted to being fired in particularly negative ways involving arson and knives. I was not eager to have to fire another employee, but what I was seeing on the screen was garbage.

I clicked on "Review" and started making notes.

My seatmate said, "I really don't care about honor codes. But you know that."

I stifled an annoyed, "Excuse me?" and didn't respond. I've had enough of guys on airplanes trying to strike up conversations. My motto is: don't encourage them. I could have said that I hoped everyone cared about honor codes. Instead, I went on making notes, trying not to let this work product upset me. We had given her samples, and I had given her specific advice about the project at hand. You wouldn't know that from the page I was reviewing. Was it possible she'd sent the wrong draft? I couldn't ask her that right now. I'd send an email when we landed.

I closed my eyes a moment and suppressed the wish to be back home, puttering in my garden. I really wasn't much of a putterer. I was terrified to even consider what I'd do if I ever stopped being a compulsive slave of duty. My MO was to keep moving, keep skittering across the ice before I fell down, not reflecting on how my life was going to change very soon. That was something I could deal with when it happened. Meanwhile, I was annoyed and upset by the possibility that just when we thought we had finally adequately staffed the office, we were going to be back to the drawing board in a hiring climate where good people were hard to find.

So far, they don't allow cell phone use on planes, for which I am grateful. Who wants to listen to endless too loud, too boring, or too intimate conversations when you're trapped in a tin can? But there are always moments like this, when I have three questions I'd like to get answered right away, when I wish the rule could be lifted for ten minutes just for me. Trouble is, everyone feels that way, including the dull, the boring, and especially the loud.

I sensed my seatmate was about to make another comment, so I got out my noise-canceling headphones and pulled up some Lady Gaga. I was just getting into her first song when my seatmate disconnected them from my laptop and said, "We need to talk."

We didn't need to do anything, and he had just invaded my space. Another trouble with being on planes—there's nowhere to escape if your seatmate doesn't observe proper boundaries. I have trouble dealing with situations that make me feel trapped. If this got too bad, I could ring for a flight attendant and asked to be moved. I could see other empty seats. But government bullies are a species apart and I suspected Mr. "We Need To Talk" was some kind of government. That meant if I asked to be reseated, he'd flash some official-looking badge, claim it was government business, and the flight attendant would leave me to his mercy or his lack thereof.

I have my issues with authority, despite being married to someone who carries a badge and has plenty of command presence. If this fellow had wanted to speak with me, he could have introduced himself politely, shown me his credentials, and asked if we could talk. I still might not have much to tell him, but at least the interaction would have been civil. Unplugging my headphones when I was happily communing with Lady Gaga? She wouldn't approve, and neither did I.

He seemed to be waiting for my response. I didn't have one, so I waited, too. Let him play to me. Give me a reason why we should talk. Cops are good at waiting, and cop's wives and girlfriends get pretty good at it, too. So do consultants who have to deal with recalcitrant clients who think if they go silent, they won't have to cooperate or answer. I assumed my seatmate—a highly inappropriate term for someone invading my personal space in such a peremptory manner—was there in some official capacity, but maybe I was seated next to a demanding civilian and he wanted to talk about growing beans.

I waited for the big reveal.

Waiting out someone who's gone silent is a common technique for getting someone to talk. Most people are uncomfortable with silences and will chatter just to fill the gap. But I wasn't most people. Evidently, neither was he. We sat in an awkward and uncompanionable silence for quite a while.

I was about to dig back into work when he finally broke the silence. "Look. I'm sorry, Ms. Kozak. I am doing this all wrong."

He had that right.

I waited for what would come next.

"I'm afraid I've spent too much time speaking, or trying to speak, with unfriendly people. I seem to have lost my social graces. I should have introduced myself."

Then he fell silent again, while I waited for him to do just that—introduce himself. If I were a nicer woman, one of those sweet, accommodating ones people sometimes mistake me for, I would have smiled and invited his introduction. But that would also have meant dismissing his rude behavior and giving him the impression that all was well. I didn't yet know if all was well. I had no information beyond his behavior on which to base any opinion. Yes. I suppose I could be considered stubborn, perhaps too stubborn, but really, all the guy had to do was tell me who he was and what he wanted. How difficult was that?

Well, not all. There were also those 'how did he get here' questions. How did he know who I was? That I'd be on this plane? What manipulations were necessary to get the seat next to me? He had to have some kind of pull to get that information. I sighed. I was just a poor consultant, on the way to do a job. I did not need a lot of mysterious nonsense distracting me.

Of course, he *was* distracting me. After last night, the presence of another intrusive and pushy stranger who seemed to think I owed him answers made me very nervous.

I put a hand on MOC, losing the patience game. A large man leaning into my space was not helping with my stress levels. I said, "Well, *are* you going to introduce yourself?"

To my amazement, he blushed. An actual, red-in-the-face blush. Then he rubbed his face and ducked his head like a middle school boy, and said, "Oops."

Funny how a single word, a word and a very human action, can change the tone of a conversation. Or an interaction. So much for the big, tough exterior. It looked like I was going to have to help him out.

I held out my hand. "Hi, I'm Thea Kozak. I'm an educational consultant. And you are?"

He took the offered hand. His was big and rough, and his handshake suggested he rarely shook hands with women, only with Godzilla and grizzly bears. "Malcolm Kinsman."

I said, "Oh," and shifted in my seat to get a better look at his face. Shifting in an airplane seat in my condition, even in a seat with extra legroom, was a challenge. My legs weren't where I needed the room.

Cut so short, it was hard to see if he had Charity's straight black hair, but he definitely had the same eyes and cheekbones. "You're Charity's twin, aren't you?"

He exhaled like he'd been holding his breath for a long time. "At least you aren't going to pretend you've never seen her," he said.

"I'm not pretending anything," I said. "You need to tell me what's going on, Mr. Kinsman."

"Malcolm," he said. "I need your help."

I politely refrained from saying he had a pretty weird way of asking, and tried to explain why I couldn't help him. "Malcolm, I don't know why you're following me. You must have gone to lot of trouble to get on this plane and seated next to me, but I really don't see how I can help. I've seen your sister exactly three times, the third time only to give her a pot of flowers. I know nothing about her or about her situation and I have no idea where she is or why a man who claimed he was a private investigator from Boston was looking for her. I can tell, from the trouble you've gone to find me, that you're expecting more. But there is no more. I'm sorry."

In minutes, he'd morphed from stiff and aloof to drooping and exhausted. He looked like someone who really did need help. Unfortunately, despite all the trouble he'd gone through, I wasn't the right person to help him if his goal was to find his sister. Probably that was someone with the Marshals Service. Only their person on the ground, if Jessica Whitlow was genuinely what that ID said she was, was beyond help. I had no idea whether she'd sent Charity on to another hiding place or if Charity had fled when she sensed danger. It might be that Charity escaped while Jessica was being killed. Faced with it now, in a new life where I was trying to avoid death and danger, the memory of last night and two people dead hit me like a blow. So did the possibility that whoever had killed Nathaniel Davenport and Jessica Whitlow might have also taken Charity.

ELEVEN

"You don't know where she is?"

He sounded disappointed, and accusatory, as though he was sure that I had more information to share but was refusing to share it.

I shook my head.

It was clear that I wasn't going to get any work done on this flight, so I put my laptop away and stowed my tray table. Then I countered his question with some of my own. "You've gone to a lot of trouble to find me and ask about your sister. Why didn't you just go to the police and ask them for help?"

He said, "I'm trying to stay under the radar. The same people who are looking for Charity would be just as happy if they found me."

It wasn't a helpful answer. "Who is looking for her? And why?"

"It's complicated."

I was trying not to let him raise my stress levels. His crap answers sure weren't helping, so I tried out one of my whacky theories. "Is Charity's husband in trouble? Is whoever is looking for her doing it to get leverage of some kind?"

He had kind of a panicked look, glancing around to see if anyone had overheard, so I knew I was close. I also knew from his tight lips that he wasn't going to answer. Just like many of the cops I've dealt with, it was all pumping me for information but always a one-way street.

I said, "What makes you think I might know where your sister is?"

He was silent so long I thought he wasn't going to answer that, either. Then he said, "When we spoke, Charity and I, she said she'd met a new neighbor, you'd gone shopping together, and while she didn't know you well, she thought you could be trusted. That if she asked you for help, you'd help. She said you had a reputation as an excellent detective and—"

Oh, dear, not that detective crap again. A few years ago, when I was working on a death at a private school, a news story had called me a detective and stuff online never dies, however inaccurate it is. "I don't know where she got that idea, but it's not true. My work is with independent schools and crisis management." I gestured toward my briefcase. "Honor codes. Cheating scandals."

I took a breath. It wouldn't do me or MOC any good if I lost my temper. "The fact that your sister misunderstood something she read online can't have been enough for you to pull whatever strings you pulled to find me and get on this flight today. So who are you and why are you really here?"

He rubbed his chin thoughtfully. I tried to remember whether, in Andre's informal classes on interviewing and interrogation, he'd said anything about the meaning of that particular gesture. I came up blank. I didn't know what else to say. I wasn't sure I should tell him about the packet of information Charity had left, but without it, I would have had no idea who Charity and the woman who'd called herself Jessica Whitlow were. Besides, he was her brother. Maybe if he could help her, I could stop worrying about her.

Before I spilled what little I knew, I asked him to show me some ID.

He produced a Texas driver's license.

I told him about finding Charity's note, and the contents of the small box. About Charity's evasiveness and unease about the protection she was getting. About seeing her putting a bag in the Volvo. Then, because I wasn't sure how much he was in the picture, and anyway, it was, or would be, public knowledge, I told him about Nathaniel Davenport, who claimed to be looking for Jessica Whitlow, and about the woman's body that I'd found in the cottage, which almost certainly was the real Jessica Whitlow. "And that's all I know. I have no idea how it might be helpful."

I leaned back in my seat and closed my eyes. This conversation, with him leaning into my space and scrutinizing my every word, was exhausting. I needed to save my energy for the work I was flying down here to do.

"So the car is gone? The one you saw with Virginia plates? And you found no sign of Charity in the house?"

"I didn't find Charity in the house," I said, without opening my eyes. He was so intently focused on his questions, on his own mission, I doubted he'd even noticed.

"Did you find anything to indicate where she's gone?"

"Mr. Kinsman, I am not a detective. I did not search that cottage for signs or clues."

"But did you—"

I opened my eyes. He clearly wasn't going to let me rest. Probably hadn't even noticed my condition, or, being a mission-driven male, didn't see it as a possible issue. I wondered how he'd feel if someone was doing what he was doing to his very pregnant sister?

"Please stop questioning me as though you think I'm withholding information from you. I do not have any more information." Getting angry was starting to upset MOC, and I was supposed to stay calm and stress-free and try not to raise my blood pressure.

He reached in his pocket and took out a photograph which he handed to me. "Look at this. This is why I'm here."

Much like the photo that had been in Charity's bedroom, this was a picture of men in full combat gear. Two men, this time. It's hard to identify people when they have combat helmets on with chin straps and are swaddled with gear, but I thought one of them was my interrogator, Malcolm Kinsman. I guessed that the other was Charity's husband, David Peckham, but I really couldn't tell.

I pointed to the one I assumed was Malcolm Kinsman. "This one is you?"

He nodded.

"And the other one?"

"Charity must have told you. That's her husband, David Peckham."

I shook my head. "Two conversations," I reminded him. "All she told me about her husband was that he wasn't in the picture. No name. No further information except that she's supposed to name the baby Amaryllis, Amy for short."

"Exactly," he said, pouncing like I'd just revealed a highly guarded secret.

I checked my watch, hoping we'd be landing soon. Sure enough, as though the pilot had read my mind, he announced that we'd be landing in twenty minutes. I restrained myself from cheering, but I was relieved. Once we landed, I'd be meeting LaDonna and rushing to rent a car, so I pulled out my breakfast bar and stripped off the wrapper. Airplane food, when there is any, has gotten worse and worse. No way MOC and I could get through the morning on a handful of blue potato chips or a packet of mostly chemical cookies.

I was two bites into the bar when he said, "I don't know how you can eat when my sister is in such trouble."

Ignoring the provocation, and the temptation to say he'd given me no information about Charity's trouble, I got out another bar and handed it to him. "Eat this. Maybe it will improve your disposition."

I was truly surprised when he took it and started eating. I should know by now—even the nicest men, which he was not, get crabby when they're hungry. When he was done with the bar, I gave him another, which disappeared just as fast. I'm a sucker for hungry guys, but that was all I had to give him. I had to save my last one for MOC.

"Don't know what else I can do to help you," I said. "Maybe if I'd had a chance to get to know her, she might have given me some clues. Though honestly, I think she was planning to settle in there in the cottage until Amy was born. The place is pretty shabby, but she was trying to make it nice. And she was putting a crib together."

He studied me and then studied his hands. "She didn't tell you anything about David?"

"Not even his name. Just that he wasn't in the picture. I got the impression that made her sad, but there was something fatalistic about the way she said it, like it was just something she had to accept."

I searched my memory for anything else I could tell him. "She was very nervous, like she was afraid of someone or something. During our conversations, which were mostly about our babies, she was careful to not reveal anything about herself. Not where she was from, nor why she was in Maine. Nothing. It was unusual."

"David is missing," he said. "There's suspicion that he may be a prisoner, held for information. There has been concern that the people who are holding him want to use Charity as a lever to persuade him to...uh...talk." He shrugged, like these weasel words were enough. "It's concerning that the agent in charge of protecting her did such a poor job."

Concerning to whom? And I thought he knew damned well what was going on with the missing David Peckham. "If that agent was Jessica Whitlow, she died on the job," I reminded him. "So what kind of work was David doing? Where was he? Who is suspected of holding him? And if the Marshals Service is already involved, what are you doing here?"

I know. It was a lot of questions, but it seemed like the answers were critical to explaining his presence and possibly figuring out how to find Charity.

He blew me off. "Not authorized to tell you any of that. What matters now is finding my sister and making sure that she's safe."

Even as I was thinking *don't get drawn in*, I found myself saying, "And how do you propose to do that?" I didn't want to know the answer. I was afraid, given his distrustful nature and poor listening skills, that his answer would involve me. I'd already given him everything I had. Plus, few things push my buttons like people who demand my help but refuse to offer anything in exchange.

"I'll have to talk to some people at the Marshals Service. Learn more about the man who called himself Nathaniel Davenport. And talk to your local police."

I refrained from telling him the local police included my husband. If he'd done his homework, he'd know this anyway. I also refrained from asking why he wasn't doing this back in Maine instead of bothering me.

"That note will have to be examined to determine if it truly is Charity's handwriting. To see if there are messages a civilian like yourself might have missed."

And only moments ago, hadn't he thought I was a detective? I didn't mind being demoted to civilian, though. Every now and then, someone asks me if I'm a cop. Probably being around them so much rubs off. But for today, I was very happy to be a mere civilian, getting off this plane and heading out to do my job, leaving this aggravating and desperate man behind.

He was kind enough to get my suitcase down, and when we got into the airport, he vanished. I hoped he had vanished for good, but thought it unlikely.

It was only when I was heading to the place I'd agreed to meet LaDonna that a scary thought occurred to me. If bad people were looking for Charity—if they didn't already have her—they might have seen me talking with her brother. After all, if he could find me, so could someone else. Had he just pointed a big red arrow at me—the detective she had confided in? And had that been a mistake, or was it deliberate?

TWELVE

LaDonna was waiting for me near the exit, and we hopped on the shuttle to the rental cars. We must have made a very odd pair. LaDonna is a petite, African American/Asian mix with pixie-cut black hair, and she dresses like an 1890's newsboy, with cropped pants and a short tight jacket. When it isn't summer, she adds a little cap that matches the jacket and truly awful shoes. People stare at her because she looks so young. When she starts to speak, their stares change to looks of disbelief. If STEM education routinely leaves girls behind, LaDonna didn't get the message. She's unabashedly smart and absolutely confident. At more than one school where she's joined me for a consultation, someone on the faculty has tried to send her back to class. She thinks it's hilarious.

Since my pregnancy began to show, she has addressed me as, "Your Roundness," which I don't mind. Right now, I am round. When people we don't need to impress aren't around, I refer to her as "my pixie."

Right now, Pixie and Roundness were trying to rent a car that would allow me to fit comfortably behind the wheel. I'd reserved a Jeep. I know I can easily fit into a Jeep. I do it every day. What they tried to give me was an SUV, but one much smaller and tinnier than

I wanted to drive on the crowded roads around Baltimore. Too often these days, what counts for service is whatever is convenient for the folks behind the counter. It took a certain amount of firm pushback before I got the vehicle I'd reserved. I may sometimes suffer from pregnancy brain, but the people behind the counter are not entitled to assume that I'm an idiot who can be given any set of car keys and sent away.

By the time we were on the road, their uncooperative idiocy was threatening to make us late. They'd probably counted on that, too. The pregnant lady will take whatever car we give her because she's in a hurry. Not in too much of a hurry to worry about MOC's safety and her own comfort, thank you very much.

"Ha!" LaDonna said when we were underway. "I guess you told them."

"Would you have done it differently?" I wondered how a woman frequently mistaken for a child gets things done.

"Depends on where I am. Sometimes I just fold my arms and wait. Waiting without speaking drives them crazy. Sometimes I just look at the car they want to give me, say 'No,' and wait. Sometimes I pretend to call my dad. It's a fact of life—I'm short. I can't drive every car they want to give me."

LaDonna's father is a bigwig in the government.

"I do a lot of different things," she continued. "Depends on how annoying they are and how much they make me want to mess with them. And how much time I have. So, these folks at Eastern Shore. What will they be like to work with? Am I gonna have to prove I'm smart before they give me what I need?"

"Don't think so. I gave you a pretty big build-up. We'll just have to play it by ear. Watch out!" I swung out a protective arm as a black SUV suddenly swerved into our lane. If we were in Maine, a black SUV would be concerning. In the DC area, which includes Baltimore, they're common.

"Thanks, Mom," she said. "I think you broke my nose."

"Sorry," I said. "I'm practicing for the real thing."

"Breaking noses?"

I handed her the directions, and she instructed Siri to find the best route. Seemed like only yesterday I was learning to read a map. Now I'm usually trying to fumble the phone out of my purse while I'm in awful traffic, and then Siri doesn't understand a word I say. The joys of progress. That joy had recently been complicated by Maine passing a hands-free driving law, so I have to be sure I've entered the necessary info before I set out. So far, it doesn't seem to have affected those phone-addicts who fail to go when the light turns green, or who absently drift out of their lanes. I never used to be someone who used her horn.

The directions were easy to follow. Siri didn't once send me weaving through a strange neighborhood or strand me on a dirt road. Yes. She's done that. We pulled into a parking space outside the administration building with exactly two minutes to spare, grabbed our briefcases, and headed inside.

We were immediately conducted to a conference room where four people were waiting for us. Dr. Kingsley, Leora Simms, and their IT guy, Luke Bascomb, I was expecting. The fourth person turned out to be Jesper DiSantis, the instructor whose tests had been the subject of the hack. DiSantis was a young, handsome African-American man who looked very uncomfortable.

I introduced myself and LaDonna, and we were off to the races.

Things went smoothly while they brought us up to speed on the situation. There were three students involved who had achieved remarkable turnarounds on their test scores. When the three were interviewed, all of them admitted to receiving the test questions in advance of both tests. All three said they had no idea who had sent them.

"Did you get the students' permission to access their computers?" LaDonna asked.

After an odd hesitation, Bascomb said, "We've traced the emails to a computer in the school's library, but the library, as a matter of policy, does not keep records of who uses their computers, and no one on staff remembers who was using the computers at the time the emails were sent."

LaDonna looked at me. Bascomb hadn't actually answered her question. She asked Bascomb a few more pointed questions he was unable to answer. Maybe thinking he'd do better one-on-one, Dr. Kingsley suggested that he and LaDonna adjourn to his office to dig into the matter further. She left swinging her briefcase like a happy school kid. He left like someone going to his execution.

There was a vibe in the room, a sense of the unspoken I was picking up on. An extension of the conversation I'd had with Dr. Kingsley. It seemed clear to me that they knew more than I'd been told, and part of the game we were playing was a form of "let's see if Thea can guess our secret." Well, Thea, with her able sidekick LaDonna, would certainly try. Thea has guessed people's secrets before.

Once they were gone, Jesper DiSantis asked if we needed him anymore. Since he hadn't yet contributed much, I wondered at his eagerness to be gone, but Dr. Kingsley was a rather fierce presence and Leora Simms, in her few remarks, had demonstrated that she was good at asking insightful questions. Maybe he was uncomfortable being on the hot spot. Though if a few mild questions constituted a hot spot, it was a wonder he could stand up to a classroom full of adolescents. They can be a very tough audience.

Dr. Kingsley said, "Sure, Jesper, we'll let you know if we need you—"

I stopped her. "Before you go, Mr. DiSantis, I have a few questions."

He was already halfway out of his seat. With a sigh, he sat back down. I wondered why he would have been so relieved to be off the hook, and what that hook was, exactly.

"How many students are in the class where the suspected cheating took place?"

"Uh. Fourteen. There were fifteen, but one of our students has left."

"Of that fourteen, the three who showed remarkable improvement, the ones who admit that they received the test questions in advance, were they the only students who were struggling in the class?"

He shrugged. "To some extent, all of our students are struggling.

That's why they're in this summer program. I guess you'd say they were doing the least well."

"And the fifteenth student, the one who left. Did they leave before or after the tests in question?"

He hesitated, then said, "After."

"And did he or she also show marked improvement, suggesting access to the test answers?"

He glared at me like I was uncovering a dark secret, then mumbled, "Yes."

This should be routine. These questions should already have been asked and answered.

"I'm sure LaDonna will ask Mr. Bascomb this question as well, but was your computer searched?"

He nodded.

"Did they find any evidence of an intrusion?"

"You'll have to ask Bascomb. Computers, other than as tools to assist my work, are not my area."

"Thank you, Mr. DiSantis. Just a few last questions. The test questions were on your computer?"

He nodded.

"Personal computer or one that is owned by the school?"

"School," he muttered, as sullen as a teenager.

Was I getting too close to something or did this guy have issues with authority? "And were the test questions stored on the school's server?"

He shrugged. "Like I said, I don't know much about computers."

I looked at Dr. Kingsley and Leora Simms. "Would you know the answer to that?"

Either they didn't, or they weren't telling me. Maybe this was part of why LaDonna was going to get her big bucks.

"Do you use email to communicate with your students? Do you have an on-line group they can use to ask questions, get assignments, etc.?"

An unelaborated "yes."

Dr. Kingsley said, "We have a text messaging program for all of our instructors. Luke can give you the details."

I nodded and finished my questions for Jesper DiSantis. "Is this the only class you teach?"

"No. I teach two others."

"Are any of the students we're concerned about here in those other classes?"

"They are not."

"Have there been any issues with students in your other classes also showing the kind of remarkable improvement which concerned you?"

"No."

"Until you began to suspect there was something concerning about these students' remarkable improvement, did you have good relationships with them?"

"Of course. I always get along with my students. They like me and I enjoy teaching them."

"So there wasn't any animosity toward you? Your students weren't taking out their frustrations that they were failing on you?"

His "of course not" was awfully defensive.

"One final question. When you became concerned about unrealistic test performance and learned your students had been given the test questions, was there anyone in particular whom you suspected might have hacked your account to obtain those test questions?"

He shook his head. I refrained from saying, "We need a verbal answer for the tape." There was no tape, just my curious and suspicious mind at work.

"Thank you. I won't keep you any longer."

He was out the door almost before I'd finished speaking, leaving me wondering if I was being too cop-like again. Was he touchy about his teaching because he was insecure? Because he identified with those students who were in the remedial program?

"I apologize, Ms. Kozak," Dr. Kingsley said. "Jesper can be a bit touchy at times. I know that he is taking this very personally."

"Please. Call me Thea. I hope we can get to the bottom of this quickly and get things settled down again. I'm sure it's making your students very tense."

She nodded. "Making us very tense, as well."

"How did the matter first come to your attention?" I asked.

"Leora can answer that," she said, nodding at the dean of the summer program.

Leora Simms reminded me of my friend Jonetta Williamson, who is headmistress of a school for underprivileged Black girls in New York City. Like Jonetta, Leora Simms was a woman of size and color and had a commanding presence. She said, "I imagine Grace, Dr. Kingsley that is, has brought you up to speed on our program. We offer a gap year for promising students who have been under-served by their schools. This summer program is kind of a pre-gap tutorial for promising students who are even farther behind. Much of what we work on are the basics—reading and analyzing materials, understanding grammar, developing some basic writing and communications skills, remedial math with approaches to problem-solving. Little of it actually lends itself to cheating on a test, except for the reading and analyzing portion."

I nodded. I'd been wondering about that. "It wasn't Mr. DiSantis who brought the issue to your attention?"

She and Dr. Kingsley exchanged glances. If looks had words, she would have been saying, "I told you we couldn't keep this under the rug."

"I was the one who noticed it. Because this program is intense, and it's all aimed at giving these kids a shot at success in the fall, we monitor their progress closely. I already had my eye on those three students based on their performance when their test scores suddenly improved. Well, four. We were sorry to see that student go." She shook her head. "Jesper misspoke when he said they weren't in trouble in other classes. Or if he gave that impression. We have forty-five students here in three sections of fifteen. He teaches the reading and analysis sections for all three groups."

"Just so we're clear, you didn't spot similar issues with his students in the other two groups?"

"No. But this is the weakest group." She halted and sighed again. "I think you know where we're going with this."

"You think he's involved somehow and you want us to be the ones to uncover it?"

"Right."

"You don't think the school's computer system has been hacked?"

Dr. Kingsley answered this one. "No. We don't."

"And why can't you do this yourselves? I understand the delicacy required if Dr. Kingsley is concerned about the school labeling some of its students as cheaters, possibly even discovering one is a hacker. Why do you have the same hesitation challenging Jesper DiSantis if you believe he gave the test questions to his students?"

Another exchange of looks. "I'm afraid we've gotten you here without the full story," Dr. Kingsley said. "Yes, we suspect it was Jesper who dispersed the information. And yes, we want you, EDGE Consulting, to discover that this is the case. Because, as you probably know, nepotism is not uncommon in hiring situations in independent schools. In this case, Jesper is the nephew of the chairman of our board. We were pressured to hire him even though we had doubts about his qualifications. Now we also have doubts about his honesty. But we can't go forward without concrete evidence. Evidence that your computer expert, LaDonna Marquis, is perfectly situated to provide."

"So I'm just window-dressing?"

"No." She gave a decisive nod. "May I speak frankly?"

"Of course."

"You're here to lend the imprimatur of EDGE Consulting to the situation when we're ready to take this to the trustees. You're also here to help us craft an updated honor code, and to speak to all of our assembled students about the importance of honor codes and the risks of violating them. About the long-term effects of cheating in college and in their future employment. These kids, as is common with high school students, think only in the short term—this paper, this test, this summer. We're trying to get them to take the long view. To take some responsibility for their futures."

Almost noon. Lunch time. And MOC was getting restless. I was getting annoyed. No, I already was annoyed that they had brought me here to make what I considered an important speech and failed to give me advance warning. I tried to channel my partner, Suzanne, who is all about handling clients with kid gloves and keeping them happy. When I come in, it is usually to bring my big guns and shoot troubles. Sometimes there is collateral damage. I hoped LaDonna and I would get out of here without having to use our guns.

I smiled. "Sounds like a good plan, though I can't promise much of a speech. I'm not the world's best extemporaneous speaker."

Dr. Kingsley smiled back. "You know your stuff, and you know your audience. You'll be fine."

Returning to the matter of DiSantis and test scores, I asked, "So, is Bascomb in on this and able to direct LaDonna, or is she supposed to find this on her own?"

"On her own. We hope."

LaDonna was good. If she hadn't already figured this out, she would soon.

"But Bascomb knows?"

Leora answered this. "We believe he does. He's kind of timid. He doesn't like conflict. Likes to stay in the background and play with his machines."

"And when am I giving this speech to your student body?"

"This afternoon. We'll be having lunch soon, right after we have you go over our draft honor code, then you'll have an hour of prep time—we've reserved you a nice quiet office—and then we're having our assembly," Dr. Kingsley said.

Is it flattering or merely misguided when your client has more faith in your abilities than you do? I might be about to find out. I can advise. I can help with important documents like crisis plans and honor codes, and I can assist a school in a crisis. Making speeches? Not so much. But I did know this stuff, and if I really was going to have a quiet hour to prepare, it should be fine. One thing was clear: this school definitely wanted to get its money's worth.

"All right," I agreed. "Now, your honor code?"

Dr. Kingsley produced some papers and gave copies to me and

to Leora. I shared some of the samples I'd brought, and we were off to the races. As we bent over our papers, I hoped that in another part of the forest, LaDonna was worming her way through the computer system, or Jesper's computer, and finding the digital trail or the smoking gun, or lack thereof. Whatever computer experts called their discoveries.

I had one question that I'd failed to ask earlier. I didn't know if it made any difference, but I had to know. "Backing up for a sec. The students who got the exam questions. Male? Female? Or both?"

There was that exchange of glances again, and Leora Simms said, "All three were female."

"And the student who left?"

"Female as well."

THIRTEEN

The founders of Exeter and Andover had it right when they defined character as including both goodness and knowledge, saying, "Goodness without knowledge is weak and feeble, yet knowledge without goodness is dangerous." Nationally, we were in the midst of a crisis of character in many arenas. Students in the pressure cooker of high school facing the challenge of getting into a good college were reported to be cheating on a shocking scale. It was important for schools to develop honor codes and educate their students about the impact of violating those codes. Lately it was looking like there should be honor codes for the parents, as well. Sadly, schools didn't have much control over them.

I was glad to be sitting with two smart women working on a code for the school that recognized it wasn't enough to be smart. It was important, as well, to be cognizant of every person's obligations of citizenship and service. With the teaching of civics on the decline, it became a challenge for every school to find ways to convey to their students—and enforce—the message that good character was an important part of their education. Honor codes might begin at home, but increasingly they were necessary for schools to protect themselves against cheating and plagiarism when it happened. When every student and his or her parents were required to read the honor code and sign a form, affirming that it had been read and agreed to, enforcing the rules got easier.

That was pretty much what I said to Dr. Kingsley and Dean Simms as we got underway. Then I climbed off my soapbox and we dug into their draft, adding what needed to be included to make it a strong and effective code for their student population. More important, perhaps, was how to best explain the concepts to students in a way that helped them apply it to their everyday lives.

"You might say that the credo many of our students arrive with is that they have to do whatever is necessary to get ahead," Dr. Kingsley said, "without anyone ever asking what that means. Plus, often they have a chip on their shoulders because they've been shortchanged in school, so they know they're behind. It can make them feel angry and stupid and that anger can cloud their judgment."

She sighed in frustration. "So while we're trying to give them the tools for academic success, they have life skills learned from doing whatever they have to to survive. Life skills that say if they need to cheat to get ahead, cheating is okay."

"Right," Simms said. "They're about survival and getting by, and then even as we're piling on the work, trying to get them ready for an academic year, we're telling them they have to follow a bunch of rules that may feel foreign. May even strike them as unfair if they've seen a lot of cheating without consequences at the schools they've attended."

"What we absolutely can't do," Dr. Kingsley said, "is have our faculty helping them cheat. It underscores the message that cheating is okay. It normalizes it."

It looked like I was going to give my extemporaneous speech to an audience that would be cynical about my message. Statistics show that between fifty and ninety percent of students engage in some form of cheating or plagiarism. Damned discouraging. But that didn't mean educators should just fold their tents and steal away.

Honor code editing done and the draft given to Dr. Kingsley's assistant to type, we adjourned to lunch in Dr. Kingsley's office. It was a beautiful office with a view out over a broad body of water. I could see several species of birds, including large and small herons.

Dr. Kingsley checked her messages. "LaDonna says she can't join us for lunch, so I'll have a sandwich sent to her. Maryland crab, of course."

"Of course," I agreed. Every place that has crab believes their crab is the best, but I wasn't about to engage in 'my crab is better than your crab' contest. I thought all crab was delicious.

Spotting binoculars on the windowsill, I said, "If I had this office, I'd never get anything done," I said. "I'd just become a bird-watcher."

"Why I sit with my back to the window, Thea. Chesapeake Bay. There's a wildlife refuge nearby. The view is lovely, though, isn't it?"

Lunch was lovely, too. A crab salad with mango and avocado and some amazing warm bread. "This is delicious," I said.

"We are fortunate to have an excellent cook," Dr. Kingsley said. "And we praise her to the skies so she'll stay. She even makes special dishes for homesick students. And Thursday night is fried chicken and biscuits."

"You're lucky," I said. "No. The students are lucky. Speaking of students, are the students in this summer program all from Maryland?"

"Mostly. Our funding for the program is from the state and from a handful of nonprofits. We're one of the few such programs in the country, though, so we do get students from other areas if they are lucky enough to hear about us."

Something EDGE could help with. "Do you want to expand the program? Are you looking to attract more students?"

Leora took this one. "This summer is our trial run," she said. "If it goes well, we'll be looking to expand. If we go that way, we'll be looking for your help."

We watched a group of students walk past the window. They looked happy and carefree, as students should in the summer, and both women smiled as they watched the noisy, jostling group go by. We were all thinking the same thing—ah, to be young again, when summers meant you didn't have to work. These kids did have to work, though. And still looked happy. It was a beautiful place to spend the summer.

Then Dr. Kingsley and Dean Simms went back to work, and I hunkered down in a small office to work on a speech. I'd been there all of five minutes when there was a sharp knock on the door and LaDonna called, "Thea. Open up. We need to talk."

I knew what we needed to talk about. It had been hanging in the air since we arrived this morning.

I called "Come in," and she dashed in, shutting the door quickly behind her like she was being chased.

"Everything okay?" I asked.

"Hardly. They do know they're going to have to fire his ass, don't they?"

"They do. They're just using us to do the dirty work and provide the proof they need in order to justify his dismissal to the board. Turns out he's the board chairman's nephew."

"Ah. Spare me from nepotism. We see enough of that in politics."

"We see enough of that everywhere. Did you get some lunch?"

She smiled. "Yummy crab sandwich and homemade potato chips and a great big gooey brownie."

"Other than that?"

"Other than that, Jesper DiSantis seems to be a rather clumsy fellow. He not only set up a fake account through his school-issued computer, an account he accessed from the library to send the test questions to certain favored students, he had been carrying on a very romantic set of chats with each of the three girls in question. Well. There were four. The fourth seems to have dropped off his radar."

"As we suspected." I sighed. "The fourth one left the program."

"Right. What we might not have anticipated is that all three girls are aware of the others, and they're playing him like a fiddle. So they're not off the hook, cheating-wise, because there are emails in which they are asking him for those test questions."

"So he's dumb and they're both manipulative and naïve?"

"Something like that. Well, I'd say two of the girls are more sophisticated, and the third plays at playing along but actually imagines herself in love with him. In short, an ugly mess he, as the adult here, is almost entirely responsible for."

She settled back in her chair with a grin and said, "So how's the speech on cheating and the honor code coming?"

"Slowly but surely, despite getting blindsided. What do you have to give our employers so they can move ahead with solving their cheating problem?"

She waved the papers she was holding. "Bunch of stuff I printed out, here. But I think it will help if I write up an explanation of how I followed the trail of information and traced it to the particular computers. I'll throw in lots of big words and computer terminology so they'll feel like they are getting their money's worth."

There was another desk in my little office, so LaDonna settled in to write while I worked on my speech.

After a while, she paused in her typing and said, "Pity we don't need to stay overnight, it's so pretty here. I'm not looking forward to going back to the city."

"You should come to Maine and visit us. We have a big house with a guest room."

"You should be careful with invitations like that. Everyone wants to come to Maine in the summer."

"Then I should tell you about the mysterious murders across the street. That might be a deterrent."

"Murders? Plural? Seriously?"

"It's my fate, LaDonna. I'm like Jessica Fletcher. Everywhere I go, somebody dies." I joked about it not because it was funny but because joking was part of keeping it at bay. When I got home, the decrepit cottage and worrying about Charity would all come rushing back. I hoped the crime scene vehicles would be gone and my street would be quiet and empty again. I hoped I had no further visits from Malcolm Kinsman. I doubted that I'd seen the last of him, but if he showed up in Maine, I planned to make him Andre's problem.

"More like somebody dies and then you go," she said. "That's what you get for being Jane Wayne."

I was sure I'd never used that expression with her, though I did sometimes think it to myself. "Jane Wayne?" I said.

"Well, sure. The tall, fearless troubleshooter who rides into town and shuts those bad guys down."

"I am planning to reform," I said.

"I've heard you say that before."

I patted the basketball. "Reforming. This kid is going to take all my energy."

She pantomimed shock. "You'd leave all these poor schools in the lurch? Leave them to wallow in cheating and drugs and campus scandal?"

"That's the plan. I have had my fill of dead bodies."

She shook her head. "Never happen. You were born to rescue people."

"How about you take a turn? I am going to devote myself to diapers and onesies."

She shook her head again. "In your dreams. Little MOC is going to be tucked into a baby carrier and the two of you will set off to right the wrongs of the world." She grinned. "I hope MOC is a girl. Mock Kozak, girl detective. Or will be she be Mock Lemieux? Nah. That doesn't sound right."

We really hadn't figured out what the kid's name would be, but Claudine Lemieux was a fine name. Better than Claudine Kozak. So were Mason or Oliver. The brat, who I am convinced can read my thoughts, kicked me.

I went back to my speech and LaDonna to her report. It was quiet in the room except for the tapping of keys until she said, "Did you locate a printer we can use?"

I hadn't. "Try hitting 'print' and see what happens. There's probably a network. I saw a printer outside Dr. Kingsley's office."

She shrugged and did. I followed shortly after with the text of my speech. Moments later, there was knock on the door, and Dr. Kingsley's very efficient assistant was there with a handful of papers.

"Got them just in time," she breathed. "Kiara, one of the girls mentioned in your report, is helping out in the office today. That would have been a heck of a mess."

"Sorry." LaDonna ducked her head like a chastened twelve-year-old.

We took our papers, and she left.

I scanned my speech. LaDonna scanned her report. Then we gathered our things and went to Dr. Kingsley's office. Leora Simms was with her, and both women looked stricken.

"What's wrong?" I said.

"It's Jesper," Dr. Kingsley said. "Security says he left campus half an hour ago and he had one of our students with him. Her roommate says she packed her things and left without an explanation."

"Is she over eighteen?" I asked.

Leora shook her head.

"So that gives us some leverage," I said. "Has anyone tried calling him?"

"We have," Dr. Kingsley said. "He didn't answer."

"Give me his phone number," I said. "And you'd better get in touch with his uncle. Your board member. Maybe he has some sway. At this point, things can still be worked out, but if he doesn't come back, admit what he's done, and get himself quietly fired, he's ruined his chances of ever getting another teaching job. Possibly any good job."

Okay. Yes, I can be a weasel sometimes. As an employer, I get as annoyed as anyone when I hire someone with a checkered past because former employers fudge their references. But right now, our goal was getting him—and the student—back here, using whatever promises we had to make. The man was obviously a self-centered idiot with no impulse control. Running away with a student did harm not only to himself and the girl's future, but to the future of the program, and it was an important program. After the girl was safely back and the immediate situation dealt with, they could let him go under any conditions they chose.

I put his number in my phone and sent him a text: Bring that girl back right now and things can be worked out. Otherwise, we'll contact the police and accuse you of kidnapping and violating Maryland law. Do you really want that?

I waited to see if he'd respond while Dr. Kingsley made a call to the uncle who'd pressured them to hire this idiot. As she quietly explained the situation, my phone buzzed with an incoming text that read: Who is this?

I showed it to LaDonna, then texted back: Your worst nightmare.

His text: What law?

My text: The one forbidding relationships between teachers and students. We have your emails, BTW.

His text: WTF?

I put my phone down. I wasn't playing this game because it wasn't a game. He'd been warned. If he wanted to throw his future away for a seventeen-year-old hottie—his future and possibly hers— that was on him.

"Jesper's uncle is going to call him," Dr. Kingsley said. "He did not sound happy. I got the impression he thought we should have found a way to cover it up. But that's not how we do business, as he should know." She looked at her watch. "Should we go ahead with the assembly?"

I shrugged. "Why not? Seems like emphasizing the honor code and responsible behavior is more important than ever."

I showed her the texts on my phone. "Either he comes back, or he doesn't. We have given him fair warning."

"Right," Dr. Kingsley said. "If he's not back by the time we finish the assembly, we *will* call the police."

So I gave my speech, which LaDonna said wasn't nearly as incoherent as it felt, and I saw a lot of surprise and the dawning of understanding on some of the upturned faces. By the time the speech was done, I was done. Ready to head home and put my feet up while Andre reheated more of Rosie's great food.

Luckily, when we got back to Dr. Kingsley's office, security called to report that Jesper DiSantis's car had just arrived back on campus, and the missing student was with him.

"I think we've got this from here, Thea," she said. "Without too much damage to our program, I hope. Thanks for everything. When we get the final honor code put together, I'd like to run it past you before we send it to our trustees."

That was fine with me.

Dr. Kingsley turned to LaDonna. "Your report is excellent. Exactly what we needed. I…we all so much appreciate your taking the time to come today and help us out." She gave LaDonna her card. "So you can send us your bill."

"Glad I could help," LaDonna said, tucking the card away. As we headed out to my car, we paused to watch two serious-looking men in security uniforms escorting Jesper DiSantis into the building.

"What was he thinking?" she said.

"He wasn't thinking, LaDonna," I said. "He was panicking. Once he realized that you'd be able to trace the leak to him, and get his emails to his female students, he didn't know what to do, so he just acted on impulse. Very stupid impulse. What was he going to do with no job, a ruined future, and an adoring seventeen-year-old high school drop-out?"

"None of that is fixed by his coming back, either," she said.

"Well, in my experience, schools are big on avoiding negative publicity, so I expect he'll quietly resign and his doting uncle will find him a job somewhere else. Hopefully, the girl can continue with the program."

"I hope it's someplace where he can't do much damage," she said. "I think he was counting on the fact that Luke Bascomb has the computer skills of a well-trained retriever."

"That's unkind."

"That's reality. Anyone with good computer skills would be somewhere pulling down the big bucks."

"Like you."

"Yup. Like me. I'm so cool."

"That you are. Thanks for doing this."

"Always happy to help out my big sister Thea."

I felt a pang at that. LaDonna would make a great little sister. I'd been a real big sister once, and I still missed my little, lost adopted sister, Carrie. Investigating Carrie's death was how I met

Andre, but that silver lining would always be surrounded by a big, dark cloud.

As we headed back to BWI, LaDonna said, "I know I said I'd like to stay here, but actually, I was afraid we would get stuck here overnight. Or you would, and you're my ride. I have a hot date waiting for me at home."

"Hot date?"

She grinned. "I got a dog. A Jack Russell terrier. She's the cutest thing ever, and she has a lot of energy, which means I get regular walks."

So we headed back to the airport, LaDonna babbling happily about her brilliant and adorable dog. I was glad she was carrying the conversational load. I was toast. I hoped that when I got on the plane, no strange men would plop down in the seat beside me and attempt a useless interrogation. Of course, remembering Malcolm Kinsman brought back all my worries about his missing sister, worries I couldn't successfully push away.

Luckily, by the time I was on the plane and heading back to Portland, the day's adventures had left me so worn out, I slept all the way home. I was excited about being the mother of MOC, whoever he or she might be, but the demands of pregnancy on top of a more than full-time job were not my cup of tea.

FOURTEEN

I paused in my car before driving home to check the emails, texts, and voice mails that had been piling up while I was snoozing on a plane. There was a cryptic text from Suzanne that just said, "Call me." An email from Bobby saying that the King School board wanted to meet with me tomorrow to discuss what he and Lindsay had found, and develop a media strategy to parallel their legal strategy. Bobby said the meeting was tentatively scheduled for ten-thirty and hoped that would work for me. He thought I should take Lindsay along.

Oh goody. A more than two-hour drive in Massachusetts morning traffic. I sighed and sent him an email saying that would be fine, then called Lindsay to see if she wanted to come along. Wanted? She was thrilled. I said I'd meet her at the office, and also gave her numbers for Emmett and the King School's main office, in case she had a problem or wanted to drive herself.

Then, though Suzanne's ominous 'call me' messages always involve a complication in the lives of EDGE Consulting, I called her. "What's going on?" I asked, when she answered.

"Jason disappearing and inappropriate behavior with Lindsay. And Marlene was crying in the bathroom."

"I thought we vetted these people? Did you talk to them?"

"Marlene admits she fudged her experience and confessed that she has a problem with deadlines. She freezes and can't do the work."

"Did you suggest a good therapist?"

"I suggested that she keep trying, that she's not on a deadline, she has great samples to work from, and you gave her the necessary feedback. I pretty much pitched it as fill in the blank. I even asked if she'd ever played those kids games where you put a word in the blank—a noun, a verb, and adjective, what are they called? Ad Libs? I pretty much treated her like Paul, Jr. when he's having his four-thirty tantrum. In short, I am trying not to have to go back to the pool of appalling applicants quite yet."

Ah. The life of a consultant is never dull.

"What about Jason?" I asked, unsure that I wanted to hear the answer.

"Girlfriend trouble. She was having a meltdown. He thought he could sort it quickly, then was afraid to leave her."

"I don't believe it."

"Neither do I. More likely something he didn't dare tell us about. He showed up today like nothing had happened. Let's see if it happens again. Or if he even shows up tomorrow. Because if we lose him, we risk losing Bobby as well. When Bobby gets stressed and overworked, he begins to listen to Quinn, and we both know what Quinn thinks. We can't let that happen. I'll keep a close eye on Jason tomorrow. I hope it doesn't come down to monitoring his social media."

That was something we put in the employment contract. A lot of younger people don't yet understand that work hours belong to the employer, and do their shopping, chatting, and monitoring their friends' social media posts while they're at work, carrying over habits from college. A small amount, during breaks or lunch, wasn't a problem. Checking in twenty or fifty times a day was.

"We can talk about the Lindsay thing when you're back in the office. You're lucky you're working from home. Things around here are feeling more than a little anxious," she said.

"Who's working from home?" I said. "I was at Eastern Shore Academy today and it looks like I'll be at the King School tomorrow. What am I going to do when this baby comes?"

"Love it. And keep working from home."

"Right now, working from home means looking at the house across the street, where two people were murdered."

Suzanne decided to ignore that. My proximity to violence and death makes her nervous. "Not your problem," she said. "Go sit on the back deck where you can't see that house."

I chose not to share my involvement in those murders, such as it was. Suzanne is always counseling me to avoid getting involved. She seems to believe I bring these things on myself. I don't think that's fair. I may have a soft spot for vulnerable people, but I didn't ring Charity's doorbell. She rang mine.

"King should go smoothly. I understand Bobby and Lindsay found some very useful material on social media. Let's talk tomorrow," she said.

"In case you didn't know, here's a bit of good news. Lindsay will be finishing her senior year in December, and would love to come and work for us."

Suzanne was silent for a moment, then she said, "That is beyond wonderful."

I absolutely agreed.

The drive home was uneventful, if slow, and I was back in time to enjoy the last of the day's light on the back deck. Summer evening light is so soft and lovely, and the air was full of flowers and the green smells of cut grass and hay. Also, the impassioned noises of insects looking for love. I'd never lived in the country before. Never expected I would. And here I was, loving it.

Andre had something warming in the oven that smelled delicious, and he was sitting with me in the adjacent Adirondack chair. He was drinking beer, a locally brewed IPA he'd recently discovered. Seems like there is a brewery on every corner these days. Regular, micro, or nano. I don't know who drinks all that beer.

I had iced tea and lemonade and wished there was a bit of

vodka involved. I used to like to unwind with a glass of wine or a drink after a long day.

We were watching mama deer and her baby puzzling at the deer fence, looking longingly at my lettuce and chard and other yummy things on the other side of the barrier.

"She makes me feel mean," I said.

"Mean enough to let her eat your garden?"

"Nope. Just a twinge of meanness."

We watched the two of them turn away, discouraged, and trot back to the woods. Someone else would have to provide tonight's salad.

"What's happening with the...uh...with your investigation next door?"

"He was stunned with a rock, then shot. She was shot."

"Witnesses? Weapon? Prints? Evidence?"

"You sound like a detective's wife."

"Am a detective's wife. One who is sometimes mistaken for a cop herself."

"Poor thing."

"That's it? The bad guy or gal didn't leave a note? Footprint? Carelessly discarded cigarette butt?"

"We've got some stuff we're looking at." He reached over and took my hand. "This is supposed to be our home, our place where the world of crime doesn't intrude."

"Except by phone."

He sighed. "Except by phone."

"No sign of Charity Kinsman?"

"Not yet. She was there. You saw that. But she seems to have vanished. For now. Of course we've got the feds breathing down our necks, doing their self-important thing like we're the ones who killed their inspector and lost the woman they're supposed to protect."

"They tell you why she needs protection?"

"The feds? Be serious, Thea. They don't share information, they just demand it."

"Just like on TV?"

"Worse than on TV."

"So I had a weird thing happen today."

He sat up straighter and took my hand. Far too many of the weird things that happen to me are of the dangerous variety. "What?" he said. "Something at the school?"

"Something on the plane."

He waited, veneering a husband's impatience with a cop's ability to wait, while I figured out how I wanted to tell the story.

"I was in my seat on the plane. An aisle, you know, since I hate middles and windows and having to climb over people to use the restroom. Which in my current state is all the time."

He nodded.

"A guy got on and sat in the middle seat. The plane wasn't that full. He could have had the window. An obnoxious guy. He was looking at my work, and made a disparaging comment about honor codes. He was annoying me, so I put on my headphones to shut him out, and, quite abruptly, he disconnected them and said 'we need to talk.'"

"Mmm hmm. A jerk," Andre said, giving off a protective husband vibe. "And?"

"And I tried not to get drawn in. You know that MOC and I are trying to live a stress-free life."

He laughed.

I was trying to remember the sequence, which weariness and my hormone-soaked brain wasn't making easy. "Then he didn't talk. Didn't introduce himself. He seemed to think I'd know who he was and why he was there. So I challenged him, and he still didn't introduce himself, and suddenly, looking at him, I realized that he was Charity Kinsman's brother. Her twin brother, it turned out. He wanted to know where she was and didn't believe me when I told him I didn't know. He said he and Charity had talked and she'd told him she thought I could be trusted."

"Trusted with what?"

I shrugged. "I don't know. Her secrets? Only she didn't share any. Keeping her safe? I never knew she needed to be. He said that she'd told him I was an excellent detective."

"You would make an excellent detective, you know. Except maybe for your too-tender heart."

"Like you don't have a tender heart?" I said.

"Only for you. Go on."

"I told him she'd made a mistake. I was a consultant, not a detective. I told him everything about my contact with Charity. All two times of it. I even told him about the pot of flowers. He didn't believe me."

"How did he know you'd be on that plane?"

"I have no idea, and he wouldn't explain. He never explained anything. But you know that picture I gave you last night, the one I found in Charity's room of the guy in uniform? The one of the guy who is named David Peckham, who is Charity's husband?"

He nodded, and politely didn't ask how I knew about David Peckham.

"Well, he showed me another photo. This one of himself, his name is Malcolm Kinsman, with David Peckham. But I still don't know how he found me. Or anything about Peckham. Or why he is missing. Well, except some very vague speculation."

"What was his vague speculation?" Andre interrupted.

I tried to remember what Kinsman had said. "My vague speculation. He said David is missing and there's suspicion that he may be a prisoner, held for information. He said there's concern that the people who are holding him want to use Charity as a lever to persuade him to…uh…talk. But he didn't tell me who might be holding him or what he or they were doing that got Charity's husband into this situation, so I have no idea who might be looking for her."

I sipped my drink and longed for that bit of vodka. "I asked some follow-up questions and got nothing. He said he wasn't authorized to tell me."

"I wish I did have some idea where Charity might have gone. If that ratty house is the best the government could do, I couldn't imagine what they'd have for backup, if they even had a backup. Do you know if they're sending someone to take their dead agent's place?"

I stopped babbling. I'd been eager to spill out the unpleasant encounter and hold it up for scrutiny by someone who scrutinizes for a living. While I'd been talking, MOC had begun the nightly ritual, and it was hard to talk while taking sharp blows. I knew this exercise was preparation for life on the outside, but I *was* on the outside. I patted the aggressive little bugger and said, "So get born already, if you're so bored in there. I promise mama will take you to gymnastics as soon as you're old enough to walk."

Andre burst out laughing. "I'm sorry," he said, "but you, pregnant, is one of the funniest things ever."

"Thanks a lot, Mister. It's no walk in the park. You swallow a basketball with more limbs than an octopus and then try to use an airplane toilet."

That made him laugh harder, which made me laugh. I never did get any useful advice about the mysterious Malcolm Kinsman, but we went in to dinner in an excellent mood. Our good mood was not diminished by Rosie's shells with meat sauce, nor by more of her tiramisu. She must have been cooking for a week to produce this feast, and I was not complaining. Except for a few times when I'd been flattened by bad guys and Suzanne pitched in, I couldn't recall a time when anyone had arrived on my doorstep with food.

Except for Andre, of course. We'd reached our first cautious détente over a bag of groceries he'd arrived with while I was cleaning out my sister Carrie's apartment. Unwanted and unwelcomed, he'd proceeded to cook me dinner, and the rest—anger morphing to attraction followed by a series of dramatic ups and downs—was history.

I guess we're still history in the making and MOC will begin a new chapter.

As dark settled in around us, a question about the guy on the plane floated into my mind like words in a Magic 8 Ball. If he had spoken with his sister, why hadn't she told him her plans? Because she believed she was safe? Or believed telling him was unsafe? Even if she had had to leave suddenly, she would likely have taken her phone. She could have updated him. There must have been a reason she didn't. Had he focused on me because of my stupid internet search? His surprise suggested he hadn't known about the two people found dead at his sister's house.

There had been hours between when we found the detective and the woman we believed was Jessica Whitlow dead and when I got on the plane. Hours when Charity could have called him. Why hadn't he come here to look after his sister instead of somehow finding me and getting on my plane? It didn't make much sense. I asked Andre what he thought, and he agreed.

"Nothing about this makes much sense," he agreed. "Like why, if Jessica Whitlow was here with her, was Charity using Whitlow's name? Surely figuring out Whitlow was a federal agent would have a piece of cake for someone who's internet savvy."

"There weren't signs of a second person staying in that house. Not that I saw," I said. "So was Whitlow staying somewhere else and just dropping in to check on Charity? Did she inadvertently bring trouble with her?"

It was a puzzle too big for my tired brain. I said, "Did I tell you I have to go down to Massachusetts for a meeting tomorrow?"

He shook his head. "Did I tell you I have to go up to Bangor for a meeting tomorrow?"

"Nope."

"Just don't have that baby in Massachusetts," he said. "I want MOC to be a Maniac right from the start."

"Fear not. Our child is going to be a maniac."

"You know what I mean."

On the plane, I'd been looking forward to a warm bath and an early night, and that's where I was heading after we finished the dishes. But quiet and the job of homicide detective, never mind the job of a crisis consultant, was often not in the cards. I was upstairs, gathering nightgown and robe, visions of lavender bubble bath in my head, when someone knocked on the door.

"You go ahead with your bath. I'll get it," Andre said.

After nine was not a proper hour for visitors. That meant we were likely receiving a visit from some form of the constabulary, never mind that we *were* some form of constabulary. I lingered in the bedroom with the door open as he answered the door and admitted a man and a woman. I could tell that much from their voices.

"Is your wife home?" the female voice asked.

"She's gone up to bed."

"We need to speak with her," the man said.

There was no reason for them to be here. I held my breath, waiting to hear what Andre would say.

"And you are?" he asked.

I could hear the rustle of IDs being produced. A long silence while Andre examined them.

"What's the nature of your business with my wife?" he asked.

"It's about Charity Kinsman," the man said. "It is urgent that we find her."

Send them away. I beamed the thought to Andre. He knew everything I knew, and none of it would help find Charity.

He must have been seeing something I wasn't hearing, because he said, "Let me see if she's still awake. Why don't you go sit in the living room and I'll be right back."

I quietly closed the bedroom door. Why was he doing this? It was late. I was tired and in no mood to speak with more people who would act like Malcolm Kinsman. Demanding. Skeptical. Unbelieving. I was too tired, and I had to get up early in the morning.

MOC agreed. It was the baby hour, when the little beast got to frolic. To be sure I understood, I was given a couple of hard kicks. I grabbed my side, groaning, trying not to curse my child. That's when Andre opened the door, and immediately went into dad-to-be mode. "Is it the baby?" he asked.

"Not getting born. Just kicking. This may not be an acrobat. It may be a kickboxer."

"What joy," he said. "I'm afraid we have visitors."

"What do they want?"

"You."

"Who are they?"

"Marshals Service."

I dropped onto the edge of the bed, shaking my head. "Tell

them they can't have me. Tell them I don't know anything. You know I don't have anything to tell them."

"It's important," said a voice from the doorway. The two pushy, impudent SOBs hadn't bothered to wait downstairs. They were right there in my bedroom door.

FIFTEEN

L iving with Andre, watching him struggle to solve cases and get justice for victims when witnesses aren't forthcoming, has given me a lot of incentive to cooperate with public safety when they need my help. But not right now. Not when they've barged into my bedroom and invaded my personal space.

Andre read the situation and wisely got out of my way.

"You were asked to wait in the living room, weren't you?" I asked.

The man didn't respond. The woman nodded.

"So go back down there and wait."

The woman looked at the man, who said, "Look, Ms. Kozak, it's urgent. We need—"

"You need to go back downstairs and wait in the living room. I am not having this conversation, or any conversation about death or violence or Charity Kinsman in my bedroom."

Andre probably didn't care so much. He was willing to interview anyone, anywhere, that would advance an investigation. I was sure these two were the same. But I was a woman whose last dream house had been tainted by a body in the living room. I was not tainting this bedroom with an interrogation. I just wasn't.

MOC, who didn't want to be left out, delivered a solid kick that made me gasp.

"Are you all right?" the woman asked.

Through gritted teeth, I said, "Go. Downstairs. Now."

I dropped onto the edge of the bed, feeling ridiculous having to argue with intrusive strangers while clutching my frilly blue night-gown. I watched my chances of a soothing bath vanish.

When they finally left, it felt like there was more air in the bedroom. Between Kinsman on the plane and my work at Eastern Shore, I'd had enough human contact. Or conflict. Or demands. I dumped my things on the bed and stood up. "You didn't have to let them in," I said.

"But you might be able to help," he said.

That didn't improve my temper. "How? I don't know anything I haven't already shared. You could have told them that. Are they legitimate? Did you check their IDs?"

His sigh might have been prompted by our unwanted guests or by my stubbornness. I really didn't care. "They have Marshals Service IDs," he said. "And they did apologize for the intrusion."

"Not to me." I glanced down at my bare feet. It seemed almost indecent to entertain agents of our federal government in bare feet, but putting on shoes was too hard right now. I put them on in the morning when I had to, and took them off when I got home. That was enough. I gestured toward the door, "Lead on," I said. I let him go first, and heard him offer them coffee as I followed him down the stairs.

One of the agents was in "my chair" and the other seemed to be taking up most of the couch, which didn't seem very friendly to me, given that they were invading my house. I settled for Andre's chair. He invited them in, he could shove the couch-hog aside. I held out my hand to the woman who'd had the temerity to barge into my bedroom.

"Your credentials."

For a moment, I thought she was going to refuse, that showing them to the man of the house should have been enough. Then she pulled out the folder and gave it to me. Her name was Alice

Harmon and yes, it appeared that she did work for the Marshals Service. Of course, I didn't know how easy it was to fake such documents. I gave it back and got his. Frederick Olson. Alice and Fred sounded so small-town and old fashioned. Harmon and Olson like a law firm.

"So why are you here?" I asked.

"We already told your—"

"Don't do that," I interrupted. He looked surprised, so I explained. "I have no idea what you told my husband, do I?"

Gad. Did they think we were living in the nineteen fifties? Even back then, when Andre would have been the anointed head of the household and I was just the little woman, I still wouldn't have known what they'd told Andre.

The woman. Alice. Maybe thinking a softer, gentler touch was called for, said, "We need to speak with you about Charity Kinsman."

I waited for a question. My silence seemed to puzzle her, which was odd, because she was a professional with a government agency and I a mere consultant. But silence was a powerful thing, and I didn't surrender mine easily.

Finally, she said, "About what Charity has told you regarding her situation, and about where she has gone."

What was it with these people? Why did everyone think I was Charity's confidant and knew where she'd gone?

"The only thing I know about her situation is that she was moving into the cottage across the street and fixing up for herself and her baby. That she's having a girl and plans to name her Amaryllis and call her Amy. That the baby's father picked the name."

I stopped because that really was all I knew.

"You never met Jessica Whitlow?"

"I was never introduced to Jessica Whitlow. I did meet someone who may have been Jessica Whitlow in the driveway when she helped Charity and me get a crib off the roof of my car."

"Did Charity tell you anything about her?"

"No."

"Did you ever see Jessica at the cottage?"

I couldn't see how this would help, but I said, "Besides her helping with the crib? From my window, I saw the woman I now believe is Charity Kinsman standing in her driveway appearing to be having an argument with a taller blonde woman. There was a black Honda parked in the driveway."

"What were they arguing about?" the man asked.

Cripes, I was missing sleep for this? I decided to go with silence again. Then, figuring a demonstration was best, I said, "Come with me."

I led them back upstairs to the big window in the hall that looked down over our rolling lawn to the street. I pointed at the window. "I saw them from here. Obviously, I couldn't hear what they were saying. Only that the woman who had introduced herself as Jessica, who I now believe is Charity, seemed angry."

I went back downstairs. My feet hurt. My back ached from the airplane seats.

In the living room, we took our places again as Andre came in with coffee and a plate of cookies that Rosie must have brought. I had the mean thought that I didn't want to waste her good food on these two. Coffee was handed around, and then the man said, "Did Charity tell you about her situation?"

"She was very careful not to reveal anything about herself, other than what I've already told you about her and the baby."

I looked at Andre, unsure whether I should tell them about the note and the little box of IDs.

He nodded.

"When I came back from my doctor's appointment two days ago, there was a note on the floor of the hall that had been pushed under the door."

"We need the note," Alice said.

"We have it. The state police," Andre said. "Part of our homicide investigation. We also have the box mentioned in the note and its contents. I can give you photos, or if you want to come to the crime lab, we can show you the actual items."

"We need it all," the man said.

Now Andre was also being quiet.

This was getting them nowhere and I needed sleep if I was going to function in the morning. A functioning brain is what they pay me the big bucks for.

"I'm sorry," I said, "but we don't have anything else for you. I have to sleep. I have a meeting down in Massachusetts in the morning."

Neither of them appeared to have heard me.

"Why were you searching Charity's name on the internet last night?" the man said.

"Because I was worried about her. And curious about who she was and why she was here."

"Are you aware that other people are also looking for her?"

I considered that. "Not aware, as in having any knowledge of her situation, but my instincts and experience suggested she was in trouble, and I was worried about a woman as pregnant as she is on her own. I wondered if she, or she and Jessica, had a back-up plan for her. I hoped they did. I don't really know what I was looking for. Maybe just some clues about what her story was. Is."

"You may have tipped off some very bad people about her whereabouts," the man said unpleasantly.

I looked at Andre again. "Look," I said. "Don't try and guilt me. There were two men in a black SUV looking for her long before I went on the internet, and one of them ended up dead along with Jessica Whitlow right across the street. If there are ill-intentioned people looking for her, they may have already found her. For all I know, they might have taken Charity and stashed her somewhere. But instead of looking for her, you're here asking me useless questions when I don't know anything that can help."

Talking to them—so expressionless and unresponsive—was like talking to cardboard cutouts instead of humans. Did they seriously think I knew anything that could be useful, based on a few brief encounters?

Unmoved, the man reached into an inside pocket of his jacket, crossed the room, and tossed a photograph in my lap. Tossing it? Seriously? Their behavior didn't make sense. It was almost as if they were trying to act the part of tough government agents.

Without touching it, I looked down. It was the same picture Malcolm Kinsman had showed me this morning on the plane.

"Do you know who these two men are?"

I nodded.

Andre gave me a funny look. Didn't he remember me telling him the story of the annoying man on the plane? "You should look at this," I told him. He picked up the photo.

Now Fred, pinch-faced and zeroed in on me, was the one who waited. He looked like he was springing a "gotcha!" though I didn't yet have any idea what he'd got.

"Charity's husband, David Peckham," I said. "I learned it from my internet search after I found a picture of him in the cottage."

Fred nodded. "And the other man?"

"Charity's twin brother, Malcolm Kinsman."

He hadn't expected me to know the second man, I realized, as he sprang out of his chair and leaned right into my face. "How the hell do you know about Malcolm Kinsman?"

SIXTEEN

A ndre got him out of my face with two words and an ungentle hand on his shoulder. His "Sit down," was not a request, it was a command. There were paragraphs about how they'd misread the situation in those two words.

Maybe they hadn't done their homework and didn't know who they were dealing with. Maybe his accommodating invitation to come in and how he'd gently pushed me to cooperate had misled them, as had his polite offer of coffee. Maybe they had no manners or social proprioception and thought nothing of bullying a pregnant woman in her own home.

The guy sat.

"Now it's your turn to answer some questions," Andre said. "We've had enough bullying about Charity Kinsman's situation, first from a Boston detective who claimed to be working for the government, and now from you two. My wife has told you what she knows. It's time we got some background on the situation. Who is Charity Kinsman, why is the Marshals Service involved, and who, besides you, is looking for her?"

The woman, Alice, got as far as, "We can't..." before Andre held up a hand.

"We've got two homicides connected to Charity Kinsman, one body found in her driveway, the other in her house, so don't play the 'government secrets' card with me. Your information is critical to our investigation."

Alice said, "It's confidential and…"

She looked at Fred, and there was something in that look. Maybe he was her boss and she was looking for direction, but I thought it was something else, though I didn't know what. Maybe the real detective in the room had some thoughts.

Andre looked at the two of them. "We've been trying to get information about Jessica Whitlow from the Marshals Service and getting stonewalled. You're here. You can share information with us, or you can go."

"But…" Fred began.

"No buts."

Neither of them volunteered anything.

"We're all in the business of protecting people," Andre said. "It's not a one-way street."

They sat there like two lumps.

Andre stood. "This is a waste of time. I'll show you out."

I stood, too. "And I'm going to bed. I'd say good luck, because I believe Charity needs some luck, but your attitude and approach couldn't possibly help anyone."

Fred started to say something about Malcolm Kinsman, but it was a question, not an answer. I went upstairs.

I heard the door shut and a car start. Then Andre's feet on the stairs. The thump and creak reminded me that we still needed to get them carpeted before MOC arrived. Old houses have many charms, but creaky stairs are not among them.

He was shaking his head as he came into the bedroom. "I shouldn't be surprised at that, yet I am. There's something off about those two."

"And you're the cool-headed professional," I said from my cocoon in the covers. "I'm just the little woman."

"Little?" he said.

I started to giggle, which was something I rarely did, especially when I was tired and annoyed. But it was funny. "Little whale," I said. "Whale with sore feet and a backache."

"Poor whale."

"So you'll check them out, right? See if there really are two Marshals Service agents named Alice and Fred?"

"I will."

He undressed and got into bed, snuggling against me.

Watching Andre undress is delicious. I'm sometimes almost overcome by the urge to throw open the window and yell to the world at large, "And he's mine. All mine." I am good at repressing such idiotic impulses, though.

"You okay?" he said. "Sure you should be driving to Massachusetts tomorrow?"

"I am a slave of duty," I said. "It's just outside Boston. Not a big deal. And I have to do what I can to haul Denzel's ass out of the fire."

"Not literally, I hope."

"Not in this condition. One of these days, I'm going to let him crash and burn."

"No, you won't. You're a rescuer, even of those who shouldn't need it."

"I'm trying to reform."

He laughed.

"I won't be driving alone. We've got a great intern, Lindsay, who will be coming with me."

"Makes me feel better. Be sure to text me her number so I can send her a thousand texts checking up on you." He put a big hand protectively over MOC, and seconds later, he was asleep.

I was envious. Sleeping was hard these days. Tonight it was especially hard. I couldn't stop thinking about Charity. Whether she was okay. Wondering why Fred and Alice had had such a dramatic reaction when I identified Malcolm Kinsman. Was it possible he was an estranged twin? That his interest in finding Charity wasn't fraternal but malevolent? I couldn't answer that question, but before I finally fell asleep, I spent some time berating myself for doing an internet search that might have put Charity at risk.

But she'd already been at risk. Already found by people willing to commit murder. Where had she gone? Was it voluntary, or had she been taken? Why weren't Fred and Alice more focused on that, and if they were truly concerned, why not share information that might help find Charity?

I hated information voids. I liked solving problems working with data and people's stories. But unless I learned something new, there was nothing I could do to help her.

I finally fell asleep, a delicious, restful sleep that was interrupted by MOC, whose nocturnal activities seems to be getting longer and more frequent. It's a weird feeling to be occupied by another human, especially one who was so willful. I know. My mother would say I deserved it because I'd been busy and difficult. That really didn't help.

All too soon, my melodious alarm was summoning me to the day. I put on the clothes I'd laid out and went downstairs, carrying my shoes. I made a cup of the half-caf I was allowing myself and poached an egg while I made toast. In the back yard, mama deer was staring hungrily at the lettuce again, her woeful face making me feel guilty. But dang it, it was summer. The world was full of tasty things to eat. I went out to tell her that, but she skipped away in a few graceful bounds. I lingered to inhale the fresh green scents of summer, then ate my egg and sat to put on my shoes.

I won't describe the comic antics involved. Suffice it to say, by the time I got them on, I was sweating, and my back hurt.

Andre appeared, freshly showered and shirtless, and I fought the temptation to blow off Denzel and The King School.

"Team meeting today about those murders," he said. "My boss isn't going to be pleased that I couldn't pry anything out of Fred and Alice."

"You weren't allowed to use physical force," I said. "Think you'll be home for dinner?"

"That's the plan." He carried his coffee out to the back deck, and I followed.

"You love this house, don't you?" I said.

"I do."

"We need to carpet those stairs."

"On my list."

"Soon," I said. We were getting so domestic.

"When do you have to leave?"

"Ten minutes."

"So sit for a minute and tell me again about your encounter with Malcolm Kinsman."

I sat and I told, but the useful stuff was what we didn't know— what his relationship with his sister was, his relationship with David Peckham, what Peckham's situation was, and how he knew I was going to be on that plane. It seemed like such an elaborate way to ask about what I knew, and Andre and I both agreed the little I did know wasn't much help in locating Charity.

"If he wanted to find her, and he *could* find me, why not come here?" I said.

"I don't know. But I don't like it. I don't like the idea of you here alone with so many people targeting you for information."

His concern was disturbing. "You're scaring me, Andre. What am I supposed to do? Stay at the office until you get home? What if you get caught up in an investigation?"

"Sorry," he said, patting my hand. "I didn't mean to scare you. I guess we'll just play it by ear."

It was time to go. He carried my briefcase to the Jeep and gave me a kiss that made me not want to leave. The man knows his power.

I made an affirmative effort to put my concerns about Charity, and murder, and people driving black SUVs out of my mind, and moved on to the subject of the day—pulling Denzel's ass out of the fire.

I picked up Lindsay at the office and hit the road. Until we left Maine, the bad traffic was coming north, but as soon as we crossed the bridge in Kittery, we were in the perpetual sludge of New Hampshire and Massachusetts traffic.

Lindsay was quiet at first, but after a bit, she said, "Bobby thinks that stuff I found online will be really helpful. Do you?"

"I do. So, you want to know who will be at the meeting today?"

"Please."

"Okay. We're going to The King School. Did you read up about it? An alternative private school founded for the specific purpose of giving young Black males a chance to succeed. The founder and inspiration—and the subject of today's meeting—is the headmaster, Denzel Ellis-Jackson. His right-hand woman is Yanita Emery, assistant head. She handles a lot of the day-to-day business and does some of their PR work. The lawyer helping to sort this mess out is also on the King board. His name is Emmett Hampton. Arleigh Davis, who is head of the board, may also be there. All four are African American."

"What should I know about these people?"

It was a good question. I considered. "Well, for starters, prepare yourself, because Denzel is a gorgeous man and as charming as he is good-looking. He's a visionary, and the energy behind the school. He's had a few problems with the ladies. We were called in once before when he was accused of assault…"

"You defended a man accused of assault?" she said, and I was reminded how young she was and that her world was permeated with Me Too issues.

"No. I helped a client school handle a potential scandal that could have affected their image and impair their ability to raise the funds to pursue their mission of giving boys without a chance that chance."

"But if he…"

"But he *didn't*. An accusation is the beginning, not the end. It's an assertion that needs investigation. It's not proof or a conviction. So we investigated. Found that the young woman who had accused him had a history of doing this. A history in which her false accusations had done serious damage to people's careers and families."

She got as far as another "But…" when the car in front of me suddenly slammed on its brakes, and I hit mine, missing their bumper by inches. Lindsay gave a screech and curled into a ball.

"Hey," I said. "Are you okay?"

From behind her arms came a tiny, "No."

Okay. I knew what this was. I'd been there myself. "You were in an accident pretty recently, weren't you?" I said. "A very scary one. Do you want to talk about it?"

We drove on, the traffic just as crazy and me being more careful. Gradually she uncurled. She said, "I've never really talked about it, except to the police."

"Your call, but I've been there. I know sometimes it helps to talk about it."

She sighed. "My ex-boyfriend, Devon. He…"

Siri announced our exit was coming, and Lindsay stopped.

"Go on," I said.

"We were at a party, back in the spring. An off-campus party at someone's house. They had a pool and a big yard. It was great. Only Devon…he liked to drink, and he'd had too much. When we left, I asked him to give me the keys and let me drive. But he was… uh…he was into this macho thing where he had to prove he was fine to drive, wasn't some wimp who couldn't drink and drive. I was terrified, but stupidly, instead of insisting that I drive, or getting a ride with someone else, I did what he wanted and got in the car."

Siri announced another turn. In half a mile, we'd be heading up the long drive to the mansion that formed the central building at the King School, a gift from a successful Black entrepreneur who supported Denzel's mission.

"We're almost there," I said. "Guess we'll have to finish your story on the way home. If you still want to talk about it."

She sighed. "I was just getting to the part where he hit the kid."

SEVENTEEN

A power quartet—Arleigh, Denzel, Yanita, and Emmett—
awaited us in what had once been a mansion's grand dining
room and now served as the school's board room. I introduced
Lindsay as our new social media maven, Yanita offered coffee and
muffins, and we sat down and dug in.

It seemed like my girth had expanded overnight. I could barely
get my chair close enough to the table to reach my papers. No one
tells you about these things when you read about what to expect
when you're expecting. I'm not sure how it would help anyway, since
getting longer arms or suddenly acquiring a servant to tie my shoes
weren't possibilities.

They were all looking to me to take the lead, so I dove in,
starting by asking Emmett for his opinion on the rap song and other
video footage and social media postings that Lindsay had found.
"Would it be useful to broadcast it, use it to create a counter-narra-
tive about the events, or do you want to keep it to use in court?"

Then I realized I needed to back up. "Yanita, you've seen the
song, and some of those posts boasting about what they were going
to do. Have you been able to identify the actors, and are they the
same boys involved in the altercation?"

"Yes. And yes. The boy whose parents are threatening to sue is the—I'm not sure what to call him?—lead singer? Head rapper? I'm afraid my rap and hip hop days are pretty long ago."

To the four of them, I said, "Have the boy's parents seen the video? Has his attorney?"

They hadn't, yet. Emmett planned to sit down with the police later today, and with the boy's attorney after that.

"Now, we've had some back and forth, and I've seen the videos and photos, but I haven't heard Denzel's personal account of the event." I looked at him. "Could you?"

"I was a fool to let myself get sucked in," he said. "But I couldn't just stand there and let him hit me, and if I'd walked away, I would have lost my credibility. This is a boys' school, Thea, and these boys are big on image and respect. As they...or my younger self...might have put it—I couldn't let them disrespect me without responding."

He then launched into a description of the fight that was not what it seemed from the brief clips that the media had shown. The bottom line was that he'd raised his fist to hit back, thought better of it, and pushed his assailant away. The video that was being shown was edited to show his raised fist and the boy staggering back.

I looked at Lindsay. "Do you have video that confirms Denzel's version?"

She nodded. Just as the plotters had been careless about posting their plans, they'd posted longer videos that showed the lead-up and provocation as well as Denzel's hesitation and then the attacker being pushed away.

Sounding aggrieved, Denzel said, "Teenagers or not, my students or not, I should be able to defend myself."

Arleigh raised an eyebrow. Denzel shrugged and fell silent.

"So," I said, "legal strategy is Emmett and Arleigh's department. Protecting the school's image and reputation is mine. I think we've all agreed that much as Denzel wants to go public with his side of the story, maintaining a dignified silence while others speak for him is the better approach."

"Look," Denzel said. "It's my reputation at stake. It's my school that's being impugned. I have to be able to..."

"Sit quietly and listen to what others have to say," Arleigh said. "Much as I wish you hadn't pushed back, I understand the provocation. We've got witnesses. We've got visuals. Your job is to regret an unfortunate situation with an out-of-control student who has impulse-control issues, and get on with running the school."

"But…"

Instead of speaking, Arleigh put a finger to her lips.

Denzel could be a handful, but his team seemed to have developed a system for calming him and moving forward that was impressive. He settled back in his chair, arms folded across his chest, subdued and frustrated. For now, his body language said he'd go along. But he was still something of a wild card.

"If I might…" Lindsay said tentatively.

Everyone's attention switched to my intern.

"One of the problems with cell phone video is that it lacks context. It can focus on a piece of an event without showing all the angles. All the expressions. Often without quality sound, so what the actors are saying is absent. I was…" She looked down at her lap nervously. "I majored in media studies with a minor in film. I could…uh…if you'd like…take the videos that are online, as well as anything you'd like to share, and put together…well, it's not exactly a hot reel. I guess it's more like a movie trailer. A video that shows the premeditation and then gives a fuller and fairer view of the fight. I mean…I don't want to be pushy here. But you're dealing with a population used to getting their information that way."

An intriguing idea, but I envisioned weeks of work and hiring an editing studio, which would be both too late and too expensive for the school. "What equipment would you need to do this, Lindsay?"

She smiled. "My computer? It won't be TV quality, but it will tell the story."

Doable, then. Only part of what we'd have to do, but it was brilliant, and I felt momentarily brilliant for having invited her along. Like me, the King School quartet were hesitant. It's hard to embrace new ideas and approaches. But as part of our messaging, it could be very effective. After some discussion, Arleigh gave Lindsay's suggestion the nod. Then we moved on to the rest of our communication strategy, via press releases and the school's website, as well as a letter to the parents.

"One question," I said. "The boys who were involved, the ones that video evidence shows planning this thing—how are you going to deal with them? I know you have a rule book and an honor code, and I'm sure there are rules about fighting. Have some of your rules been broken?"

"It's a dilemma," Yanita said. "We don't want it to seem like we're retaliating."

"How would you handle this if it were boys fighting among themselves? Or if one of the boys hit another adult on campus?"

"I'd like to get the criminal matter settled first," Emmett said.

"And what about the boy who punched Denzel? You say his parents have filed a lawsuit. Under the circumstances, have you assessed whether they understand he's at risk of being expelled?"

It was leverage. I was sure Emmett was already thinking about it. I just wanted to be sure holding hearings for the involved students on violating the school's conduct code, with the potential implications including suspension and expulsion, was on the table. I wasn't being a weasel. The school couldn't let fighting go unchecked. These students needed to get the message that fighting was unacceptable. Ignoring it risked creating a negative atmosphere for all the students and risked giving them permission for future misbehavior.

Our respective assignments clear, and after I'd gotten a copy of the student conduct manual for Lindsay, I gathered my papers to leave.

It remained to be seen whether the rest of his team could keep Denzel in check. That wasn't EDGE's department, but we'd pulled him out of the fire before. I hoped we could do it this time.

I took a quick bathroom break before we got back in the car, and we headed home. I used to be able to skip from meeting to meeting, all day and all night. Now, a two-hour drive and a two-hour meeting, and I was ready to recline on my chaise and eat bonbons. Too much sitting and my back starts to ache. It didn't look like bonbons were in my future, though. Suzanne needed the two of us to get together as soon as I got back, and then I had to review the questionnaire she'd cajoled Marlene into finishing.

From time to time, I imagine life as a hermit, without the calls and texts and anxious clients and the challenges of staffing our office. Now the hermit option was off the table. The reality was that if I retreated to my mountaintop cave now, I'd have to bring onesies and pacifiers and diapers and swaddling wraps and a whole host of other baby gear. I might as well stick around.

Once we were back on the highway, I said, "That was a great suggestion, Lindsay. You really think you can do it?"

"I know I can," she said. "Actually, I've already started."

"Any chance we can clone you?"

She grinned. "I like to think I'm one of a kind. Glad you liked the idea, though. And can I tell you something?"

I said, "Sure," without wondering what it was. I figured that she was going to finish telling me the story of her drunken boyfriend. Instead, she said, "It's uh…about Jason."

Maybe she knew why he'd disappeared?

"Okay. Unless you're not comfortable, or you'd be betraying a confidence."

"It's not like that. It's…uh…I mean, it's really not my business. He didn't tell me. He was on the phone and I overheard."

I waited, unsure whether she wanted me to pry it out of her or if she was just formulating the story.

"He's got another job. I mean, he has a website design business which he does from home, only I guess he had a client who wasn't happy, or a client that he had to have a meeting with. That's why he disappeared for the afternoon—to go see a client. He didn't want to say anything about where he was going, so he just left. Which, in my opinion, is really dumb. If he's going to keep running a personal business, he needs to do it outside of his hours at EDGE."

She went silent. Then, "I'm not wrong, am I?"

"No. You're not."

"But should I be telling you this? I mean, it's not really my business Only I know it upset Bobby, because he was counting on Jason for something, and then Jason blew him off and…" She stopped.

"It's just...you know...I really like working at EDGE. Bobby is a prince, and I don't think Jason's being fair. I feel kind of like I'm tattling, though, especially after I already told you about the...uh... him touching me."

"Thanks for telling me. It's not your job to worry about us. We're supposed to be worrying about you. But the information is helpful."

I wondered if she had some useful insights into Marlene as well, but asking her wouldn't have been right. She was an intern. We were supposed to be guiding her. Training her. Teaching her about the working world. Encouraging her to gossip about fellow employees should not be part of that training.

———

We rode in silence for a while until I said, "Did you want to tell me the rest of the story about your accident? It's fine if you don't."

"I...uh...well, I guess I do. I mean, I started to, so I should finish."

"There's no 'should' here, Lindsay. It's what you want to share. What you're comfortable with. How we handle our traumas is up to us."

"Yes, Dr. Kozak," she said.

"I'm not trying to analyze you. It's that I've been in a traumatic accident. I know how hard it can be to get back in a car."

She didn't need to know that in my accident I'd been forced off the road by someone trying to kill me. Nor that a lot of my trauma was because people wouldn't believe me. I was met with a wall of disbelief and people judging me for being careless. Nor that there had actually been two such times. Two accidents, two traumas, due to my unfortunate habit of trying to get answers that lead me to bad people.

She stared straight ahead, not looking at me. "Devon was driving too fast. I kept begging him to slow down, which only made him drive faster. He put his hand on my leg and was squeezing it. He had a huge grin on his face, saying how he couldn't wait 'til we got home. We were driving through a residential area, and there was a kid, a teenager, out walking his dog. He was in the crosswalk, and Devon was looking at me instead of the road."

She stopped to catch her breath. "I yelled, 'Devon, watch out! Stop!' but it was too late. He swerved, but he still hit the kid. He wasn't going to stop. Thea. It was so awful. He was just going to drive away and leave that kid and the dog lying there in the street. I grabbed the key, turned off the car, and jumped out. I ran back to help the kid, and he was really messed up. He kept asking if his dog was okay, and I didn't want to tell him it was dead."

She mopped at her face with a tissue. "I called 911, and I sat down beside the kid. I was talking to him and holding his hand. I still had the keys in my other hand, and Devon came up and snatched them and got in his car and drove away."

"Did the kid survive?"

"He did."

"And Devon? What happened with him?"

"He lied to the police. Said I was driving. It was awful. They were able to establish that he was lying, but..." She sighed. "You know what it's like the first time you realize how utterly dishonest a person can be? It's like a trap door opens under your feet, and you never quite trust solid ground again."

"I do." Which was so true. There had been the accidents—like my own, and my husband David's friend driving drunk and killing the man I loved. There had been people I'd trusted who'd turned out to be far from who I thought they were. In fact, too much of my life had involved working with the dangerous and dishonest. That was how I got my white hat and my reputation as the person called in when trouble struck school campuses, as well as within my own family.

"It's hard to know who to trust, difficult to rebuild after your trust has been betrayed," I said.

She nodded. "Here's a good thing, though. There was a cop... uh...police officer who showed up at the scene, and while everyone was treating me like a suspect while they checked out Devon's lie, he believed me. I mean, you know, he didn't say a whole lot. He was kinda far down the pecking order. It was just the way he was there, kind of a comforting presence, and he'd kind of keep me up to date on what was happening when no one else would. And then when it was over and I was cleared, we…uh…we started dating."

I usually liked to use these long drives to think. Mull over what I've heard and plan out where to go next. I used my phone to take messages and memos. I could get a lot of work done while I was driving. Today I wasn't going to get any work done. It was clear that Lindsay needed to talk, and so Dr. Kozak was in.

"Are you still seeing him?"

"I am."

"Your parents know?"

She laughed. "I guess you know what that's like, telling your parents you're dating a cop? I'm not sure I knew what snobs they were until I brought him home to meet them."

I flashed on multiple conversations with my mother. She kept hoping I'd dump Andre—she insisted on calling him Andy—and marry a suitable man.

"Yeah," I said. "I've been there."

Traffic was heavy. The Maine turnpike in July and August is packed with people heading for vacationland, their cars crammed with recreational gear—kayaks on the roof and bikes on their tails, along with boats and jet skis in tow, and giant motorhomes. Oblivious to the challenges of driving these vehicles, drivers were happily chatting on phones or changing lanes without looking. It made driving such an adventure.

Amidst this normal summer chaos, a black SUV came up behind me way too fast—unnecessary since the passing lane traffic was already going over eighty. I moved over a lane to let it pass. I did not have anything to prove out here. It flew past, then braked and jammed itself into the lane in front of me. "Hold on!" I said, hitting the brakes.

I changed lanes and floored it. The Jeep, with its gas-guzzling V-8 engine, responded with a delicious burst of speed just as an 18-wheeler rolled up beside the offending car, trapping it. Truck drivers can often be white knights on the highway.

I kept my foot down for the half-mile until the next exit, then got off and promptly hid myself in a Walmart parking lot. If this was another one of the people looking for Charity Kinsman, they were going too far. I would not tolerate anyone whose behavior threatened MOC.

EIGHTEEN

As soon as I got my breath back, I got on the phone to Andre, telling him what had just happened. "Lindsay and I were rescued by a truck."

"But you're okay?"

"I'm okay. We're both okay."

"You get the plate?"

I gave him what I had. "It happened so fast I didn't get it all. I was focused on getting out of there."

"Where are you?" It was almost a growl, though I knew his anger wasn't meant for me.

I told him where I was, which was about fifteen minutes from the office, that I'd stay off the highway, and that I would be there at least for the next few hours, meeting with Suzanne.

"Call me when you're ready to leave," he said, from which I inferred that I would likely have a police escort for the journey home. I was grateful. I could be both brave and foolish when it came to protecting myself. I wasn't taking chances with MOC.

Well, I suppose someone might think excessive speed constituted taking chances, but I've been trained in getaway driving by the best.

"Whew!" Lindsay said, when I was off the phone. "That was

scary."

"The black SUV or my driving?"

"Both."

"I'm sorry. Something weird is going on with my new neighbor, and scary guys in black SUVs are involved." That was enough explanation. Maybe more than enough. I could have left her thinking it had just been a bad driver.

I took the back roads to the office, and though I vigilantly watched my mirrors, no racing SUV appeared. Before I parked, I drove around to be sure there was no one lurking in the parking lot. We went upstairs, Lindsay eager to dig into her new project, me for a sit down with my partner. What I wanted, and could not have, was a stiff drink and lots of chocolate. Well, I suppose I could have chocolate, if there were some around, but my traitorous companion MOC doesn't always like chocolate.

Suzanne was looking flustered, which wasn't like her. She is the most controlled and composed person I know. Her clothes are always impeccable, and her hair is never out of place.

"Shut the door," she said.

I shut the door and sat in one of her comfortable guest chairs. "What's up?"

"It's Jason. Or it's Jason and Marlene." She sighed. "We were careful. We took our time. Vetted them. Did good interviews. So how could we get it wrong twice?"

"I haven't had a chance to look at Marlene's draft yet. Is it awful?"

She shook her head. "There's hope. But it's not good, and neither of us has time to train someone who claimed to already have the skills we need."

"So mostly it's Jason? Did he disappear again?"

"He's here. But when I asked him what happened, he said a bout of stomach flu, which I don't believe. And he's spent a lot of the day on the phone and hunched over his computer looking devious, so when he went to get lunch, I checked. It's not our work he's doing."

"I thought it was a girlfriend having a meltdown. You

confronted him yet?"

She shook her head. "Wanted to talk to you first."

"Lindsay says he's still running his own web design business. That he had to leave to meet with a dissatisfied client."

"Not on our dime," she said.

"I'll get him," I sat, heaving myself up. "We might as well get this over with."

I crossed the room to where Jason was hunched over his desk. When I got close, he blacked out the screen.

I reached past him and opened what he'd been working on. It was a website for a pizza restaurant. It looked pretty good and reminded me that I was hungry. I was supposed to eat regular meals to keep MOC—and me—from getting cranky. A scone several hours ago wasn't enough. Now food would have to wait.

"Really, Jason?" I said. "Remind me. Which one of our client schools also runs a pizza business?"

"I'm on a break," he huffed. "I'm entitled to work on my own projects when I'm on break."

"No," I said. "You are never entitled to use EDGE computers or the EDGE office to run your personal business. Can you come to Suzanne's office now, please? We need to talk."

"Right now is not convenient."

He'd been so polite and businesslike during the interviews. Where was this Jekyll and Hyde stuff coming from?

"I'm confused," I said. "You're doing someone else's work on our time, but it's not convenient for you to talk about that?"

"Oh, all right," he said, as though he was doing me a big favor. "But..." He checked his watch. "I've only got a few minutes."

"Before what?" It was only two o'clock.

"Before I...uh...have to get back to what I was doing."

Which thing, I wondered. *His or ours?*

I shook my head. It was bad enough to trouble-shoot at client schools and deal with thuggish people in black SUVs at home and on the highway. I didn't have the patience for dealing with childish and unprofessional behavior in the office.

Together we walked to Suzanne's office. He sat. I shut the door and took the seat beside him.

Suzanne gave him her deceptively sweet, warm smile. "Jason, do we have a problem here? We were so excited by your credentials, so pleased you were coming to work here."

A pause. "Just so we're clear, you did understand that this is a full-time job? A professional job?"

He shifted in his chair like something was poking him in the ass. "Of course."

"So why do you feel entitled to do other work while you are here?"

He shrugged. "I was in the middle of some projects when I got the offer. I need to finish them."

"You didn't think that you should have informed us about that? Discussed them with us when we were finalizing the details of your employment?"

"It was my personal business."

"I see." Suzanne waved a hand, indicating her office. "And this is my personal business. Where I expect my employees to be doing my work. Leaving abruptly during the workday without telling anyone where you're going, and pursuing your private business while you're here, do you understand that is not acceptable?"

"Hey," he said, like he was disagreeing with one of his buddies and not speaking to his employer, "I told that woman out there, the one with the accent, where I was going."

"You told her you were leaving to spend the afternoon meeting with a client from your side business?"

Jason didn't answer.

Suzanne looked at me. "Can you ask Magda to step in?"

I asked Magda to step in. She brought her straight back and her dark-eyed glare. Jason hadn't been with us long enough to realize not even Suzanne or I messed with Magda.

"Ah. Magda," Suzanne said. "Jason says he told you he was leaving for the day when he disappeared for the afternoon two days ago. Is that the case?"

She had such a talent for keeping it friendly and light when her stiletto was poised.

"That boy?" She glared at Jason. "He didn't say a word to me, he just walked out. I doubt that he even knows my name." She leaned toward his chair, those fierce eyes looking directly at him. "Do you know my name?"

Like many others who have skated on charm and looks and rarely been challenged, who've spent their lives being patted on the head and told they're special, who figured if it was important to them, it was important to everyone else, he was nonplussed. Secret confession: I love the word nonplussed. Like seeing it in action. Suzanne, Magda, and I waited to see what he'd say. He didn't disappoint us.

He said, "It doesn't matter. I don't work for you."

"Ha!" Magda said. "Good luck with that." She looked at Suzanne. "I may go now?"

"You may go now."

When the door closed behind her, Jason said, in a mocking tone, "May *I* go now?"

"I have a question," Suzanne said. "Why did you take the job if you didn't want to do the work?"

"I did want to do the work. Your work. I just have to get this other stuff done first."

"Do it on your own time," Suzanne said.

She surprised me. I thought he was going to be sent packing. She was sensing there was more to this than loutish youth.

"Can you do that? Because otherwise, you might as well leave now. Bobby needs someone to pick up the slack and to train to work with client schools. If that's not going to be you, because you're too busy, then leave. We have too much going on here to put up with an employee who doesn't want to work."

Jason sat there, looking at her like she'd spoken in a language he didn't understand. After a minute, he said, "But..."

"There are no buts," she said. "Work? Or leave?"

He mistook graciousness for weakness. She hadn't built this business by being soft.

"But I..."

Suzanne looked at me. I nodded. She was giving him a second

chance, and he was totally missing it.

She sighed. We both sighed, because we really needed someone with internet expertise and the ability to write short and punchy material for client media.

Then she waved a hand. "Go."

"But…"

She and I were already mentally reviewing our resumes, wondering if we had any other promising candidates.

"Jason," I said, "just checking. You do speak and understand English, don't you?"

He nodded.

"So you've just been asked to leave. Do you understand? And don't say 'but' again. Just get your stuff and go."

He shook his head, like he was dizzy or stunned. "But…"

Suzanne and I burst out laughing.

"I don't get it," he said. "It's just for a couple weeks, until I get some things done…"

"Can't you do them at night? When you're done here?" I asked.

"Yeah, but…"

He should be gone already, but I was curious about his thinking. Still, inspired by Suzanne, I was looking for something redeemable in the kid.

"But what? What is keeping you from finishing your projects in the evening?"

He looked at the floor, like answers were written on the carpet. "Uh. It's a personal thing."

"Maybe we understand personal things," I said. Sometimes people could be too proud to share information that made a difference. It might be something he could have told us at the start, but thought he couldn't. Or something that had come up since?

"It's…I…"

We waited.

"My mom's in the hospital. My dad works nights. I have to take care of the twins."

"How old are the twins?"

"Eight. Cassie's easy, but Moira…she's disabled. And…"

He shrugged like he didn't know how to explain it. "When I took the job, I thought I could finish at night. And then this happened."

Suzanne and I are both pretty good truth barometers, but Jason was a hard read. I didn't know if we were hearing truth.

"And you didn't tell us this because?" I said.

"I didn't want to look unprofessional. I've been told you don't bring your personal life into the workplace. And I didn't want to lose my job, because I need it. I..." He stopped. "I was just trying to be a guy, you know? But it's all so overwhelming, and I got scared, and I got stupid, and I'm sorry. I'm uh...sorry about Magda, too. Of course I know her name. It's just...uh...she scares me to death."

That we could both relate to.

"Try getting your personal work done at lunch and after work," Suzanne said. "If you need more time, our time, talk to me. Now get out. Go back to work. Our work. Going forward, if you have issues, tell us. We're not dragons. You need to be able to talk to the people you work for and with."

He started for the door again. I said, "Jason. One more thing we need to be clear about."

He froze.

"You don't touch other people without their permission. Not your bosses, your co-workers, the interns, our clients. No one. We work for schools that serve a teenage population. Me Too is a big issue. Consent is a big issue. Maybe at college you developed a bro mentality that said touching people is okay. I don't know. But if you're going to work in a professional setting, you need to lose that behavior. Okay?"

He looked like I was speaking a foreign language.

"So you didn't give Lindsay a casual pat on the butt?"

His red face said it all.

Suzanne said, "You are on awfully thin ice here, Jason. Do you think you can conform your behavior to the norms of an office and the work world?"

"It was just..."

"There is no 'just,' Jason," I said. "Now get out. Go do some of our work before we change our minds."

He left her office dazed.

"You're a kinder person than I would have been," I said.

"We take turns. Sometimes I'm overwhelmed or intolerant. Sometimes you are. And I hadn't focused on the business with Lindsay." Switching gears, she asked, "How did it go at the King School?"

"Pretty well. Lindsay had a rather brilliant idea, if she can pull it off." I told her about the short video. Then I switched to the next matter on the table. "So. Marlene?"

"I never thought I'd say this, but I'm starting to feel like a babysitter. Between his dumb dishonesty and her insecurities. Gad. Makes me feel like an old fogie to say this, but I'm worried about the next generation."

I said. "You and I, we're millennials. Behind us, it's Gen Z. But Marlene is no kid."

"Well, whatever the designation, do you think they take classes in how to lie creatively on their resumes? So Marlene? There's hope, but I was expecting more. We need to have a chat with her. After you look at her work product." She sighed. "I think I'm done nurturing employees for the day. I've got two more people to nurture when I get home, and we've got a faculty do tonight. By nine, my face will ache from smiling."

"Don't you owe us a full day's work?"

"Stop. Just stop. Go back to your office and do something productive," she said.

I went. Suzanne balanced work and motherhood with calm and grace, most of the time. I didn't expect to do as well. I also didn't expect one of our client schools would as readily produce a nanny for me as they had for her. But while I knew I was supposed to have detailed plans in place, I wasn't ready to think about leaving MOC when I hadn't even met the little creature yet.

As if in agreement, MOC gave me a few gentle "I'm right here, Mom," kicks.

I went to my desk to look at Marlene's questionnaire, and any feeling of satisfaction or accomplishment flew out the window.

NINETEEN

My plans to leave work soon, or to grab a late lunch, disappeared as I dug in. I was elbow-deep in revisions and trying not to curse when Sarah brought me a handful of messages. "Sorry," she said. "I got caught up in Lisa's proposal and your draft honor code and forgot to give you these."

"It's okay," I said, hoping there were no emergencies hiding in the thin pink stack. "Just don't send me home again, all right?"

A compulsive spurt of work and some Braxton-Hicks contractions had seemingly scared my coworkers.. Actually, the contractions had scared me, too, even though my doctor had told me to expect them. I now knew not to let the people around me know if something was happening. I wanted to be here at my desk, not at home, where I could stare across at the cottage and worry about what had happened to Charity or the possibility of more unwanted visitors.

"You can stay as long as you don't go into labor or give me more than a day's worth of work," Sarah conceded. "Are we clear?"

It was bad enough that Magda had us all terrorized. Now Sarah wanted to do it, too?

"We're clear."

I sorted through the messages. A small nudge from Eastern

Shore about their honor code, which was puzzling since, as I remembered it, they were supposed to send their draft to me. I sent a quick email to clarify. Got back an almost instant "Oops" with their draft attached.

There was an invitation to speak at a conference far enough in the future that I could probably accept. A school that had ignored us for months was now anxious about when they'd get their crisis management plan. I'd need some details from them; otherwise, it was mostly boilerplate.

And there was another call from Jameson Jones. Not a client. I had no idea what he could be calling about. I picked up the phone, hoping he wasn't in trouble again.

He answered on the first ring, that stunning, deep voice. "This is Jameson Jones."

"It's Thea Kozak," I said. "You wanted me to call?"

His sigh *wasn't* stunning. It was despair. "It's Shonny," he said. "Again." His sister Shondra. Ace basketball player, difficult, chip-on-her-shoulder personality. "She's supposed to start college in a week, full basketball scholarship, and she doesn't want to go."

I'd crossed paths with Shondra and Jameson when they got in trouble at their boarding school. The school didn't believe she had a stalker, and his efforts to protect his sister got him arrested. We'd gotten it sorted, but it hadn't left her with positive feeling about the school, though that was somewhat mitigated by her love of basketball and her loyalty to her team.

"Did she tell you why?"

"I think she's afraid of more of the same."

The same being a community suspicious of her since she was undeniably angry and Black. And an angry Black six-foot-three woman was hard to dismiss.

"I doubt that she'll listen to me," I said. "But I might know someone who can help. Let me give Jonetta Williamson a call. What's Sondra's number?"

"We don't know her, do we?" Experience had taught him to be skeptical, but he should know I wasn't one of those people who tried to hand off problems.

"Come on, Jameson. You know me, right? You called me for help, so if I offer help, you need to trust me, okay? She runs a school for underprivileged Black girls in New York City. She's smart. She's fierce. She's tenacious. And she's connected. She knows about talking insecure young women into trusting opportunity when it's offered. Believe me, she's the right person to talk to your sister."

Ordinarily, I would have waded in myself. I *did* have a relationship with his sister. But I wasn't going to New York to talk an angry and suspicious young woman into taking advantage of a great opportunity. If Jameson, and their grandmother who'd raised them, couldn't do it, it was too hard a job for me, even if I am a chronic rescuer. I said goodbye to Jameson and called Jonetta.

"Hey, girl," she said. "What you doing at work? You should be home getting ready for our baby. You even got a room for that child yet, or is the poor little thing gonna have to sleep in a box?"

Our baby. I was lucky to be bringing this child into a world where so many people waited to love it and help raise it. Jonetta was one of them. If Dom and Rosie were my surrogate parents, Jonetta was my righteous godmother. She was one of those rare people whose presence in the world made everything better.

"Relax. Yes, MOC has a room. And a crib. And a rocking chair. And a stack of adorable little clothes. And a kick that has us expecting a soccer star or a football player. Now I have a problem child for you," I said.

"Oh, honey. I think I've got enough of them."

"Well, you're getting another one. I've told you about her—Sondra Jones, tall, angry teenage basketball player? She was in that mess I sorted out at the school in New Hampshire, where she had a stalker?"

"I remember. And what seems to be the problem now?"

"Her brother says she's ready to give up on a full-ride college basketball scholarship because she's feeling uneasy about the school." I told her what school and she laughed.

"Doesn't that girl know almost the whole team is gonna be Black? She needs to talk to her coach."

She launched into a whole set of questions I had no answers for.

In the end, I gave her Shondra's number and said she could call me if it didn't work out, though what I could do if a miracle worker failed, I didn't know.

As I put down the phone and leaned back in my chair, I realized what I was doing. I was avoiding the issues I'd face when I left here. Even with a police escort, the drive home would unnerve me, as would seeing Charity's cottage. I wouldn't be able to stop puzzling about her welfare, about why people were after her, and which side Malcolm Kinsman was on. It made no sense to me that he had gone to such elaborate lengths to ask me what I knew but hadn't shown up at her house to find out for himself.

This wasn't supposed to be my problem, but how could I ignore the plight of a pregnant woman who'd knocked on my door? How was I going to not worry about a pregnant woman who knew no one in the area who was being chased by people who were willing to kill to get to her? I would have felt a lot more comfortable about the possibility of a Plan B if Jessica Whitlow hadn't been killed. If Nathaniel Davenport hadn't found them both so easily. I wondered if anyone else in town had known Charity. If Jeannine, our librarian, knew more about Charity or had suggested she meet anyone else, another person Charity might have turned to for help. Did someone else in town have her stashed somewhere safe?

Maybe I should have wondered if Charity had killed Davenport and Whitlow before she fled, but I couldn't see how she'd managed to hit someone as tall as Davenport over the head with a rock, and she didn't seem like the type to shoot someone, never mind doing that in her baby's room. Besides, Andre-the-expert hadn't raised that possibility. I believed she was the victim here.

I reminded myself that Thea the Human Tow Truck had been retired. I wasn't going to take chances. But another big thing loomed that made it impossible to forget about Charity. Like her, I had once loved a man named David. Loved him. Married him. And lost him. If I hadn't been hooked before, knowing that she had a husband named David, who was in danger, that her flight was both to protect her unborn child and to protect him, I felt too many connections to Charity to let my worries go.

I scanned the remaining messages. All work-related. No mysterious government agents or private detectives were looking for me. I called the school that wanted its crisis plan done asap, gathered the necessary information, and carried my notes and some samples out to Marlene's desk.

She cringed and dropped her eyes. I suppressed a sigh.

"Parker-Adams Academy wants a crisis management plan in place before school starts, which is in two weeks. It's pretty much boilerplate, except for a few school-specific details, which are here." I put down the sheet with my notes. "Here's a sample. You can pull it up as a document and make the necessary changes. Then send it to me for review. I'd like it tomorrow by noon. Think you can handle that?"

Sarah could have handled that. I just wanted to try Marlene out on something very straightforward.

She hesitated, then shook her head. "I'm not sure..."

I faked a reassuring smile. "You can do it. It's pretty ABC. Have it on my desk by noon."

I left before she started offering excuses. Then I called Andre.

"I'm heading out in about twenty minutes. You going to be here to watch my back?"

He didn't respond.

"You said..."

"Something came up. I've been trying to reach Norah. It's only ten miles. If we can't be there, just be careful, okay?"

Until he said that, I hadn't realized how much I'd counted on having him watch my back, ironic since I've always been fiercely independent. MOC changes everything. Also ironic since I've never thought much of women who make everything about themselves and their pregnancies. I was still me. Still very capable of taking care of myself. Still furious that I let some guy in a black SUV rattle me like this.

"Hey," he said. "Are you okay?"

"I'm fine. Just surprised to find myself being such a wimp."

"You're no wimp. Quite the opposite. You don't know how to be a wimp even when you should be."

I could hear commotion in the background, voices and radio chatter. He was definitely at a scene.

"Call me as soon as you are home," he said. "I'll let you know when I'll be home. It won't be for a while. Lights on. Lock the doors. You know the drill."

Yup. I didn't want to, but I knew the drill.

"I will."

"Eat something," he said, because he knows my habits so well.

I'd already loaded my briefcase. If I was going to be sitting home alone in a spooky old farmhouse, I would need work to distract me.

Funny how on a sunny summer day, the house seemed happy and safe, and when faced with the prospect of solitude and darkness, it seemed threatening. I was sure I would jump at every bump and creak, which, since it was an old house, it had in spades.

I said goodbye to my husband, reminded myself that I was Thea the Great and Terrible, and headed home. Well, headed out to my car. I didn't head home until I'd checked inside the car, and under the car—that must have been hilarious to anyone watching—and scanned the lot for lurking black SUVs.

The coast seemed clear.

I put my briefcase in the back, checked my pockets for my phone, my pepper spray, and my alarm, and started home. No car seemed to be following me, and no one passed me except a hippie-looking guy in a rusted Volvo. In my experience, the bad guys never drive Volvos.

I was driving through the town center, past the common and the bandstand and the Civil War memorial, when I decided to detour to the grocery store for basics like bread, milk, and whoopee pies. Despite their lack of anything resembling nutrition, MOC and I are very fond of them. I wanted to go easy on all that pasta, so I also got a rotisserie chicken, a bag of green beans, and some fresh corn.

I was checking out with my nutritious and unnutritious finds, wondering if I could wait 'til I got home before I tore into the chicken, when the man behind the counter, an avuncular fellow named Bob who always wore a crisp white shirt and jeans held up with suspenders, said, "You aren't in some kind of trouble are you? Because there was a guy in earlier who looked and acted like a cop asking about you."

"How could I get in trouble with Andre for a husband?" I asked.

"What I thought, too."

He grinned at the basketball and said, "Anyways, looks like you're already in trouble."

We both had a laugh about that.

There was no one behind me, so I said, "The guy asking about me. What did he look like?"

"Tall. Got one of them military haircuts. Sharp features. And really blue eyes, kind you notice because they aren't common. Wearing a goddamn suit in August. Pardon my language."

Malcolm Kinsman.

"What did he want to know?"

"Did I know you. Where you live. Did I ever see you with another pregnant woman. Kind of strange questions. I figured he didn't need to know your business, so I didn't tell him anything except that you and your husband, who is state police, live somewhere here in town, but you're new, so I don't exactly know where."

"Thanks, Bob. That's perfect. He doesn't sound like anyone we know. I wonder who he is?"

"Dunno," he said, bagging my purchases, "but I seen him heading across the common to the library, so you might check with Jeannine. She's a pretty good reader of people as well as books."

I carried my goodies out to the car, then started across the common to check with Jeannine. Damn Charity Kinsman anyway. I'd already had one house ruined by a crime victim, and now, even if it was inadvertent, she was bringing more trouble into my life.

By the time I'd passed the bandstand, I was feeling guilty about those thoughts. Whatever trouble I was having with nosy people snooping around, her situation was far worse.

TWENTY

Jeannine was checking out a freckled, red-haired boy named Albie. Albie was twelve and wanted to be a detective just like Andre when he grew up. I'd met the boy when the chain came off his bike while he was out collecting returnable bottles and cans, and he'd come to the door for help. I gave him lemonade while Andre fixed the bike.

"Be with you in a sec, Thea," she said.

Albie turned and said, "Hi, Miss Thea."

It made me feel like a schoolteacher from the nineteen fifties. Unless it was the eighteen fifties.

"Hi, Albie." I looked at the books he was taking out. One about detectives, a Harry Potter book, and a kids' book about the FBI. "FBI, huh. Given up on the state police?"

His grin was adorable. "Just keeping my options open," he said. "I saw a guy earlier today snooping around your house. He looked kind of official, and I wondered if he was from the FBI."

"Out hunting bottles again?"

"Gotta buy a new bike," he said. "I'm close."

"Well, we've got a couple bags of returnables in the barn. I'll drop them off at your house if you tell me where you live."

"That would be great," he said, and gave a careful description of the route from my house to his, including landmarks like Henry's Farm Stand and the road into the girls' camp out on the lake. It was such a Maine thing, giving directions this way. Andre says he was once directed to a crime scene by being told to "turn right at the refrigerator, and it's just past the rusting red tractor."

Such delight at a few bags of cans and bottles. I wished more of the people I dealt with were so enthusiastic. "Oh, and thanks for telling me about that man at my house. I don't like the idea of anyone snooping around when I'm not home," I told him. "Can you describe the man you saw?"

"Tall and…uh…strong-looking. You know." He spread his hands. "Big shoulders. Dark hair. Gray suit. Sunglasses. And instead of those shiny shoes they wear on TV, he was wearing cowboy boots."

This kid *would* make a good detective. "Did you see his vehicle?"

"Yes, ma'am."

Ma'am makes me feel ancient, but I liked that Albie's parents had taught him such good manners. "Car or SUV?"

Another of those fabulous grins. "Black SUV, like you see on TV. It didn't have government plates, though."

"Did he see you watching him?"

"Nope."

"You did well. Thank you for the information, Albie."

Albie, short for Albert, gathered up his books and left.

"I'm glad you're here, Thea," Jeannine said, giving me a curious look. "I've been so worried about that poor girl. The pregnant one who was moving into that cottage near you. Jessica. Did she ever come and introduce herself? She looked awfully forlorn the day she was in here. I thought she could do with a friend, so I suggested you. Believe it or not, she was looking for a book about plumbing, which, given what a wreck that place is, shouldn't have surprised me. Only I was trying to imagine her working under a sink in her condition."

"You won't find me under any sinks, that's for sure. I did paint the baby's room with some supposed to be nontoxic paint, and even that was a challenge. Andre was not happy about me being up on a ladder."

I realized I hadn't answered her question. "I did see her a few times. She stopped in. Told me you had suggested we meet. I liked her. We had tea and made plans to go shopping for baby things, which we did, and had a great time. Then those two people got killed at her cottage, and she has disappeared."

"You don't know where she's gone?"

Why did she sound so suspicious? Jeannine and I usually chatted in a very comfortable way. I shrugged. "No idea. I don't think she's familiar with the area. You have any thoughts about that?"

Jeannine looked uncomfortable. "You really don't know where she is?"

Now *I* was uncomfortable. Why would she think I knew Charity's whereabouts? I studied her face, wondering what was going on, and whether a visit from the mysterious fellow Bob had described was behind this.

I decided to lob the ball back to her. "Was she in here a lot, enough for you to get to know her? There must have been some reason, other than we're both pregnant, for you to suggest she get to know me."

I waited. Silence makes people uneasy. Often, when people don't want to tell you things, silence will get them to talk.

Although, of course, she was a librarian. They're supposed to like silence.

After a pause awkward in its length, she said, "I just figured, since you're a detective, that maybe if she was in trouble, you would help."

"Gosh," I said, carefully picking such a girly word, "Jeannine, I had no idea poor Jessica was in trouble until...well, until those awful murders happened and she'd disappeared. Before that, we were just two women having our first babies, having fun shopping for baby things. It makes me awfully uneasy, thinking there might be strangers around here bent on doing harm. Especially in my condition."

I gave it a beat and said, "You know I'm a consultant to private schools, right? My partner and I run a business called EDGE Consulting, which keeps me plenty busy. I have no idea why anyone would think I'm a detective."

I shook my head in wonder and said in a puzzled voice, "Did someone tell you I'm a detective?"

It sounded like something the soft, pathetic heroine of a book might say. I had to suppress adding a breathy giggle. I watched her face as I said, "And then that nice young Albie says there have been strangers around my house. Andre's out on a case, and I'm almost afraid to go home if he's not there. Jeannine, you are pretty plugged in to what happens around here. Have *you* seen anyone strange around town?"

I knew she had. Bob said he'd seen that guy heading for the library. Again, I waited. Was she going to lie to me? If so, why?

"No. Not other than the summer people who are renting camps. They come in for books and videos when they realize those rentals don't have cable."

I kept my sweet, girly avatar as I asked, "I'm curious though, really, why you would think I'm a detective." I repeated my unanswered question. "Did someone tell you I am?"

She blushed. She actually blushed and looked down at her feet. Of course, she deserved to be embarrassed, since we'd had multiple conversations about my job and the challenges of working with teens and young adults and helicopter and snowplow parents. We'd even talked about young adult books and how to communicate with a population raised entirely in a digital world. She'd shared her challenges trying to attract teenagers to the special area she'd set up for them and how to get them to use the library for anything beyond logging into social media.

Clearly, she wasn't going to come clean. Maybe the mysterious guy had scared her? I stopped waiting for revelation and asked a direct question. "Bob over at the market says there was a man, a stranger, in earlier today asking questions about me. Did he stop in here as well?"

Confronted with the choice of believing a pushy stranger or a friendly new neighbor, she became the Jeannine I was used to. "There was a man in earlier asking about you."

She described a man I suspected was Malcolm Kinsman. I was puzzled. He couldn't have been looking for my house. If he'd found me on the plane, he clearly had resources behind him that could locate me. Was he checking to see what he could learn about me from my neighbors? Trying to learn whether I had other properties where I might have stashed Charity?

Whatever he was up to, it was disturbing.

"I thought it was odd," she said, "and you know, we librarians have a code about protecting the privacy of our patrons, so I didn't tell him anything." She paused. "What would I tell him anyway? That you're new in town and fixing up a house and having a baby and your husband is with the state police?"

"But something he said made you suspicious, didn't it?" I suggested. "Made you wonder if I was somehow involved in Jessica's disappearance." Charity's name hadn't been reported anywhere. I wasn't about to call her that, despite the two Jessica problem.

"I'm sorry, Thea," she said. "He was kind of a scary guy, and he showed me his government ID and made it seem like finding you was critical to finding a missing woman."

Government ID, huh? He'd showed me a Texas driver's license. "They can be that way, people who work for the government, can't they? Do you know what agency he's with?"

She was almost wringing her hands as she said, "I didn't look that closely. Just that it was an ID card and it said U.S. Government. I guess that was pretty trusting of me, wasn't it? I suppose he could have gotten something like that on the internet."

"What Jessica's story is surely is a mystery," I said. "All you did was suggest she meet her pregnant neighbor. All I did was invite her in for tea and take her shopping. Both times, she was very careful not to reveal anything about herself. Now we've got strange men going around town asking questions, and if Albie is telling the truth —and he seems like a truthful boy—and his description is accurate, there's another strange man besides the one who spoke to you prowling around my house while I'm at work. Unless your stranger was wearing cowboy boots?"

She shook her head.

I dropped my voice. "This isn't good, Jeannine. Andre is gone a lot and I'm home alone. I'm going to give you my number. Please call me if you see any more of these strangers, or if the man comes back. Can you do that?"

Jeannine didn't say anything. She seemed to be debating about whether she should tell me if strangers were asking about me. I didn't think there was anything to debate about. I lived here. This was my local library, while a transient man asking questions about locals was owed nothing. I wasn't sure what was bothering her— maybe she was intimidated by authority—so I decided to pull her into my camp.

I put my hand protectively over MOC. "Frankly, Jeannine, this whole business is frightening me just when my doctor says I'm supposed to be avoiding stress. I saw that woman, Jessica, exactly three times. Once for tea, once for shopping, and for one minute to drop off a pot of annuals from Agway. It spooks me to think anyone believes I might have had something to do with her disappearance. I mean, you've seen her more than I have. It's like saying that she came into the library a few times and spoke to you, so you must know all about her. Like *you* must somehow be involved in what happened to her."

She was still wavering. I doubted the guy would be back, but something in my perverse nature made me need to win this thing. Guess I'd reached my quota of liars and suspicious people. I dropped into a chair, cradling my basketball, and lowered my head. "Jeannine," I said, "Please. Two people were just murdered right across the street from me. That makes it hard to feel safe. It would help if I knew I could count on you."

"Sure," she said. "Yes. If anyone comes asking about you, I'll call you."

"Thank you."

I took a breath. I needed to get home. It was summer, and hot in the car, and I'd left my groceries there. But I had one more question for her. "I'm really worried about her. Jessica. Can you think of any place around here where she might go? To hide out? Were there any places the two of you discussed?"

I was ignoring what Jeannine had said about librarians keeping their patrons' secrets. She'd been hesitant about keeping mine, hadn't she? But Jeannine knew the ins and outs of this town in a way I didn't.

She shook her head. "Not really. When she told me where she was living, I was surprised. It's not a nice place. It has been kind of a bottom-of-the-market rental and hasn't been taken care of. There are other, better places to rent. I may have suggested some of them —some cottages out on the lake with weekly rentals, things like that. Sylvia Harris's cute B&B where at least she could stay until she could make the cottage livable. There are those new condos down on the river. I don't think they're all rented yet."

She shrugged. "It just bothered me, you know, thinking of someone bringing a newborn to that place. Have you seen it?"

"I was only in the driveway when I picked her up and when I gave her the plants. It looked awfully rundown." She didn't need to know I'd been inside when I found the real Jessica's body.

"Right. You said. Maybe I was too pushy. She was so upbeat about the place when it needed so much work and…well, frankly, she didn't look like she had that much time left before the baby. I told her my husband's cousin has a little A-frame up on Morse Mountain that he rents. I think I even gave her his name and number. But that's all. Nothing she couldn't have found in an internet search. Except for Brad's place."

I was trying to think of a way to ferret out Brad's last name when she said, "And in case you really are a detective, despite what you say, or you just care about finding that poor girl, Brad's last name is Twitchell."

I still thought she was holding something back, but nothing in my toolkit was prying it loose. She'd patted her pocket a few times, which made me wonder if she had someone's business card in there. I gave up. I wasn't about to tackle her and wrestle it away from her. It was only speculation anyway. Or my suspicious nature, honed by years of dealing with liars and bad guys. And bad gals. The bad world is an equal opportunity place.

I didn't bother to ask her why she thought a detective would buy a house in rural Maine. Or what kind of detective she thought I was.

A mother and two small children came in, and Jeannine used them as an excuse to end our conversation.

I took my cue and left, puzzling over whether Jeannine was still suspicious of me. Maybe she'd pull out the mystery man's card and call him as soon as things quieted down.

A younger, more energetic me who didn't have groceries waiting in a hot car might have done some driving around, looking for a gray Volvo with Virginia plates. I was going to go home and order a batch of tee shirts declaring, **I Am Not A Detective.** If they arrive and I get to wear them before MOC is born, people are going to wonder what the heck they mean. I guess they will anyway.

I doubted they would do much good. A newspaper article once labeled me a detective, and the label is harder to shake than a burr.

I went back across the Common, looking left and right, half expecting Malcolm Kinsman to leap out from behind a tree.

I reached my car unscathed.

TWENTY-ONE

I am not a detective, but I do have a tendency to get involved in matters that affect my life. Otherwise, why would I have tangled with a northern Maine militia group? Or tried to comply with my mother's request that I get her protégé, the young woman who was everything she wanted me to be, out of jail after she was accused of murdering her husband? So despite not being a detective, I stopped in at the post office and asked Barry, the regular guy behind the counter, for an address for Brad Twitchell's A-frame.

I wished I could avoid thinking about Charity or her husband, David, who might be in serious trouble. Her beyond-irritating brother. And people like Fred and Alice, people who kept turning up and asking intrusive questions. But how could I, when strangers were snooping around my house and even my local librarian was acting odd and evasive? If I ever wanted my peaceful life back, it seemed like the best course was to find Charity myself. Not that I knew what the heck I would do with her when I found her.

Bless Barry, he bought my story of a friend looking for a place to rent without a blink. I drove home with no idea what I was going to do with my new information. No one followed me, and I found no suspicious cars parked in the yard. By the time I got inside, my feet were screaming to be released. I dropped the groceries on the counter, wiggled my shoes off, and searched the house.

I was alone.

I stowed the food in the refrigerator, exercised willpower and didn't immediately gobble the whoopee pie, and put on flip flops. Despite visions of sinking into a chair on the back deck, I found myself picking up my purse, locking the door, and heading back out to my car. I knew where those condos out by the lake were, and cruised past them first. No gray Volvos with Virginia plates. Searching summer rentals was best done with the internet and some calls, so I saved that for later and plugged the address for Twitchell's A-frame into my phone.

Morse Mountain wasn't a mountain, of course, it was just a high hill, but as I rose higher on a winding road with crumbling tar that was not much better than gravel, I felt like I was far from civilization. I passed a rusty trailer with three dead cars in the yard, and an abandoned farmhouse with a half-collapsed roof and a spooky barn.

By the time Siri announced I'd reached my destination, I was feeling uneasy. The A-frame was set in an untended clearing. The small, brown structure was surrounded by a deck perched in the air with no railing. There was no car in the drive, but I parked and climbed the steps to the deck, peering in the large windows. The inside was pleasant, decently furnished, and clean. A lot better than the cottage, except for being so isolated. There was no sign that anyone was living there.

I went around the back, but the curtains were drawn, and I couldn't see in.

The trash barrels were empty.

There were no clothes on the line.

Disappointed, I trudged back to my car. For no good reason other than intuition, I thought I'd find her here. On the gravel where I'd parked, I found a crumpled receipt from the local market from three days ago. It might be a clue, but it was for two six-packs of beer, and a handful of scattered cans suggested someone had parked here to drink.

I looked for tire tracks, but the gravel was thick and dry and showed nothing.

Not finding her had amped up my anxiety level. Reminding myself that I was supposed to avoid stress, I started the car, rolled down the window to let in some warm summer air, and headed home. Silly me. I hadn't wanted to look for her, felt compelled to, and was now genuinely depressed that I hadn't found her.

Mentally I put away my magnifying glass and hung up my deer-stalker hat and went inside.

I poured myself a glass of lemonade, tied on an apron, and shredded the rotisserie chicken into a bowl. I added walnuts, celery, and cranberries, and stirred in some mayo. It would be a perfect dinner for a warm summer night. Then, because I hadn't eaten since my morning scone, I fixed myself some cheese and crackers and carried them out to the back deck.

I set my phone on the wide arm of the Adirondack chair, put my feet up, and looked out over our back forty, actually more like two acres before the open space ran into woods. I grew up in the suburbs, and it still seems odd to own so much land. I like it, though. I could already imagine MOC toddling across the lawn on chubby legs, bent on escape. My mother says that I was always trying to escape. Given the lifelong difficulties in our relationship, I can understand why my baby self wanted to get away.

MOC gave me a few "notice me, Mom," kicks before settling down, leaving me to doze peacefully in the sun. Before I'd been out there twenty minutes, I'd dropped off to sleep. I woke with the eerie sense that someone was watching me. When I looked around, though, I was alone, except for that frustrated mama deer and her baby. They were peering through the deer fence like they were visitors to a zoo and I was the exhibit.

I clapped my hands, and they skittishly moved a few feet away. But only a few feet.

Wondering how long it would take them to accept the fence as a deterrent, I settled back and closed my eyes.

My phone rang. Andre.

"Hey," I said. "No bad guys around here. It's a perfect afternoon and I made us a delicious salad for dinner."

He sighed. I can read his sighs so well he didn't need to say what came next, which was that he wouldn't be home for dinner. He didn't know when he would be home, but would I please keep my phone with me, just in case.

The life of a cop's spouse. The phone rings. Your heart skips a beat. You wait for the news about when he or she will be home. The news is bad. You turn off burners. Put the food away. And dig into work.

I wasn't digging into work yet. I was enjoying my perfect August afternoon. Blue sky. Gentle breezes. No work that couldn't wait. I put Charity Kinsman out of my mind and was feeling totally relaxed.

My phone rang. I'd already spoken to the only person I wanted to talk to. I gave it a dirty look, then picked it up with two fingers, cautiously, the way you might pick up a suspicious thing stuck to a shoe.

Jonetta's voice burst out of the phone. "That Shondra girl needs someone to whack her upside the head."

"I can't argue with that," I agreed, "but were you able to set her straight?"

"Did my best. Did my best. But she doesn't want to listen. I called her coach. I know her coach real well. I've sent her some players. She's going to call your girl, see if that will do any good."

Damn. I had hoped Jonetta could work her magic. "Well, if she won't listen to her coach, the opportunity is wasted on her anyway."

It made me sad to say it. Sondra Jones was a very talented girl. But she was not my problem. If all of the people I'd rescued over the years—the ones Suzanne calls my 'waifs'—suddenly reappeared, my life would be too full and my head would explode. MOC needs a mother with a working head.

"Thank you for trying, Jonetta. When are you going to leave that miserable, hot city and visit us in Maine?"

"Didn't know I was invited."

Oh dear. Someone was in a bad mood. "When are you *not* invited?" I said. "We have a guestroom."

"With walls and windows? A floor and a door?" she said skeptically. She knew we'd bought a place that needed work. "Does your house have working plumbing?"

"All of those things," I said. "You'll even have a bed."

There was a long silence, like she was actually thinking it over, which would be a surprise since Jonetta is even more wedded to her work than I am. When she said, "Would tomorrow be too soon?" I almost fell off my chair.

"Tomorrow would be fine. It would be wonderful."

"Great. E-mail me directions. I haven't had a vacation in six years, and if I don't come now, the school year will start and I'll be up to my ears in these girls and their problems."

I put the phone down gently, like a small, grumpy Jonetta might still be trapped inside it, and shook my head. She was orderly and overworked, and the lead-up to a new school year is always hectic. I couldn't imagine how she would—or could—take some time off. Couldn't imagine her being willing to. But she'd said she was coming. Having her here was fine with me, especially if Andre was swamped.

Lying back in the chair, I reviewed the state of my pantry. Jonetta is a generously-sized woman who loves to eat. I still had a few trays of Rosie's food left. One day we'd have to go over to the coast for lobster, and my garden would give us salads. Broccoli. Beans. We needed a coffee cake or muffins. A steak for the grill. Red wine. And chocolate cake. There were no food delivery services operating this far from the city. I would have to go to the store. A big store, not my local market.

My watch said it was only six-thirty. I had time for a provisions run now that what counted as rush hour outside Portland died down. Or I could go in the morning. My tired feet said, "Tomorrow." My husband wasn't coming home anytime soon. My default mode was work.

I went to my desk, sent Jonetta directions, and pulled out my work. The phone rang. I have such a love/hate relationship with phones. They're essential for my work. The rest of the time, all the calls seem to be from the IRS or Social Security, computer scammers or bogus credit card companies. I think it should be a national priority to get rid of spam and free us from these constant intrusions, but our government doesn't seem to have any priorities. Maybe if a few spammers are captured and put into stocks in the public square? Personally, there are days when I'd vote for beheading, so it's probably good we don't do that here.

It was the time when schools geared up for fall, and I am a slave of duty, though, so I answered. Shondra Jones's anger and paranoia burst into my ear, a loud mélange of why didn't I stay out of her life, and what did I know about basketball and scholarships anyway?

All I'd said was "Hello," and all I'd done was try to help her. If she wanted to wreck her life, that was up to her. When she paused in her rant, I said, "That's enough, Shondra. More than enough. If all you can do to the people who try to help you is abuse them, when instead of saying 'thank you' you curse and yell, you don't deserve my help or anyone else's. Just get this one thing straight—if you pass up this chance to go to college and play basketball, which you know you love—you aren't likely to get a second chance. Blow it off, screw it up, insult and alienate all the people who care and are trying to help, and we won't be here when you realize you've made a big mistake."

She started up again and I cut her off. "I don't want to hear it, okay? It's a great school and a great team. You're damned lucky, and you should be grateful. If you have genuine concerns, talk to your coach. And get your head straight. Or don't. The choice, and the responsibility, are yours. Jameson has tried to help you. I've tried to help you. Jonetta Williamson, the best person you could have in your corner, was willing to help you. You aren't going to find a better team to have in your corner. No buts. No maybes. No whatever else you've got to complain about. You blow off the school and the coach, word will get around, and you won't get a second chance. Okay?"

She started in again and I hung up. Life had given Shondra

plenty of reasons to feel aggrieved. She still had to take responsibility for her life choices. We all have to grow up sometime.

Darn it, I thought, as I settled back in my chair, I was supposed to stay calm. Avoid stress. Keep my blood pressure low. I'd already had a tense time with Jeannine. Arguing on the phone with an obstinate girl who risked wrecking her future chances wasn't good for me. I needed peace and calm.

Someone knocked on the door.

A cautious little voice in my head said, "Don't answer it."

Another knock, more vigorous this time. Whoever was there was persistent. From my office door, I looked to see if there was a vehicle in the driveway. Maybe another of those damned black SUVs. There was no vehicle. Maybe Albie had biked over to get our returnable bottles and cans. The kid was a real go-getter.

Before I could decide what to do, the kitchen door opened and a man walked in. Well, more staggered than walked. I'd forgotten to lock it when I came in from the deck.

As I stood in the doorway, stunned, a battered and bleeding Malcolm Kinsman collapsed onto one of my kitchen chairs. Blood from a cut above his eye had slicked his face a gory red. He looked like something from a horror movie.

"I need your help. Please," he gasped.

"You need an ambulance. A hospital. A doctor," I said. "I'll call…"

"No!" He was struggling to hold it together. "No ambulance. No one can know I'm here. It's too dangerous."

I handed him a clean kitchen towel, and he started mopping the blood from his face.

"You need a doctor," I repeated.

"You've got to help me find Charity before they do," he said, ignoring what I'd said.

Of course I still had no idea who "they" were. But before I probed for answers, if he was at risk I had to get him out of my kitchen, where people could easily see in, to a place where I could pull the blinds—the couch in my office—and see how badly injured he was.

I am no Thea Nightingale. I don't like blood and I don't have much in the way of first aid skills. He needed professional help. I knew if I insisted, rather than risking harm to his sister, he would stagger out of here and hide himself somewhere. No use to yell at him that his methods were ridiculous. If my guesses were right, this guy could slither through villages in Afghanistan and probably spoke Arabic. If the bad guys could get to him, he was facing some seriously dangerous opponents.

I wasn't liking Charity's chances.

"Come with me, away from the windows," I said. I got him to his feet, tucked my arm under his arm, and half led, half carried him to my office. I settled him on the couch and asked what I could do to help.

He muttered, "Find Charity before they do."

"Who are they?" I think I yelled it. I was so frustrated by all these strangers and the information void.

He said, "Cartel," like I was dumb for not knowing, and faded. Unconscious or asleep, I didn't know.

WTF? Cartels operating in our small Maine town? This was way beyond my job description.

I pulled the shades and went to look for first aid supplies. I found some butterfly bandaids and used them to stick the cut on his forehead together. Best I could do. I wasn't going to try and sew him back together. I covered him with a blanket, and went to call my husband. However busy he was, he was needed at home.

TWENTY-TWO

Despite our understanding that he would always answer except in a dire emergency, I went to voicemail. I wasn't sure what message I should leave—that Malcolm Kinsman was lying unconscious in our house? Or just the more cryptic he needed to come home? But that would bring him racing to take me to the hospital, and I didn't want him racing anywhere. Andre is a cool and collected character, except about MOC. I just said that Charity's brother had shown up unexpectedly, he was injured, and I needed Andre's help.

While I waited for him to call me back, I got a washcloth and warm water and cleaned Kinsman's face and hands. With the blood gone, I could see how pale he was. "You'd better not die on me," I told him, like that would do any good. I sat down in my desk chair to watch him.

Watching the facial tics of an unconscious, injured man is excruciating. It seemed so wrong not to call for help, to let him suffer, perhaps risk his life. I had no way of telling if someone finding him could actually be a threat to Charity, but being found was clearly a threat to him. When I'd last seen him, on the plane, he hadn't known where she was. Since then, had she gotten in touch? And how, in the few hours since he'd been going around town asking about me, had he run into the people who'd done this to him? Where were they now? Where was his car?

A chill ran down my spine. What if they'd followed him here? Or been following him earlier today and then spoken to the same people I'd spoken with? What if, in a semi-conscious and injured state, he'd led whoever had bad intentions regarding Charity right to my door?

"Damn you, Malcolm. Why did you come here? Have you put us both at risk?" I said to his unconscious body. "And why does everyone think I know where Charity is?" I liked her. We'd had so much fun together. But I had no idea where she would have gone or even if she was still in Maine. My only comfort was that she'd appeared to be very competent and able to take care of herself.

Then again, so was I, and yet I wouldn't want this baby to arrive in a strange place without help. Could I hope that she'd gone home? Back to where there were people who could care for her? Or, given that it appeared people with bad intentions were looking for her, would that be too dangerous?

The kitchen door. I still hadn't locked it. I went out to take care of that, knowing that Andre was going to ask why I'd locked it *after* Kinsman was inside. There was some expression about locking the barn door, wasn't there?

Andre didn't call me back, which could only mean he was deep into something that couldn't be interrupted.

Kinsman didn't wake up.

It began to get dark. I left Kinsman—I wasn't doing him any good anyway—and walked around the house, pulling shades where there were shades to be pulled, and turning on the lights. My house looked so pleasant in the soft light. The first thing a person would notice was not the splotches of repaired plaster on the walls or which of the floors still needed refinishing or that many of the windows needed replacing so they didn't rattle or leak cold air when winter came. It looked cozy and welcoming, and still I felt awfully alone. No neighbors on the left—that was an open field—and the neighbors on the right spent the summer out at their camp on the lake, only coming back to check on the house and do laundry. That wouldn't be until Monday.

From the upstairs hall, I looked across the street to Charity's cottage, unlit and still behind the dark hedge. The next house down from the cottage had lights on, and I felt foolishly grateful to see signs of other humans.

MOC was tuning up to begin the evening acrobatics. They always began with little stirrings, as though my baby had to stretch its tiny limbs before it could start the workout to strengthen itself for its eventual appearance in the world.

I never watched TV, so that couldn't distract me. Besides, it seemed like every time I turned it on, it was either bad news or right in the middle of a sensationalized true crime program. My own life had had enough true crime. I didn't need to invite more into my life as entertainment. I felt like I had two choices. I could work, or I could sit and watch Malcolm Kinsman to see if he was still breathing.

As I gathered up my work to move it to the kitchen, I checked him. Still alive, his breathing now deep and steady like he was asleep. I left him to it, avoiding doing one of those annoying hospital things where they constantly disturb healing rest to record vital stats proving that the patient is still alive.

He was lying half on his side, and something was sticking out of his pocket. His wallet. Yup. Of course I snagged it and took it into the kitchen with me.

I was not surprised to learn that he was, indeed, Malcolm Kinsman, nor that he was active military. Nothing there told me why he was here in Maine or whether he was acting on his own, which his ability to find me on a plane suggested was not the case. I did find the photo of him and Charity's husband. I got my magnifying glass and studied it to see if it would tell me anything useful.

All a mystery to me, but after an internet search, it looked like special forces badges on their fatigues. Or whatever their camo outfits were called.

Without any actual information, I began to develop a theory. It was that a foreign operation had gone wrong and someone, somewhere, presumably not someone friendly to the United States, was holding David Peckham hostage and wanted to find, and abduct, his pregnant wife, Charity, to use her as leverage to learn whatever confidential information he had about the operation. His buddy, Malcolm, had not been captured or had escaped and was here trying to find his sister and protect her. Malcolm had said cartel, so did that mean David Peckham was somewhere in South or Central America? Mexico? Did we even conduct operations in Mexico? No way I would know.

Who hired the private detective? The cartel? And why was he killed? Who was the guy in the cowboy boots? How was the Marshals Service involved, and why would someone looking for Charity have killed both Jessica Whitlow and Nathaniel Davenport if they were working for opposite sides? Was there some third party involved?

If I were to tell this story to someone, based on my woeful lack of facts, they'd say I've been watching too much television. But I don't watch television. Nor am I a cop, though I've been accused of being one, and I'm not a detective, though I've been accused of that, too. What I am is a woman who's been thrown into many situations where people are lying, where someone has malignant intent or doesn't mind killing to protect themselves, and where finding the answers involves sorting out lies, getting enough information to build the right picture, and understanding people's motives.

Here, aside from my whacko theory, I had nothing. Well, I had a special forces guy named Malcolm Kinsman in the next room. Bad guys were presumably after him. And I was alone in a charming but isolated house.

I got the key from a package of frozen peas, went upstairs to the gun safe in our closet, unlocked it, and took out my adorable Barbie special handgun. A gift from my loving and protective husband who also took me to the range and made me learn to shoot it.

Actually, this was not the gun I'd learned to shoot with. That gun had been taken by the police after I shot someone with it. A most righteous shooting, necessary to save my husband's life. I'd never asked for it back, though. I'd never wanted to see it again.

The only thing connected with that night that I wanted in my life was my husband. Andre had gotten me this gun instead.

I loaded it, relocked the cabinet, and went back to the kitchen, returning the key to the package of peas.

Andre says when he searches a house, he always looks in the freezer, but we still do this. There's another key upstairs, just in case. Just in case bad guys bent on stealing our guns also think to look in the freezer.

I shrugged, even though there was no one around to observe my gesture. Then I sat at the counter and made a list for my grocery run, a chore that would complicate my day tomorrow. I would have to get up very early to get to the store, get back and put the food away, then spend some time at work before I had to be back here for Jonetta's arrival.

Thinking about work nudged me to do some now, starting with a review of Eastern Shore's honor code. At this point, dealing with a world awash in cheating and campuses living in fear of a shooting or other threatening event, honor codes, and crisis management plans have become our bread and butter. Not the kind of bread or butter I'd ever wanted to have in my life. Bread and butter sounds so benign, and this was anything but. At least I wasn't living on some campus where I had to conduct active shooter drills or deal with the news that someone on campus had a gun. Ironically, I'd learned that there was an active-shooter simulation video schools can access called EDGE.

Sigh.

If I'd ever entertained the idea of becoming a head of school or working in private school administration, this job had dissuaded me. A significant proportion of the student body was on medication for something. Helicopter parents were morphing into snowplow parents, unless it was lawnmower parents or bulldozer parents. Maybe I should be grateful that my parents hadn't hovered. My mother had been judgmental, and my father had hidden himself in work to avoid crossing her. My brother Michael had been Mom's favorite and my sister Carrie had had a gift for rubbing Mom the wrong way, forcing me to act as the family peacemaker. I was eight when Carrie was adopted, and I'd practically raised her myself.

I sighed again. I needed to think some happier thoughts. Between my work and Andre's, MOC was going to be born a pessimistic depressive unless the kid was surrounded by more positive examples. How did someone who grew up in a tense and difficult household raise their child differently? Was it possible not to revert to the patterns I'd known?

Andre's family was more tight-knit. Nosy, quarrelsome, religious. Very certain that their way was the right way and unselfconscious about imposing their views on others. His sister Aimee had too many out-of-control children, and none of the women were ambitious.

Ugh. I did not want to think about families and how much could go wrong. I wanted to think happy thoughts. As I sat in my bright kitchen, child-to-be acting like a Kung Fu fighter, husband unreachable, and a badly beaten man slumbering or unconscious in the next room, I couldn't find any happy thoughts.

Wait. There was Jonetta on my horizon. What she dealt with every day put my pity party in perspective. Wow. There was a line: Putting pity parties in perspective. That, at least, made me smile.

I forced myself to work. Work could always fill my time. When the clock said nine and Andre still hadn't called back, I realized that I'd once again skipped a meal, and that just because he wasn't here didn't mean I wasn't supposed to eat. I got out the chicken salad, filled a bowl, and started to eat.

There were stumbling steps from the hall, and a pale and shaky Malcolm Kinsman appeared in the doorway.

"You really don't need that gun," he said.

His eyes fell to my salad. "And would you mind if I had some of that?"

Like everything here was perfectly normal.

TWENTY-THREE

He limped to a chair at the table and kind of fell into it. "I didn't mean to scare you," he said.

"The way to hell is paved with good intentions," I said. "You're welcome to the salad, but I also have some lasagna, if you'd rather. I could warm it up and it's easy to eat? And maybe a cup of tea?"

"Tea," he said. "The universal panacea. Be better if you had some whiskey."

"Jack Daniels okay?" I asked, like I was an ordinary hostess and he was an ordinary guest. This wasn't nearly as frightening as trying to feed a hungry child in a room full of angry militia.

"Please," he said. "And lasagna would be fabulous. Salad…" He started to raise a hand, then dropped it. "All that chewing? Maybe too much?"

I took out a pan of lasagna, cut a big chunk, and put it in the microwave. Then I poured him a generous slug of Jack. "Ice?"

"No. Thanks."

I set it on the table beside him. Got a fork and a knife and a napkin and set them on the table. This all felt surreal. Why was I tending and feeding this scary stranger who'd barged into my house?

As if he'd read my mind, he said, "I'm sorry. I seem to keep getting it wrong with you, don't I?"

I didn't bother to answer.

The microwave beeped and I took out his food. Set it on the table. Retreated to the kitchen island where my gun was.

His smile was lopsided and small as he said, "I know 'I'm sorry' doesn't cut it. You need to know what the hell is going on. It's...I... I'm not in the habit of sharing my business with civilians."

"I think you've already made this my business, on the plane and now. Just as your sister did by knocking on my door. You can't hide behind that 'us vs. them' wall anymore. So tell me. What's going on with Charity's husband, David Peckham? Who do you work for? Who is a danger to Charity, and why?"

"That's a lot of questions," he said. "You got all night?"

Like what? I'd back down if it was going to take time? "I've got as long as it takes. And by the way, we had a visit from a couple of government agents last night. Their IDs said Marshals Service. Alice and Fred. I know. Sounds like a couple from a TV sitcom. Are you working with them?"

The lasagna had disappeared. So had the whiskey. This man was more efficient than a vacuum cleaner.

"More?" I said. I have a caretaking problem when it comes to wounded, hungry men, even, it seems, unwanted ones who barge into my house uninvited.

"Please."

I put more lasagna in the microwave and retreated to my island. "So? Some answers?"

Andre, blue lights blazing, flew up the driveway and rocked to a stop. I quickly unlocked the kitchen door so he didn't knock it down. My husband in impulsive protection mode is something to behold.

He burst through the door, immediately taking in the gun on the counter and Kinsman at the table. Ignoring me, he focused on Kinsman and said a single word. "Explain."

Kinsman half rose and stuck out a shaky hand. "Malcolm Kinsman. Charity's brother."

Andre, a quick reader of situations, decided despite my gun on the counter that if I was feeding Kinsman, he might be okay. He shook the offered hand and repeated that single word. "Explain."

Kinsman sank back into his chair.

And Andre waited for answers.

I took the lasagna from the microwave, gave it to Kinsman, and cut a piece for Andre. Chicken salad wasn't going to do it under these circumstances. They might be stationary instead of circling each other and growling, but there was plenty of alpha male stuff going on.

Kinsman, who was definitely subpar right now, gave up the fight pretty quickly. "Just trying to find my sister," he said.

"Before someone else does," Andre said.

"Yes."

"Who wants to find her, and why?"

The central question here. I put some silverware and a napkin down across from Kinsman. Andre sat without taking his eyes off the man.

I poured more Jack for Kinsman and some for Andre, wishing I could have some myself. With Andre fed, I retreated to my island again. I can get a bit huffy when men are doing their thing and I feel like I'm being relegated to "little woman" status, but right now, I was hors d'combat. Willing to let the guys sort it out while MOC danced and I watched Kinsman figure out how much he could share about secret government operations, even to a cop who might be able to help.

"David and I are special forces. We were coming back from Mexico. Part of a task force working with the DEA, doing surveillance on a cartel. We had a couple hours in a Texas airport before our connecting flight. David went to the restroom and… uh…he didn't come back. Two of us went to check. Found his gear and a smear of blood in one of the stalls and a janitor so scared he couldn't talk. We're looking for him…the team…uh…and…uh… we immediately were concerned about Charity since…David would never reveal operational details—the who, what, where, and what our intel is. But if…if they had his pregnant wife? If they threatened her and the baby? The leverage is huge."

"Why did Charity come here?" Andre asked.

"Some pointy-headed bureaucrat decided Maine would be safe," Kinsman said.

"If they were trying to keep her location secret, how did you find her?"

"Charity…uh…she knew she wasn't supposed to, but she was so worried about David. No one would tell her anything. She kind of got in touch."

I wondered how someone kind of got in touch? Message in the hollow oak? Cryptic ad? Maybe there was a secret code, some message the person was supposed to post on Facebook?

Andre asked my question. "How did she 'kinda' get in touch? Was that what got Jessica Whitlow killed?"

Kinsman slumped in his chair. "Jess was a friend."

Which wasn't really an answer. It was clear he would share as little as possible. Never mind that Andre had two murders to investigate and Kinsman presumably wanted our help finding Charity. I should know, from my years living with Andre, that people in secretive lines of work struggle to reveal any information. Kinsman was the operative, tough, secretive, used to everything about his work being clandestine. I wondered if he'd tell us anything that might help.

While Kinsman wrestled with that, Andre had another question. "Any idea how a Boston detective would have found her? Or who he was working for?"

Kinsman sighed. "Someone was careless. Though he may not have known it, and he may have thought he was simply working a domestic, looking for someone's wife who was hiding out, he was working for the cartel."

The thought of a Mexican cartel operating in my town, even through proxies like the rude, arrogant, and not-too-careful Nathaniel Davenport, was terrifying. We've all read in the papers about how ruthless they are. No compunction about hurting or killing women or children. I glanced around my bright kitchen and briefly wished we'd moved into a fortress instead of a house. Despite our longing for MOC and our excitement about the kid's pending debut, I sometimes wondered how anyone could make the decision to bring a child into this crazy world.

We still didn't know about the man Davenport had with him. He'd never been identified.

Once this thing was over, we were adding doorbell cameras to our renovations list. Also motion-activated lights, a moat, and a portcullis.

Right now, I had a question of my own. "You're not here with a team?" I asked. "You're doing this on your own?"

"The rest of my team is looking for David," he said.

"But Jessica Whitlow really does...did work for the Marshals Service?"

He nodded.

"With them or on her own?"

I looked at Andre. "Do you know whether the Marshals Service has people here looking for Charity? I mean, I guess I mean, are Fred and Alice for real?" I really needed to know that he'd looked into this.

"There are agents by those names," he said. "I've asked them for pictures. They aren't excited about cooperating, but they will." He sighed. "In their own time."

Because we were just a podunk Maine town and he was just a podunk Maine detective? I remembered what Albie had said at the library. "Albie says there was a man snooping around the house today."

Andre was wearing his "I'm going to lock you up in a tower" look. "Was that you?" he asked Kinsman.

Kinsman said, "No."

"Albie—he's that boy whose bike broke while he was out collecting bottles—said the man was tall and strong-looking," I said. "Big shoulders. Dark hair. Dark skin or a deep tan. Gray suit. Sunglasses. And he was wearing cowboy boots." The man who'd been with Davenport.

Andre glared at Kinsman. "You know who that is?"

Kinsman said, "Oh fuck." Eloquent shorthand for concern and despair. "Not who, but what."

Andre looked around our bright, fishbowl kitchen. If there was someone out there looking for Kinsman, we might as well have put him under a spotlight. He grabbed Kinsman by the elbow and pulled him to his feet. More dragged than led him into the hall and up the stairs where I heard him clomping around in the guestroom, pulling shades, and then the rumble of voices as he extracted the reasons for Kinsman's reaction.

I've never liked being shut out of the action, but the situation sounded dangerous. Sounded? Was. Kinsman's condition, plus two murders and Charity's disappearance, made the danger quite clear. Another time, another me, the headstrong, independent Thea I'd been before the advent of MOC, I would have charged up the stairs and demanded to be part of the conversation. Instead, I stayed in the kitchen, anxious and uneasy, waiting for Andre to reappear and tell me what the heck was going on. That anxiety was choking me, and I was ridiculously close to tears. I didn't want to be involved in this, but there was no way out. Bad enough when Andre's work or mine brought troubles. These damned people had brought their own troubles to our doorstep and made them ours.

I put dishes in the dishwasher and wiped down the counters. Stared longingly at the bottle of Jack. Put it away and made myself a cup of tea. The jury is still out on whether an expectant mother can drink at all. I wasn't taking any chances. Yes. It was pathetic to look for comfort in a bottle, but I wasn't finding it anywhere else, and besides, I tough it out plenty. Wasn't I entitled to let down now and then?

The work spread out on the counter reminded me that whatever craziness was going on here, inside this house and in this town, my work life went on as usual. I finished with Eastern Shore's honor code and started on a client's crisis management plan, thinking that it looked like the Kozak-Lemieux household needed a crisis management plan of its own.

I sipped tea, listening to the rumble of men's voices upstairs. Tea couldn't soothe me. This business with Charity and strangers and murders across the street was unleashing too many bad memories. I didn't know how Andre and his colleagues did it, dealing with people's awfulness over and over. I'd seen enough to give me four lifetimes of PTSD, and I was just a consultant.

I practiced my breathing exercises. Not the prenatal ones that were supposed to get me through childbirth, these were the ones my therapist had taught me. They were supposed to calm me and help me send those memories away. They were supposed to help me focus on the here and now. Be able to plan and act in a clear and coherent way. Tonight they didn't help. Against the backdrop of those droning voices, every creak of the house and every small noise outside made me jump.

I closed my eyes, tried to shut out my surroundings, and thought back to my conversations with Charity. Had she said anything or had I noticed anything that would help me find her now? And fast on the heels of that came the question: Did I want to find her? If people, presumably some of them with bad intentions, were focused on me to help them find her, wasn't my best course of action to do nothing that might lead them to her? Had I been the world's biggest fool today, driving around looking at places she might go?

But I was sure no one had followed me.

Then, because I'd been so focused on this town, I wondered—why did I think she'd stay around if the bad guys had found her here? What if they already had her and all this speculation was just that? I had no way of knowing whether whoever killed Nathaniel Davenport and Jessica Whitlow had taken Charity at the same time. Was the fact that I'd seen her loading things into a Volvo a clue? What about the absence of the baby things we'd bought from the cottage? Was there anything at the crime scene that gave any clues? I wouldn't know, but Andre would.

I climbed down from my stool and headed upstairs. Voices still rumbled behind the closed guest room door. I opened it and went in.

Kinsman drooped in the pretty upholstered blue armchair I'd bought to match the duvet cover and carpet. He looked ghastly, a handkerchief pressed against the wound on his forehead. Andre stood over him, close and menacing.

My husband turned as I came in and gave me the look he might give to an underling, an upstart baby detective who was interrupting an interrogation at a critical moment.

"Not now, Thea," he said.

He should have known better. "Just one question," I said, "and I'll leave. Kinsman, have you heard from your sister Charity since her handler, Jessica Whitlow, and the private detective, were killed at her house?"

Andre hissed in exasperation.

I waited.

Kinsman said, "Yes."

Which meant I had a second question and likely the wrath of my husband. "Did she say she planned to stay around here? Anything about her plans or where she'd go? You must believe she's still around, or you wouldn't be here, going around town asking questions about me. Going around pointing a big red arrow at me."

I hadn't realized I was so mad.

There was the crunch of tires on the driveway.

Andre hit the light, said, "Stay," to Kinsman, and pulled me out of the room.

TWENTY-FOUR

I t was late. My watch said ten-thirty. Not an appropriate time for visitors. Outside the guestroom, Andre pulled me against him and wrapped his arms protectively around me. "Damn the man," he said. "He's so mission-driven he didn't see the harm he was doing." He unwrapped and said, "You get ready for bed. I'll handle this."

"Shouldn't we send Kinsman to the attic?" I said.

"Whoever this is, they're not coming upstairs," he said. "You're here."

Last night he'd been okay with that, or hadn't fought it. I understood that this was different. Maybe instead of assuming I was fine —like I was always reassuring him I was—he sensed my fear. The threat was increasing. And we had Kinsman in the house. I remembered that I'd left my gun sitting on the counter. "My gun," I said.

"I'll take care of it."

"But..." I got all my sense of being unsafe into that one word.

"Trust me, Thea," he said. Then, hesitating at the top of the stairs, he said, "I'll bring it up to you."

That shook me to the core. Yes, Andre made me learn to shoot, and yes, that training had come in handy in the past, but he knows I hate guns. He wouldn't offer to get it for me if he didn't think there was a chance I might need it, even though we had no idea who our late night visitors might be.

He pounded down the stairs and was back in seconds, handing me that damned gun. The gun and I retreated into my bedroom, but I didn't undress and get ready for bed. A nightgown isn't the best outfit for a gunfight, nor for a retreat if that became necessary.

Instead, I swapped my flip flops for sneakers. Pulled on yoga pants and a black jacket. Tied back my hair. Geared up, I crept to the top of the stairs and sat down to listen. I heard a male voice and a female one, unless it was another guy with a high voice, talking with Andre in the kitchen. His back was to me, so I couldn't hear anything beyond a rumble. Even at a rumble, I could tell Andre was angry and not interested in whatever our visitors had to say.

Just a few hours ago, I'd been excited about Jonetta's visit and thinking about how I'd entertain her. I'd been thinking about groceries and my clients. Now I had a renegade special ops guy in my guestroom along with two suspected—and unwanted— federal agents in my kitchen. I clutched my gun in my lap and thought about how absurd this was. I patted the basketball. "Don't worry, baby. Mom and Dad won't let anything happen to you."

Suzanne always claims I bring this on myself, that bad things never happen to her. I wouldn't want her to trade places, but I think she was missing a couple of points. First, that I got the jobs at EDGE that involved risk and bad actors. I was the trouble-shooter, Jane Wayne, the girl in the white hat. When people called me, there already *was* trouble. Second, that my unalterable personality trait was to help people in need. In danger. I was a fixer, starting when I had to run interference between my adopted sister Carrie and my mother. If Suzanne looked at my track record, a lot of good people had been rescued, and a lot of bad people had faced justice because of me.

The flip side? I was supposed to stop all this because of MOC. No more danger. No more helping people. I would be an irresponsible mother if I didn't. But how could I have kept Charity from knocking on my door? Was I supposed to have somehow sensed danger from this smiling new neighbor in her colorful dress and slammed the door in her face?

Going forward, did I need a bodyguard wherever I went? I guess such a person would be useful for carrying heavy packages and groceries. Except, of course, that that would prevent him or her from doing their protective duties.

I sighed, resting my head against the railing. All this surmising was making me dizzy. I wanted to go lie down. But there were still strangers in my kitchen. I longed to charge down there and throw them out, but if they needed ejecting, Andre could do that. He should do it. Now.

I tried the breathing exercises again, like the therapist had taught me. It didn't make a bit of difference. I am impulsive. I wrapped my gun-free hand around the railing and pulled myself up, planning to head downstairs. I felt a hand on my shoulder, and a voice whispered, "Don't."

What the hell? Kinsman had left the guest room and reached me and I hadn't heard a thing in this creaky old house.

I shivered even though it was a warm summer night. "What the . . ?"

He held a finger to his lips. "Shhh."

He must have felt my resistance. "When they're gone, I'll explain."

"But…"

This time he put his finger on my lips. "Come with me." The hand on my shoulder wasn't gentle. I turned around and let him steer me into the guest room. In the dark I found my way to the chair, leaving the bed for him. There was a certainty about him that reminded me of Andre. Men who knew their way around bad guys and violence. Real take-charge types.

Maybe I was being too trusting, but I offered him the gun. It would be better in his hands anyway.

"Thanks." He took it. Checked it the way people who know their way around guns do.

I closed my eyes. I wanted the people downstairs gone. I wanted him gone. I wanted my happy summer life back.

No one knows better than I that wishing won't make it so.

We waited in a silence so charged the air almost crackled with electricity. I had to remind myself to breathe. After what felt like forever, the downstairs door opened and shut. Car doors slammed and it backed down the driveway.

I heard Andre's footsteps on the stairs and headed for the door.

Kinsman said, "Wait." In the gloom, I saw him get up.

I wasn't waiting. In a moment of carelessness and instinctive trust, I'd armed this man. Now he was heading toward my husband. What if I was wrong?

I am quick on my feet, and I reached the door first even though he was closer. I slipped through and straight into Andre's arms. To hell with acting like the little woman. Compared to Andre, I was little. Except in the middle.

His arms wrapped around me and he pulled me up against his chest. He has a chest like a wall. I closed my eyes and inhaled his scent. Out there in the world, I am a tough pragmatist. Here at home, I will readily admit Andre is my rock. My center. We've been through a lot to get here. It has bonded us. Just listening to him breathe is more comforting than any breathing I might do myself.

I heard Kinsman come out behind me, not moving quietly this time. He waited until Andre released me, then held out the gun to me.

Andre gave him a look. I think it was thanks, but I'm not sure.

"I could use a drink," Kinsman said, like he'd been the one down in the kitchen.

"Sure," Andre said.

"Me, too," I said. I wouldn't, though. I went to the kitchen, where they were back at the table, bent over glasses of warm brown liquid, looking like they were engaged in a staring contest. I got the key, carefully stowed my firearm, and took the key to the cabinet back downstairs. But returning it to the peas seemed ridiculous. It was an awkward method of securing the guns, one that wouldn't work very well if a bad guy entered. And Kinsman was too observant not to notice. Of course, there was a second key upstairs in an easier location. We used this one as a rule, though neither of us could probably explain why. Something superstitious, maybe? For now, I put it in my pocket.

I climbed back on my stool by the island. "Who was it?" I asked.

"Alice and Fred again."

"You tell them to stop coming here?"

Andre nodded. He got out his phone and showed me pictures of their badge photos.

He showed them to Kinsman, who sighed and said, "I don't think they're Marshals Service."

"But you don't know?" Andre asked.

Kinsman shook his head.

"Why do they keep bothering us," I asked, "when we've told them we don't know anything?"

"Because you met Charity. She lived across the street. The two of you did stuff together. And it's you she chose to leave her ID with. It all suggests a deeper relationship than you actually had. That you are hiding her somewhere or know where she's gone," Andre said. "Some feds, you know, they get so distrustful they can't see the forest for the trees." He hesitated. "Some cops, too."

Which I knew to be true from my own misadventures. "You think they're for real?"

"I don't," Kinsman said. But he didn't offer any details.

I hadn't helped her, and I had no idea where she was, though, being me, I would have helped her if she'd asked. It's damned hard to prove a negative, though.

I didn't have enough bandwidth left to try and sort anything out. Not tonight. "I've got to get some sleep," I said. Then, remembering I hadn't told Andre this yet, I said, "Oh, and Jonetta is coming tomorrow. She needed to escape the city. Says she hasn't had a vacation in six years."

"You'll like that," Andre said.

"If all this will let me enjoy it."

I was so ready for bed, but I still needed to know what was happening with the investigation into the murders across the street. I wouldn't sleep unless I did. Usually, I didn't ask about Andre's work. I let him tell me if he wanted to, and if he could. But this was different. I'd found one of the victims. "So, the murders at Charity's place. What have you learned?"

He glanced at Kinsman, a not-so-subtle reminder he didn't discuss cases in front of strangers. We would talk later, if I was still awake.

I gave up. I climbed off the stool and found I was shaking. This whole business was too unsettling. It was so damned unfair.

Andre wrapped his arms around me again. "I know," he said. "I know. We'll get it sorted out. I won't let anything happen to you."

I politely refrained from mentioning the call I'd made that had gone to voicemail. The hours I'd waited here with Kinsman, not knowing whether Charity's brother was friend or foe. He was here now, and I was almost asleep on my feet. But there was always one more question. "So, Malcolm," I said. "Who is the guy with the cowboy boots?"

TWENTY-FIVE

K insman touched the cut on his head. "Cartel. I'm sure. He's the one who did this."

I was out of questions. Andre could ask the rest—like was the guy out there somewhere? Had the guy followed him here? How did he know cowboy boots was cartel? Where was Kinsman's car? Despite the way unanswered questions swirled around me, buzzing like a swarm of bees, I was too tired to focus, and I had to get some sleep before my early run to the store. I left them to bond, or circle each other warily over their drinks, and went to bed.

When my alarm rang the next morning at six, I was not ready to face the day. I am not a morning person, yet I'm living a life that acquaints me far too much with mornings. But company was coming and groceries were required. I dragged myself from bed, wondering how it was possible that I would get any more whale-like in the next few weeks, and pulled on a baggy tee shirt and a pair of Andre's old sweatpants cut off just below the knee. I was definitely making a fashion statement, especially after I tied on a bandana to hold back my unruly hair and wiggled my feet into flip flops.

Andre didn't stir, and the closed door to the guestroom suggested Kinsman had spent the night.

In the kitchen, I made a quick cup of coffee. I grabbed my reusable bags, left a note for Andre on the counter, and headed to my car. Not in my normal, headlong way—my two speeds tend to be all and nothing—but cautiously and looking carefully around for any strange cars or unwanted visitors. Nothing in sight.

The drive to the store was soothing. The roads were empty, there were summer flowers everywhere, and it was lovely morning for a drive. Scoring food was easy. So easy that I bought far too much. Bacon. Eggs. Good bread. Lots of cheese and olives and good crackers. I got the steaks and the chocolate cake and red wine, and some brownies, and another rotisserie chicken, and ham and turkey and Swiss and deli coleslaw. Bagels and cream cheese. Potato chips for the man who can eat without worrying about his waistline.

Right then, I supposed I could, too. I didn't have a waistline.

I drove home with the windows down and the radio blaring, feeling like a successful hunter/gatherer coming back to the cave. Andre was in the kitchen when I lugged in the first load, and chivalrously offered to bring in the rest while I put things away. Sunlight and domesticity made yesterday's scary black car and last night's visitors seem far away and unthreatening. I am such a simple soul.

I was stowing the last items when Kinsman appeared. If anything, he looked worse than yesterday. The day after an injury can do that. Andre told him to sit and I offered coffee.

As soon as he'd been plied with caffeine, I said, "Charity's been in touch with you, hasn't she?"

He nodded.

"Before you appeared on the plane?"

Another nod. "She has a burner phone she's using."

"You haven't heard from her since?"

"She said she didn't feel safe with Jessica. In that house. That she was going to find another place to stay. Since then? Nothing. That's why I'm here."

"Do you know the person or persons who assaulted you?"

"The guy with the cowboy boots and another guy who sounded kinda like that guy who was down in your kitchen last night."

"Could you describe them any better than that?"

"You're not a cop," he said with a wry smile.

"I'm not. But since you put me, us, our family, at risk by coming here, I want to know everything Charity told you that led you to believe I might know where she is."

He looked at Andre, making me wonder if they *had* done some male bonding after I went to bed.

"If I were you, I'd answer her questions," Andre said.

"She called me. She said she'd met you. Said she was going to confide in you. She said that Jessica Whitlow had been assigned to get her settled here, and what she'd found was a wreck of a place that wasn't fit to live in. She said she was supposed to trust Whitlow but she didn't. She didn't feel safe."

He absently fingered the bandage on his forehead. "I asked her to hold on until I could get to her. Then she called me in a panic, said there had been some strangers snooping around and she'd also seen them at your house. She and Jessica had argued and Jessica told her not to worry, Jessica and her partner were watching out for her. Then she stopped answering her phone. I tried to reach you and your office said you were going to be out of the office at a client school. Someone gave me the name of the school. I did a little digging and managed to get on that flight with you."

He stared at his empty cup and Andre poured him more coffee. "We've got bagels," I offered, even though I didn't want to interrupt his train of thought.

"A bagel would be great," he said.

Andre put one in the toaster. We're a good team.

I waited for Kinsman to go on. He didn't.

"I told you everything I knew on the plane," I said. "But you still came here, looking for your sister. I get that you're concerned about her. Jessica Whitlow doesn't seem to have done a good job looking after her. What I still don't get is why you think I know where your sister is."

Kinsman looked away. Maybe embarrassed? "You're the only link I've got."

"What about the Marshals Service? They're looking for her, too. Couldn't you be working together?"

"If they were willing to share information. Which they're not. They're into witness protection. I'm into family protection. I gather most of the time they're protecting witnesses from their families. Or trying to isolate witnesses from their families so others can't use their families to find them. I can't convince them this situation is different, and that's true even though I know...knew Jessica. She was very by-the-book."

The toaster dinged and Andre put the bagel on a plate.

"Charity was pretty frustrated," Kinsman went on. "They wouldn't tell her anything about David and what was happening. That's why she called me. Then that private dick showed up, and that really spooked her. She said I had to come. When I got here, I called her and there was no response, and then I read about the murders..." He looked at me. "So I tried to find you."

"You did find me." I was impatient with this narrative, which didn't seem to help us solve the killings or find Charity. I looked at Andre. "You're going to work?"

He nodded.

"And I'm going to work for a few hours."

Back to Kinsman. "Are you staying here or leaving? Where's your car? Do you think that..."

Andre held up a cautioning hand. "Slow down," he said.

I felt like being a brat and saying, "What for?" but restrained myself. "You guys work it out, okay? I'm going to work. And he..." I pointed rudely at Kinsman. "... can't stay in the guestroom because we're expecting a guest."

Okay. This was bringing out my worst side, if I have such a thing. These endless conversations where I declared that I didn't know where Charity was and no one believed me made me feel like a gerbil on a wheel. I had to get out of here. Go to the office where I could concentrate on something other than Charity Kinsman.

"Go," Andre said. He was smiling, though. He knows me well. Knew this wasn't about him, but about how I can't stand it when everything is out of control. "What time are you coming home?"

"Jonetta said she'd be here by three, so maybe two-thirty?"

He nodded. "You might want to change first?"

197

I'd forgotten the tee-shirt, cut-off sweats, and flip flops. I may be no fashion plate, but I'd never go to the office dressed like this. I only went to the store this way because it was early morning and no one I knew would see me. Being pregnant has made me more concerned about comfort, even at the expense of my normal sense of propriety. I headed upstairs, slipped on one of my new tunic tops, capris, and proper sandals. I added a chunky black and white necklace and earrings and came back down. I shoved my work into my briefcase, got my purse, and left. I was sure between them, Andre and Malcolm Kinsman could figure out what to do next. They didn't need me, even if at least one of them thought a few hours spent together made me Charity's confidant and BFF.

On the drive to the office, I pondered on why Charity had left me her ID and credit cards and also Jessica Whitlow's ID. Had she just not wanted them on her person to give her deniability? I could see hiding her own ID, but why Jessica's? Surely witsec didn't give people they were protecting the IDs of their agents or inspectors or whatever they were called. Was she trying to protect the other woman or incapacitate her by leaving her stuck here without ID? Or was it a message: here's who I really am and who Jessica is and why I pretended to be her. What was she doing for money? Was that wad of cash I'd seen her using enough?

I can puzzle my way through a lot of things, but not this, and I resented having so much of my personal bandwidth taken up by Charity and her problems. My attempt to achieve a better work/life balance didn't need this thrown in. I'm a professional worrier and fixer, though. There was no way I could simply ignore Charity's dilemma even if the people didn't keep knocking on my door and shoving the situation in my face. Or, in her brother's case, simply opening it and barging in.

Despite a grocery run and an unwanted houseguest, I was at the office early. Unless there's an emergency, Magda arrives at nine on the dot, and Sarah has to wait for the camp bus to pick up her kids, so she comes in a few minutes later. Lisa was doing an on-site visit at a client school and Bobby had a dentist appointment. Suzanne had some early faculty wives' breakfast. All that was fine with me. I like a quiet, empty office.

As I parked, I saw that I wouldn't be entirely alone. Lindsay's bright blue Subaru was already there, and miracle of miracles, Jason's little Corolla was right beside it. So far, punctuality hadn't been his strong suit, so I was pleased. The little chat with me and Suzanne must have done some good.

I grabbed my briefcase and headed inside. I paused at the door, though, when I heard a woman's upset voice say, "Stop that, Jason. Take your hands off me. Right now. This is not okay."

This was not a flirtation or some goofing around. Lindsay sounded panicked and scared.

I stepped back outside, dialed 911, gave the address, and said that a woman was being assaulted. If I was wrong, I could say "my bad" later. I didn't think I was wrong.

I stepped quietly through the door, setting my briefcase on Magda's desk. Jason had Lindsay pressed up against the wall, using his body to pin her there. I recorded some video with my phone as I headed toward them, not because I'm a voyeur, but because in case he denied it, I wanted evidence. I am not a cop. I am not a detective. But I am not letting anyone get away with this behavior if I can stop it. The world is ridiculously full of people recording things. This time it made sense.

I captured Lindsay's desperate voice saying, "Don't touch me, Jason. Let me go. Don't do this. Oh my God! What are you doing! Stop!" Her "stop" ended on a frightened wail.

I didn't doubt that she could usually handle herself, but he was a big guy, she was a small woman, and he wasn't listening.

"Jason. Stop right now! Get away from her!" I yelled it as loudly as I could. A man bent on sexual assault can be difficult to refocus.

When he didn't respond, I switched my phone for my pepper spray, grabbed his shoulder, jerked him around and blasted him full in the face. He staggered away, hands clasped over his streaming eyes, moaning and cursing.

I heard sirens and then the pounding of feet on the stairs.

Ignoring him, I opened my arms, and Lindsay threw herself at me, sobbing. "Oh my God, Thea. Oh my God. What if you hadn't been here?"

The first officer through the door was one I'd met before. He gave a nod of recognition, then indicated Jason. "This the guy?"

I nodded. "And this is the victim."

"Pepper spray?" he said.

"I couldn't get him to let go of her."

"We'll take it from here."

His partner, also someone I'd met before, a woman who was quick, smart, and unflappable, approached Lindsay and said, "Officer Bonnie Martin. Ma'am, could we talk for a moment?"

Martin looked at me. "Can we use your office?"

"Of course." I kept an arm around Lindsay as I walked her to my office. Martin followed. I got Lindsay into a chair and said, "Do you mind if I stay?"

"Please let her stay," Lindsay said.

Martin nodded. I sat behind my desk, while Martin sat beside Lindsay in my other visitor's chair.

"I know this is hard," Martin said. "Can you tell me what happened?"

Lindsay shot me a desperate look.

"Just walk Officer Martin through it, Lindsay, step by step," I said, handing her some tissues. "She needs to know the facts."

"Okay," Lindsay said, her voice shaky. "I uh...Jason asked...uh, I'm an intern working here at EDGE for the summer. Jason is... uh...he just started working here." She looked at me. "About a week and a half, two weeks ago, maybe? Is that right, Thea?"

"Two weeks."

"The other day he...uh...he put his hand on my butt when I was bending over, putting something in my purse. I confronted him right away. I told him that kind of behavior wasn't okay in the workplace. He...uh...he kind of smirked, like it was all a big joke. I didn't smile. I told him it wasn't funny. And later, I told Thea about it because working near him was making me uncomfortable."

Martin nodded and looked at me. "Yes," I said, "Lindsay told me about the incident, and my partner Suzanne and I spoke with

Jason about it, about appropriate behavior in the workplace, with co-workers and with clients. We were concerned because we work closely with independent schools, and our work often involves contact with high school students. We had to know that he understood boundaries and it wouldn't happen again. We were very firm that one more misstep, and he'd be fired."

I spread my hands in a gesture of defeat. "Guess the message wasn't received."

"Were there any other instances of touching before today?" Martin asked.

Lindsay shook her head. "Except that pat."

"Any other contact? Conversations? Phone calls? Have you spent any time with him outside of work?"

Lindsay straightened up and looked at the officer. "No. There has been no contact outside of work." She sounded offended. "You're not trying to say…"

Martin cut her off. "Tell me what happened this morning."

I might be feeling protective of Lindsay, but Martin didn't need my interference. She knew what she was doing. Knew she had to test the veracity of Lindsay's story.

"I'd mentioned to Thea's secretary, Sarah, that I planned to come in early this morning to work on a video we're making for a client school. Jason must have overheard." She looked around nervously, like he might still be lurking somewhere.

"It's okay," Martin said. "No one is going to interrupt. Jason has gone with the other officers. Please go on."

"I came in around seven-thirty. No one was here, it was nice and quiet, and I was working on my video when Jason arrived."

"What time was that?"

"Maybe eight. Eight-fifteen. I didn't look at the clock. I was pretty immersed in my work. I just noticed he'd come in and he went to his desk. I thought, like me, he probably had something he wanted to finish. A few minutes later, I went to the ladies' room. When I came out, he was standing at my desk, looking at my work. He was reaching for the keyboard and I said, 'Don't' pretty loudly because I wasn't sure I'd saved everything. I mean, I thought I had, but I didn't want to take a chance. I'd put a lot of work into the video."

She knotted her hands together. "I…he…when I got closer, he turned toward me. He had this ugly smirk on his face. He said, 'You told Thea and Suzanne that I was working on my own stuff, didn't you?' and he came toward me. I backed away. He was scaring me, and the two of us were alone in the office. I said, 'Stay away from me, Jason. You're making me uncomfortable. You're scaring me,' and I tried to get around him, so I could get out of the office and find someplace else in the building where there were people around. But he grabbed my arm and he…"

She started to sob.

I handed her another tissue, but I didn't say anything. This was Martin's show. I was only here for moral support.

"Go on," Martin said softly.

"He jerked me back toward him and dragged me toward the wall. I tried to talk to him. I told him I was scared and asked why was he scaring me? Why was he acting like this? He just kept that smirk on his face, like the whole thing was very funny. It was…terrifying." She let out a sigh. "I've never been in a situation like that. Some of my friends have…have been in a situation where there's a guy who won't hear *no* and who is just determined to do what he wants. I didn't really know what he wanted. I mean, was he just trying to scare me? To intimidate me because I'd spoken with Thea? Or was he…"

She stopped and buried her face in her hands. From behind the barrier of her fingers, her words were faint. "Was he planning to assault me?"

"I know this is hard," Martin said, "but I need to hear the whole story in your words."

Lindsay dropped her hands and glared at the officer. "It's not a story, okay? I didn't make this up. Thea saw…"

She took a breath and let it out slowly. "I tried to get away, but he was between me and the door. He kept coming forward, and I kept stepping back away from him, and then I was right up against the wall and I had nowhere to go."

She shook her head. "He kept coming until he was pressed right up against me. Rubbing his body against me. I said, 'Stop it, Jason. Get your hands off me. Let me go. This is not okay.' I begged him to stop. I was yelling at him. And pleading. He put his hand up under my dress and..."

She was wearing a pretty summer dress, sleeveless and short, like all the girls were wearing this year. It wasn't tight. It wasn't low cut. No one could claim that she was being provocative.

"Go on," Martin said quietly.

"He put his hand up my dress..." Lindsay was crying again. "Uh put his fingers... inside me, and he said, 'Come on, Lins, you know you want me' as if..." She gasped for breath. "As if I'd ever want to be treated like that. And that's when Thea grabbed him."

She dissolved into sobs.

I felt like an idiot. I felt responsible. She'd told us about his inappropriate touching, and we hadn't taken it seriously enough and fired him on the spot. We'd thought counseling would handle the problem. We'd been dealing with Jason like a professional employee who'd crossed a line, not like some hormone-driven adolescent. Not like some thuggish bro with a Neanderthal view of women. He was a twenty-something college graduate. Maybe our judgment had been impaired because we really needed the help. But never in a million years, however callow and self-centered Jason's recent behavior had revealed him to be, would I have expected this.

"When I came into the room and saw what was happening," I told Bonnie Martin, "I stepped back out, called 911, then set my phone to video as I approached them."

She looked at me and quirked an eyebrow. "Really?" She held out her hand. "Let me see."

It wasn't great from a production standpoint, but it absolutely confirmed Lindsay's account.

"I can send it to your phone," I said.

She gave me her number and I sent it.

She returned her focus to Lindsay. "Lindsay, you'll need to come down to the station and give us a formal statement. Can you do that?"

Lindsay nodded. "But first I…if it's okay, I mean…I need to finish this video I'm working on."

Martin patted her hand. "There's no rush. Any time today is fine." She looked at me. "You'll come with her?"

I nodded.

"Good. We'll need a statement from you, too." She shook her head. "That boy has had more chances than anyone deserves. This is his last."

"What do you mean?" Lindsay and I said together.

"I mean this is not his first rodeo. He got the other cases filed. Good lawyer. Connected parents. The old juvenile defense, no one wanted to ruin his future. He was supposed to keep his nose clean and it would go away."

"But we…" I started.

"You wouldn't have found anything," Martin said. "His daddy takes care of that."

"So when he told me that his mother was in the hospital and his work schedule was affected because he had to take care of his twin siblings, that was just a story?" I asked.

"I'm afraid so. He doesn't have twin siblings and his mother is probably out playing golf. As I said, you couldn't know. There was nothing to find." She looked at Lindsay. "I'm sorry this happened to you. If you need to talk to someone…if you feel like you need support…we have a victim advocate you can talk to."

"I'm just…" Lindsay was crying again. "Trying to do my job."

"Me, too," Martin said. She snapped her notebook shut, then gave us each a business card. "Call when you're coming in, so I can be there."

She hesitated at the door. I thought she was considering whether to comment on the video I'd made. Or say something more comforting to Lindsay. Bonnie Martin was a good cop, but she wasn't warm and fuzzy. She shook her head. Then she turned and left.

I wondered if she, like me, was wishing she'd done something sooner, so this wouldn't have happened. As Andre sometimes says, cops do their job, but sometimes the justice system doesn't.

"Cup of tea?" I asked Lindsay.

"Unless you have a bottle of whiskey in your desk drawer."

"I'm afraid not. It's tempting though. But this early in the day, the bars aren't even open."

"S'okay. I've got work to do."

"You can go home if you want."

She shook her head. "And sit there by myself brooding on what just happened? You know how that will go. I'll start thinking it must have been my fault."

"Stop!" I held up a hand. "Don't even start with that. It's how predators get away with it, making their victims feel like they did something wrong."

"Predator? Wow. That's a strong word."

"It's a perfect word."

She considered that and nodded. "It *is* a perfect word."

She went back to her desk, and I fought my maternal desire to sit there and watch over her.

This was not how I'd planned to spend my day.

TWENTY-SIX

Magda came in as Martin was leaving, followed shortly by Sarah and Suzanne. I called them into my office and filled them in on what had just happened. Magda looked like she was contemplating homicide, Sarah was ready to mother Lindsay, and Suzanne looked disgusted.

"We warned him," she said.

"Bonnie Martin says this isn't the first time he's been in trouble, though she didn't elucidate. I guess he's one of those guys whose important daddy bails him out whenever he gets in trouble."

"Not this time, I hope," Sarah said.

I agreed.

"If he shows his face around here again, call the police," Suzanne said. "If he says he needs to pick up his stuff, that happens only if a police officer comes with him. In fact, I think we should go ahead and get a restraining order, and Lindsay should get one for herself as well."

Because we deal with vulnerable student populations, and have been writing tons of honor codes and crisis management plans, the necessary steps to protect a victim are practically tattooed on our arms. Suzanne left to call our attorney, and Magda and Sarah went back to their desks.

I was answering messages and fielding questions from client schools when Lindsay appeared in my office door.

"I've got a pretty good rough cut of the video, if you'd like to look," she said.

"Love to," I said. Her color was back and she seemed calmer. "How are you doing?"

"It was terrifying," she said. "You never think…I mean, we all talk about assaults and try to be vigilant. We're careful in bars and watch out for each other. You know. But who would expect this? In the office, when someone might walk in at any moment?" She looked down at the floor. "What could I possibly have done…"

"Nothing. You did nothing. Don't do this to yourself, Lindsay. Please. It isn't something you did, other than being young and attractive and female, which is neither a provocation nor a crime. This is all on him. Maybe it *would* help to speak with their victims' advocate."

She shook her head. "I can deal…"

"You don't have to do it right now, Lindsay. But if it stays with you and you don't feel like you can move on, it's all right to get help. It doesn't mean you're weak."

"Would you? I mean, you're so strong and tough."

"I have. I did. Actually, Andre's boss made me go see someone. I went kicking and screaming. But it did help."

I was not eager to recount the adventures that led to Andre's lieutenant, Jack Leonard, sending me for help. I would if that was what Lindsay needed. For now, I thought focusing on work would help her like it helped me. I stood. "Let's look at that video."

I stood behind her, looking over her shoulder, as she ran the brief but powerful narrative she'd put together. The boys rapping their plans. Their photos mixed with texts and Instagram postings, so the posters were clearly identified. Their own videos of the fight, quick cuts between the various phones, showing them setting up, the attack on Denzel, him trying to talk to them, bring them to their senses, the blows continuing until he was finally forced to defend

KATE FLORA

himself by shoving an assailant away. It was as riveting as a movie trailer and very persuasive.

"It's brilliant, Lindsay. You've done such a great job of telling the story. Or letting the story tell itself. It doesn't look contrived; it looks honest. I think The King School is going to be very impressed."

"Did the video of that attack on Dr. Ellis-Jackson inspire you to…uh…record this morning?"

I hadn't thought about it. It had just been instinct. The phone was in my hand and I had seem too many instances where it was his word against hers and male voices were the ones that were believed. "Maybe," I said. "It just seemed important."

She nodded. "It was…it *is* important. Can I…do you mind if I see it again?"

I wasn't sure that was a good idea, but I had to let her take the lead here. Trust her instincts for what would help. I queued up the video and passed her my phone.

She played it. Replayed it. Handed the phone back. "Thank you," she said. "Makes me want to kill him, you know? Hit him with a brick. Run him down with my car. Do something bad."

"Probably not a good idea," I said, worrying that maybe I'd misjudged her as well. Should I let Bonnie Martin know Lindsay was thinking like this? I understood rage and the desire to do something, anything, to restore the balance and reclaim a sense of personal autonomy. I had no idea how serious Lindsay was about acting on it. The fiasco with Jason had me worried about my judgment. We'd made a personnel decision a few years back that had nearly gotten me killed.

"Are you ready to send that video to our clients?"

She nodded. "I am."

"You have their contacts, right?"

"I do."

"Then go ahead. It was your idea; you should get the credit."

As I headed for Suzanne's office, I noticed that Marlene had come in without saying hi to anyone and was huddled at her desk in the corner. I headed over there to see if she was okay.

208

"Good morning," I said, trying to sound more cheerful than I felt.

She looked up nervously.

"How did you do with the crisis management plan?"

"I think I've got it. Shall I send it to you?"

"That would be good."

She looked down at her desk and said, in a low voice, "The thing with Jason this morning. I should have told you. Warned you."

"Should have told me what?"

"That he would be a dreadful employee. I live in the same town, you see, and I know his family. His history. If I'd told you what I knew, maybe I could have spared that poor girl."

"You didn't because?" I asked.

"Because I didn't want to be that new employee who tries to undercut other people. I didn't want you to think I was bad-mouthing him. So I didn't say anything and now look what's happened. The thing is that it has been such a distraction, trying to work and trying not to think about him. I'm afraid I've been kind of a mess about it."

"That's a hard call to make," I agreed. "Especially when you're new. He's gone now, so let's hope you'll be able to concentrate better."

Her smile was grateful. "I will. And of course, he made it very clear that he'd make my life miserable if I said anything."

"He threatened you?"

She nodded.

This just got worse and worse. Here we're thinking we've solved our personnel problems when our office is actually a hotbed of intrigue and anxiety. How had Suzanne and I missed all this? The answer, of course, was that we were working ourselves. Balancing home and family and trying to build and sustain a business. And if Martin was right, Jason's sordid history wasn't there for us to find. Still, we'd have to do better.

She held up some papers. "I've been working on this for Bobby, and I think I've got it right. He has been so kind to me."

Ah. Bobby. Our peacemaker. Our ray of sunshine. I wasn't

209

being sarcastic. Bobby was a treasure, which was why we worked hard to keep him happy when he was under constant pressure to quit from his husband, Quinn. Why we'd been looking for someone to help him with his work.

I took the papers she was offering. One of Bobby's projects was helping schools develop guidelines for incorporating LGBTQ history and issues into their curriculum to develop greater understanding among their students. Her desk was covered with marked-up print-outs and I was holding a draft set of guidelines. Was working on this why she'd done such a poor job on my assignment? Had Bobby and I, between us, given her too much work, and that's why she'd been weeping? Weeping instead of telling me what the problem was?

I understood that younger people sometimes had trouble communicating face to face, but Marlene was a middle-aged mom.

It felt like things were spinning out of control. Maybe EDGE needed a workshop on communication?

I gave her back the pages. "Interesting project. He should be in soon to give you feedback."

"About the other thing," she said.

I waited, because I didn't know which other thing she was referring to.

"The questionnaire?"

I nodded.

"I really didn't try. And I'm sorry. I was caught up in this. I have…my fifteen-year-old is transitioning. I guess I let myself get too excited about the idea of schools that really want to be open and accepting."

She gulped, and looked me in the eyes for the first time. She was a slight woman with an eager face, rusty red hair, and a trendy haircut that didn't suit her. We'd hired her based on good credentials and a bit of desperation. Now I was discovering more interesting things about her. We're a small office. Very much a team. Her openness and revelations gave me hope. We needed someone to work with Bobby. With Jason gone, it looked like she was eager to step into that role.

"That's good to know. We really do need someone to assist Bobby. But Marlene?"

She flinched like she was expecting criticism.

"Next time, come talk to me. I'm not an ogre."

She laughed. "It's not you, it's me," which made both of us laugh.

I headed to Suzanne's office, thinking at least this was one bright spot in a difficult day.

She was on the phone. She waved me in and I sat while she finished her conversation. Whoever she was talking to was not a pleasant person. I could tell by the squawks coming out of the phone and the way she was frowning. I wondered who it was. Suzanne is brilliant with people. She can charm anyone.

"No," she said, firmly. "No, we cannot sit down and talk about this. Furthermore, your client may not enter these premises nor approach anyone on our staff, in or out of the office. Rather than arguing with me, you should be explaining this to him. Now I have someone waiting in my office. Goodbye."

She hung up and sighed. "Jason's lawyer. She says the situation was misunderstood, and she and Jason want to sit down and sort things out. I told her there is nothing to sort out, and both we and Lindsay are getting restraining orders."

She ran her fingers through her neat blonde bob. "How is Lindsay doing?"

"I don't think it has hit her yet. We're supposed to go down to the station and give statements. I suppose we'd better get that over with so it won't be hanging over her head."

She shook her head. "I keep thinking, what if you hadn't come in early?"

I shivered.

"How did we get that so wrong, Thea?"

"Bulldozer parents who have kept his record clean. Probably leaned on people to give him good references. Marlene says his presence here made her very nervous. She lives in the same town."

"But she didn't say anything."

"For two reasons. She was trying to be a good employee and not badmouth him. And he threatened her."

We sat and stared at each other. How had it come to this?

"Guess we'll have to find someone to replace Jason," I said. "Here's a bit of good news, though. Marlene has been working on a project for Bobby. It's good. I mean, she's done a good job and he's going to be happy."

She shook her head. "If this weren't our business, I'd quit."

"Me, too. Just as soon as I finish the six things on my desk and make a little trip to the police department. Got to get moving. Jonetta's coming this afternoon."

She looked at me like I'd suddenly started speaking a foreign language. "Jonetta? Did I hear that right?"

"She said she needs a vacation."

"Right. For the last six years."

"Just what she said. So you and Paul and the kids should come over tomorrow. We'll get the big guy to make burgers or steaks or something. He's becoming a grilling champ. We've got a big back yard for the kids to run around in. And you can drink."

She eyed the beach ball. "Soon, you can, too."

"Soon, I'll need to think about a nanny."

"Right," Suzanne agreed. "In that department, I may have good news. My nanny just told me that she has a cousin who is looking for a job."

"Impossible. There are no responsible young people looking for a job."

Suzanne shrugged. "It was just a suggestion."

"Do we know anything about this girl?"

"Not yet. But I can ask. I will ask."

I wasn't ready for any of this, but it would be foolish to pass up the opportunity to at least explore. I'd found Suzanne's nanny at a client school, and she had worked out very well. "Okay. Get me the details and I'll talk to her."

I checked my watch. I had to get down to the police station soon so I could be home in time for Jonetta.

"You should take a look at Lindsay's video. It's pretty brilliant. I'll have her send you a copy."

"Too bad she has to finish school."

"Right. But it's only one semester, and then, unless that jerk Jason has driven her away, she'll be coming back to us."

Suzanne smiled. "A bit of good news in the midst of all the bad."

"We've seen worse."

"Don't remind me."

One of those casual things people say, except she really meant it.

Her phone rang. Our attorney needed to speak with Lindsay to finalize her request for a restraining order.

"I'll get her," I offered.

As I led her to Suzanne's office, I said, "When that's done, let's ask if Martin can see us. I'd like to get these formalities over with."

"Me, too," she said. "Hard to concentrate with this hanging over my head."

Officer Martin could see us, so Lindsay and I drove down to the station and gave our formal statements. I could tell, when we were finished, that she was done in. It had been an awful day for her.

"Why don't you take the rest of the day," I suggested. "Is there someone who can stay with you?"

She shook her head. "This is the summer of me striking out on my own. I don't really know a lot of people around here. And… uh…to tell the truth, my place is pretty much only somewhere to sleep. It won't be comforting. I guess…" She considered. "I guess I could go to a bar. But I'd only have to drive home after, so I couldn't get stupid drunk like I want to." She stopped, a nervous hand to her mouth. "Oops. I don't often…or ever…do that. It's just…right now, I don't feel like…"

I couldn't leave her like this. She was trying to be brave and grownup when she was clearly so in need of someone to look after her.

"Come to my house. We've got room, and I've got the best person in the world coming for the weekend. Andre will cook steaks on the grill, and we'll have salad and corn and chocolate cake. Wine or beer."

She hesitated. I thought she was going to say no. Then she said, "You mean, stay over?"

"If you want."

"Then yes. I'll go home and get my things. I'd love to come to your house." Another hesitation. "I don't care if it makes me seem like a big baby, Thea. The idea of being alone spooks me. What if he gets out on bail?"

I'd been alone after a scary experience. I knew how easy it was to dwell on it, rehash it, and begin to think it was my own fault, even when I knew that wasn't true.

"Great. Get out your phone and put in my address. Your GPS can find me easily."

Now that this was underway, I was a bit nervous about letting her go home alone, even to get her things.

"Do you want me to follow you home?"

"With your history of scary black SUVs?" she said. "That's okay. I'll see you there." She hesitated. "We will have police protection, right?"

With all the commotion of the last twenty-four hours, I'd forgotten about the car that had menaced us on the highway. I decided I'd call Andre before I left. Even if he didn't answer, it meant someone would know where I was and be concerned if I didn't show up at home. I wasn't scared, exactly, just wary.

"Cops or special forces," I said.

"Wow. You sure are a full-service employer."

"I try."

I watched her leave with a mingled sense of pity and admiration. She'd held herself together beautifully. Finished her work. Barely let us see how shaken she was. Maybe I was seeing myself in her?

I went and told Suzanne what the plan was, then I left, too, pausing in the parking lot to make two calls. The first to Andre to update him on the events of the day and tell him I was on my way home. He answered this time, said he'd be home soon.

"Will Malcolm Kinsman be there?" I asked.

"I think so. He wasn't sure about his plans."

I skipped any sarcasm. It was unproductive. For all I knew, having a highly trained special forces guy around might be useful.

My second call was to Officer Bonnie Martin to ask about bail for Jason. I thought I detected some satisfaction in her voice when she said that he'd be held at least over the weekend, and they would let Lindsay know if he was released.

I hoped she was right and strings wouldn't be pulled on his behalf. We'd all breathe more easily if there was no prospect of him appearing on the horizon. Restraining orders help, but bullies who've escaped consequences in the past have a tendency to believe those orders don't apply to them.

The drive home was uneventful. When I passed my favorite farmstand, I realized that I'd been so busy I'd forgotten to eat lunch, despite my newly reformed habits. I stopped, thinking that some fresh fruit would be nice. I ended up with a fresh raspberry pie, plus berries, a melon, and a loaf of homemade bread. Nutritional rules be damned, I got a white chocolate and raspberry scone that I knew I'd eat in the car even though it meant I'd arrive home covered in crumbs.

I drove with the windows down, the scented August air surrounding me. I ate the scone. Got covered with crumbs and didn't care. I stopped at the market and got more corn and chicken to barbeque, and gave in to the temptation of a key lime pie. In Andre's opinion, there can never be too much pie. Now we had two pies and a chocolate cake.

I arrived home in a very mellow mood. It lasted until I turned into my driveway and found a shiny black SUV waiting for me.

TWENTY-SEVEN

Fred and Alice were lounging in Adirondack chairs on my back deck, watching the deer and her fawn, who were staring at the lettuce like they were starving. There was no one on this human and herbivore welcoming committee I wanted to see, and I didn't know whether Malcolm Kinsman was somewhere inside my house.

No one can say that I am indecisive, yet at this moment, I didn't know what to do. I stood there, briefcase and purse draped over my shoulder, my arms around a cardboard box full of farmstand produce and bags from the market draped over my forearm. Tears welled up in my eyes—those darned pregnancy hormones again— as I stared at them.

A decent person, someone with manners, would have jumped up and offered to take the box out of my hands so I could let myself in. Neither of them moved. They just sat and stared at me. I sighed. Set down the box. Unlocked the door. I pushed the door open, bent awkwardly and picked up the box, and staggered inside with my burdens. They rose from their chairs, intending to follow.

They could forget that. They were not getting inside unless Andre was home. Kinsman thought they weren't for real. Andre was still checking. And I'd already had my fill of them. I had nothing to offer.

I quickly shoved the box onto the nearest surface, turned to them, and said a single word, "Stay." Then I closed the door behind me and locked it. I stowed the chicken, corn, and the key lime pie in my crowded fridge. In my office, I put down my briefcase and purse, relieved to see that even though the shades were still drawn, there was no semi-conscious man lying on the couch.

I checked the rest of the downstairs—empty—and went upstairs. The guestroom was tidy and the bed was made. There was no one in our room or the baby's room. The door to the other guestroom, the one that was still under construction, was closed. I decided that if Andre had parked Kinsman in there, I didn't want to know. That way, if I ended up having to talk to my unwanted guests, I'd have deniability.

How had my life come to this?

The clock said Jonetta was due to arrive any time now. She'd texted about forty minutes ago that she was getting off the highway. I didn't know when Lindsay would arrive, but I should be ready. I checked the daybed in MOC's room. Clean sheets and a soft quilt in blues and greens. I got a second pillow from the closet. Andre is bemused by all the pillows we have on the beds, but I like to sleep with two, and believe we should offer that option to our guests. We are not a hotel. We don't ask if people would like feather or alternative pillows. But we do have lots of pillows.

I called Andre to alert him to the presence of Fred and Alice. Then I changed back into the cut-off sweats and a tee-shirt, kicked off my sandals, and padded barefoot down to the kitchen. Alice was peering through the door like a stray cat hoping to be let in.

Right now, what I wanted was a stray German Shepherd trained in bite work eager to be let out.

Someone in the helping professions would ask where all this hostility was coming from. Probably with some questions about how I felt about these persistent intruders in an effort to make me explore my negativity. I thought the answer was embedded in that question. I was feeling hostile because my life was under constant siege. These were my last few weeks before motherhood swallowed me up. I wanted to enjoy them. I wanted peace and quiet. Instead, I had two dead bodies and mysterious twins impinging on my peace and quiet. Not to mention two annoying government agents, a sexual assault victim, and an overworked headmistress from a New York school.

I've been going ahead full tilt for years. It's still a surprise when I have an attack of "I don't wanna," but that's what this felt like. It felt like the poor mother-to-be should turn a fan toward herself, lie down on her living room floor, and close her eyes. Rude or not, Alice and Fred could cool their heels until Andre got home, and he could deal with them.

Tires crunched on the driveway and I looked out to see Jonetta's electric blue Kia Soul fly up my driveway. She parked beside the SUV, got out, grabbed her bags, and headed for the door. If she found the two federal agents lounging in chairs disconcerting, she didn't show it. She just nodded as she passed.

I unlocked the door, and she came into the room, dropped her cases, closed the door on Fred and Alice, and wrapped me in a hug. When we unwrapped, she tilted her chin toward the door and said, "Unwanted visitors? That why you've left them outside?"

"Yes. Very much so. I've decided to leave them to my beloved spouse."

"'Bout time you learned to delegate." She moved on. Jonetta lived in a world where her students, fairly or unfairly, had frequent unwanted visits from the constabulary. She recognized cops, PIs, and others of their ilk easily and was used to brushing them off like specks of dust.

After inspecting me and finding me satisfactory, she said, "Pity about those people out there. I was looking forward to sitting on your porch and unwinding." She sighed the sigh of someone who had just driven from New York in summer traffic, making me wish I had a magic wand I could wave to make Fred and Alice disappear.

"We have a front porch, too," I said. "And it is shaded. Let's get your things upstairs, and then we can sit out there."

"They won't come around and bother us?"

"I hope not."

She picked up her suitcase. "Good. Let's do it, then. I need to hear all about this house and this baby and your adventures." Her eyes narrowed. "You *are* being careful of this baby, right?"

My own mother might not be doing much to nurture me through this pregnancy, but there were good people filling her empty shoes.

"It's a challenge," I said, "but I think I'm rising to it."

She laughed, a big, full-bodied laugh that enveloped me just like her hug. Jonetta is who I want to be when I grow up.

We wrangled her luggage up the stairs and into the guestroom. She loved it. Then she had to see the baby's room, which she declared "perfect," and our room, and the giant bathroom. I didn't offer to show her the unfinished room. For all I knew, Kinsman was in there, recovering or plotting his next move.

We went to the kitchen, made Arnold Palmers, alcohol-free for me, and carried them, and a tray of veggies and dip, out to the broad front porch. We settled onto two ends of the large glider-sofa out there, and slowly glided back and forth as we caught up. We were discussing the ever-present challenge of fund-raising when Lindsay's little blue car turned up the driveway and parked behind Jonetta's, looking like baby car snuggling up to mama car. Not that the Soul was big, just taller and even bluer.

The Lindsay who got out was a diminished version of the young woman we'd hired. Her jaunty, vigorous carriage drooped and she looked so tentative as she stepped from the car and came toward the house.

My unwanted welcoming committee didn't help.

I scooted through the house to the kitchen door and answered her knock. She looked puzzled as she passed the two agents, still upright and attentive, in their deck chairs. Two people in suits don't belong on a country deck on a summer afternoon.

I gave her a hug and drew her inside. "U.S. Marshals Service agents," I said, by way of kind of explaining Fred and Alice, "looking for a missing person." I was beginning to feel a little sorry for them. I considered offering lemonade or ice tea, but it would be like giving milk to a stray cat. I didn't want them to feel encouraged. "They believe I know the whereabouts of that missing witness, which I don't. I'm tired of explaining things to them, and they won't stop harassing me."

I didn't truly understand why they stayed. Maybe because Andre had given them coffee and cookies once they figured he was the soft touch. Maybe they thought if they stuck around, Charity would arrive to join the party. Maybe they believed we had her hidden in the attic and were waiting for reinforcements to arrive with a search warrant. I wanted them gone so badly I struggled not to go out there, scream at them, and demand that they leave. Maybe I was being foolishly passive for not doing so?

Lindsay looked puzzled, but didn't say anything until the door was closed and locked. "Are you sure this is a good time to have company?"

I shrugged. "If I waited for a good time to have company, I'd never have company. Leisure and I are usually pretty distant." I opened the fridge. "Arnold Palmer?"

"Sure."

"Vodka?"

"Please."

I gave her the drink and led her through to the front porch, where I pulled up a wicker chair and introduced her to Jonetta.

Have I mentioned that Jonetta isn't shy? She took one look at Lindsay, wilted after her dreadful day, and drew my intern into a big embrace. Jonetta is a magical person. I'm a cynic and yet I believe this. Now I was seeing her in action once again. By the time Lindsay was released from that healing hug, she looked restored.

She took her chair, inhaled and exhaled, and smiled. "Wow," she said. "What was that?"

"One of my secret weapons," I said.

Lindsay sipped her drink and Jonetta said, "Do you want to talk about it?"

I expected Lindsay to say no. Instead, she started to talk. I should have known that along with her magic touch, Jonetta is like the best possible therapy. Lindsay went through the morning's events with Jonetta patting her hand and offering murmured encouragement. I sat back at watched. The soft voices lulled me into a somnolent state. Birds chirped. An occasional car whooshed past down below. If I could forget about Fred and Alice out behind the kitchen, waiting to pounce, this would be almost perfect.

But Fred and Alice were like a splinter.

Ever tried not to think about a splinter?

What did they expect to accomplish here? Were they expecting Kinsman or his sister to suddenly appear? Hoping that if they persisted, I'd break down and tell them what they wanted to know? Were they truly as hard-headed as they appeared, or did they have a different plan in mind? Did they know something that I didn't—which wouldn't be hard, since I knew almost nothing about the situation? Was it possible that they were well-intentioned, simply here in case the bad guys came back, the same ones who'd killed Jessica Whitlow and Nathaniel Davenport? If that was the case, they could have used their words and told me so.

How was I supposed to stay calm and stress-free with death on my doorstep and feds on my porch?

I felt a warm hand on my arm. Jonetta. It was like getting a transfusion of peace.

I smiled. "Thanks. Now, if you could only make those two vultures disappear."

"I probably could," she said. "I know some people."

I didn't know if she meant people highly placed in government or people adept at getting rid of problems in a less law-abiding way. Jonetta knew both kinds. Probably people in both arenas were former students.

"It's okay," I said. "Just tired of all this death, especially now that it's on my doorstep."

"Where's your husband?" she said.

"Guess."

"Investigating those deaths. That what those two out back are here about?"

"In a way, I suppose, except being government, they're about a forthcoming as my big toe. If they really are from the government."

221

Jonetta looked down at my naked feet. "I think your toes are more forthcoming. They're naked and free and happy. And you still have ankles."

Lindsay giggled. It was nice to hear.

"Andre should be home soon," I said. "He can deal with Fred and Alice. They won't listen to me anyway." I looked over at Lindsay. "Andre is my husband. Detective. Maine state police."

"Oh," she said.

Because what do you say? She'd already spent much of her day with cops.

Everyone was silent for a while, except for the crunch of veggies or the tinkle of ice against glass.

In the midst of that peaceful moment, I suddenly remembered a fragment of my conversation in the car with Charity. We'd passed one of those old-fashion motels that was a series of small cottages along a lakeshore, and she'd said, "Those are so cute. You know, I've always wanted to stay in one of those places."

I had stayed in a few, on family vacations. My mother had shared Charity's fascination with tiny cottages. She'd quickly learned that they lacked most modern amenities, and that cramming five people into a small space with partitions that didn't reach the ceiling wasn't conducive to sleep. After that, we stayed in chain motels with swimming pools.

Was it possible that was where Charity was hiding out? My first instinct was to jump in my car and go and check. But it was twenty minutes away, I had a houseful of company, and Fred and Alice on the back deck. If I left, they might follow me. Their mission might be to protect her, but I worried they'd just put her at risk.

I shelved the impulse for now, especially as Andre was coming up the driveway. I watched his SUV fly in and park behind Lindsay. He surveyed Fred and Alice's vehicle, then headed toward the kitchen door. I held my breath, hoping he would send them packing.

TWENTY-EIGHT

A soft afternoon breeze had come up, bringing with it the scents of new-cut hay and dust. I looked at my two guests. "Any bets on whether he sends our unwanted guests packing?"

Jonetta shrugged. "You aren't gonna like this, but my bet would be he invites them to stay for dinner."

I shook my head. I knew about the bond between people in public safety organizations. I believed that the bond between me and my husband would trump it. My misplaced faith was shattered when Andre appeared in the doorway, Fred and Alice behind him, and announced he'd invited them to stay for dinner.

"I'll be back," I told Jonetta. "Look after Lindsay, please. She might need another drink."

I walked inside, ignoring Andre and the annoying federal duo. I wiggled my feet into flip flops, grabbed my purse, and headed out to my car.

"Hey, wait. Where are you going?" Andre said, coming after me.

I manufactured a smile and a shrug. If he didn't know what the problem was, I wasn't going to enlighten him. Long ago, my mother labeled me stubborn. She might have been on to something. "Just going to pick up some beer," I said. A seasoned detective should have spotted the lie. If he couldn't, that wasn't my problem.

"I got some extra chicken," I said, "and pie. Is Kinsman still around?"

He shrugged. "He was still here when I left. You didn't see him?"

"Nope. I didn't look in the unfinished room, though."

He kissed me and I almost relented and told him what I was up to. Almost. No one kissed like this guy. But my failure to invite Fred and Alice in should have been a clue. Maybe he had a reason he hadn't shared; he was the wily detective, after all. Right now, I was in no mood to try and read his mind.

I climbed into my car and headed out past the barn and down the back way to the road. I kept an eye on the rearview, worried about a sinister black SUV, but spotted none. I did see a silver Subaru a few times, but since that's pretty much every third car in Maine, I wasn't too worried. Twenty minutes down the road, give or take a few doddering tourists, I turned into the place I remembered her remarking on.

Up close, it looked kind of shabby, like it was barely hanging on. Still, I parked by the office and walked in. The air smelled like lake water and I could hear small waves lapping the shore. An old woman with blue sausage curls was knitting in an armchair. She perked up when I came in, set down her knitting, and smiled. "Can I help you, dear? If you're looking for a cabin, we're full up. The weekend, you know."

I did know. Chez Kozak-Lemeiux was also full up.

"I'm sorry to bother you," I said. "I'm looking for someone. A young woman. Striking blue eyes and dark hair." I waved a hand, indicating the basketball. "Pregnant, like me. She drives a gray Volvo."

She nodded, like someone looking for Charity was the most normal thing in the world. "Oh yes, dear," she said, in one of those voices that was like a grandmotherly pat on the back. "She was here. Such a sweet girl. Her cabin was booked for the weekend, though, so she couldn't stay."

"Do you know where she went? Her brother is looking for her. He's quite concerned about her."

She looked thoughtful. "Well, there was someone looking for her earlier today. What does her brother look like?"

"Like her, only tall and male," I said, describing Kinsman. "They're twins."

"Oh." She shook her head. "No. That wasn't who was here asking about her. Actually, that was a couple. And you know…" She leaned toward me confidentially and said, in a low voice, "I didn't like them very much. Their manner was what my mother would have called 'high handed' if you know what I mean. They flashed those badges and all but they…well, I didn't get the impression they knew her or cared about her. So I didn't tell them everything."

Her smile was sly, like she'd sussed out Fred and Alice perfectly and knew better than to give them too much information. It frustrates the police, I know, but sometimes people's failure to cooperate is instinctively correct.

"Fred and Alice," I said. "They wave those badges about and don't listen to anything we say. It was them, wasn't it?"

"Oh, yes, dear. It was. I gather you've met them?"

"Unfortunately."

We exchanged smiles.

"Do you have any idea where she was going?"

"Well, I gave her a few suggestions of places that might have openings. She wanted something with a kitchenette and said she liked being by the lake. I made a few calls that didn't pan out, and then I gave her a few names back in Stover she could contact." She rattled off a few names and I wrote them down. "I didn't much like the idea of her being out there on her own in her condition." She eyed MOC. "You'll understand what I mean. But it is high season, so I don't know whether she'll have any luck finding a place on the lake."

She grabbed a brochure from a rack on the wall. "I gave her this, too, so maybe it could help her find a place. You're welcome to take it."

She gave me the brochure listing local accommodations, then

picked up her knitting again and settled into her chair. "Good luck, dear. I hope you find her."

I thanked her and headed back to my car, mentally reviewing where, on my way back, I could stop and buy that beer. I'd given it a shot. Any further searching for Charity would have to wait. I had a house full of wanted and unwanted company and no more time to drive around looking for that elusive gray Volvo.

There was no black SUV waiting for me, but I found a silver Subaru parked beside my Jeep, with Malcolm Kinsman at the wheel. He looked like crap. I knew these guys trained under all sorts of difficult conditions, and he had to be tough as nails. Maybe it was the beating, or maybe it was concern for his sister. I didn't know. He hadn't exactly been forthcoming. I still didn't know whether I could trust him, though I'd sure taken a step in that direction last night when I handed him my gun.

I approached him warily as he lowered his window. "Is she here?" he said. His voice was urgent.

I shook my head. "She was. All the cottages were booked for the weekend, so she had to leave. The woman in the office gave her some suggestions but said it would be difficult for her to find another accommodation on a summer weekend. Especially on the lake."

He gave me that skeptical look, like he didn't think I was telling him the truth. *Fine*, I thought. *So much for our cautious détente.* I waved toward the little building. "Go ahead. Go ask her yourself. And you should know that Alice and Fred have already been here."

He just stared at me, like he had some kind of Superman gaze that would penetrate and let him see into my soul. I don't show my soul to just anyone. There were no secrets to be discerned anyway, at least not about his missing sister. If he wanted to gaze into the murk of other deaths and terror, he could go ahead. If someone wanted to take all that on, it was fine with me. I would love some celestial housekeeper to come and sweep out the dark and damp, do a Marie Kondo on the ugly pictures inside my skull.

MOC kicked me and I gasped. My child did not want mama thinking like this. So much for my vow of moving on. Even though I was standing on a grassy green lawn beside a gently lapping summer lake, Charity's situation haunted me. Why couldn't I just hand it over to this guy and go back to being a happy mom-to-be with gardens and a lovely home to renovate? Peaceful and tranquil until my phone rang with the next emergency someone needed me to handle?

His look of sullen disbelief irritated me. I was sick, sick, sick of people acting like I was hiding something. "Look, Kinsman, I'm concerned about her, too. Otherwise, why would I leave a house full of guests to come looking for her? It's not because of something she told me that I've been keeping from you. I just suddenly remembered a casual remark she made when we were driving past here and thought I'd check it out. Now I've got to get home."

Why was I staying here talking with him instead of saying "screw you" and driving off? My soft spot for injured guys who soldier on? Because I understood the pain of searching for a missing loved one? I didn't know.

"I'd say you're welcome to join us, but Andre has invited Alice and Fred, who I am sure are not among your favorite people. Unless it's that you're not among theirs. Is it the truth that you're not working with them because they won't share? Of something else?"

I had another question I needed answered first. "Hold on," I said, putting up my hand like a traffic cop when he started to reply. "I need to know. Are you a threat to me? Are you a threat to Charity?"

He had an opaque face. The only time I'd seen any emotion other than exhaustion or pain was when he was sleeping. Now I saw a flash of something. Surprise? Hurt? I wasn't sure.

He sighed. It was big sigh. A heartfelt one. "Good God. No. I told you. I'm trying to find her to protect her. I promised David. You know, like a general promise. He's my best friend. She's my sister." Another sigh. "And why would I hurt you?"

I countered with my own question. "Good question. Because if you don't want to hurt me, why would you take a chance on leading someone who wants to hurt you, or has hurt you, and to find Charity, to my house?"

"You've got Andre to protect you. And I needed to know…"

"Mission-driven. I get that," I said. "Only Andre wasn't home to protect me. But right now, I also need protection. Or MOC does, which means I do. And by now, you should recognize that I am not the enemy."

Ignoring that, he went on to answer my question about Fred and Alice. "Why am I not working with the Marshals Service? Because dear Fred and Alice have got it in their heads that I somehow mean Charity harm. Or that my presence will screw up their mission— which is finding my sister. After they already screwed up. And working with me is not doing it by the book, and they're too rigid to consider doing things differently. When our paths crossed, they did not deign to explain their reasons. They told me to get the hell out of Dodge. They were handling this."

He tried to shrug, but it hurt. "Marshals Service having done such a great job so far."

Since he was in a semi-talkative mood, I ventured another question. "So who attacked you?"

"I told you. Someone working for the cartel. The guy in the cowboy boots. And another guy, one who looked a lot like Fred. Listen. We didn't exchange names, ranks, or serial numbers. They attacked. I fought back. I was outnumbered." Another attempt at a shrug. "I'm just better at hiding in the woods."

"I'll bet you are."

"I don't think they're really with the Marshals Service," he said.

I felt the depressing let down that comes from hoping the bad stuff is over and learning that it isn't. I'd been excited at figuring out a place Charity might hide. I'd been right, but I'd missed her. Now I was drained and I still had to pull it together for the people waiting at home.

He looked at flattened as I felt. Probably he'd followed me with the same high hopes. "Look, Kinsman, I'm scared for your sister, too, but what can I do? You now know everything I do about how to find her. Maybe she'll call you."

I wished I could have done more. I knew her situation would continue to haunt me. But people were waiting. The only way to explain why I'd been gone so long was tell Andre the truth. It's hard to lie to him even if I wanted to. He's too good at spotting liars, and anyway, I place a high value on honesty in our marriage.

I left Malcolm Kinsman slumped over the wheel of his car, trying to summon the energy to take the next step. On the way home, I stopped and bought beer and an assortment of unhealthy snacks.

TWENTY-NINE

Andre came out to the car to get the beer and said, "Please don't do that again." He's too good at spotting subterfuge.

"I had an idea about where Charity might be," I said.

"And went larking off on your own to check it out, right? Without telling anyone where you were going and without backup?"

He graciously refrained from saying that I was an idiot.

"Yes. And I just missed her. She's moved on." I placed my hand on the basketball. "I'm sorry. I'm not used to thinking for two. Uh. Three."

"I know that."

"And you invited Fred and Alice to stay for dinner. Without consulting me."

"I know that, too." He hesitated, warring, I could see, between the cop's reluctance to share and a husband's obligation to explain. "I'm waiting for some intel," he said. "Something about them. It just feels off."

"Wouldn't that be a reason to keep them away from us?"

He sighed, like his explanation was long and complicated and I might not buy it anyway. "Trust me just a little longer, please?"

"Okay."

I followed him inside with my bag of snacks, passing Fred and Alice and Jonetta and Lindsay, who were sitting in a congenial circle on the back deck. I poured some Doritos and veggie chips into bowls, delivered them to our guests, and returned to the kitchen. "Kinsman was right behind me. What's the story with him, anyway? Is he a good guy or a bad guy?" I said.

"Good. Mono-focused. Can we talk about that later? Right now, we've got a hungry crew and I've got chicken to cook."

Was he avoiding me? Trying not to upset me? Were his explanations really complicated? Or was he just eager to get to his grill and feed these people? Just a guess, but I thought we'd cleared the air, he'd explain everything when he could, and that it was the allure of the grill. There is a peculiar affinity between men and their grills. Some men. It was part of Andre's new-found pleasure with our house. He'd grilled at our rental, but not often. And there had been a time in our lives when the smell of burning meat had been taboo. Part of the dark wallpaper in my head.

While I was wondering when I might get his theories about Kinsman, Andre tied on his apron and assembled his tools. He goes at this like a surgeon. "Did you get enough corn?" he asked.

"We're good."

Well, good meaning we had enough food for this group, and for dinner tomorrow, when Suzanne, Paul, and their kids would be coming. I wasn't sure we were so good interpersonally. I was pondering on that when he abandoned his meal prep and put his arms around me. "We're supposed to be in this together," he said. "Then you suddenly take off with our kid like that. Thea, there are bad people looking for Charity. People who are willing to kill a federal agent. You think they'd hesitate to harm you if they thought it would help them find her?"

He pulled me tighter and I burrowed into that space where his shoulder met his neck. If I have a happy place—a concept I generally resist—this was it.

"How can I take care of you if you won't let me?" he said.

I decided not to remind him of the times lately when I'd been home with potential threats and he wasn't answering his phone. We both knew his work sometimes required that. We also knew my work could sometimes be dangerous. Our world was a dangerous place, though we were working on making it safer. Our baby would be too little to fend for itself.

"Talk to me about Kinsman. Please. I can't get a read on him, and I bet you can."

"He's kind of a fish out of water," Andre said. "He's a team player without a team. He's a man of action and he's got nothing concrete to act on."

"I though those guys were trained in infinite patience."

He nuzzled my hair with his chin. "True. So am I, but if a family member is threatened?"

I exhaled, realizing I'd been holding my breath for a long time. "So why do Alice and Fred distrust him?"

"They're afraid he's a rogue agent."

"I don't know what that means. Do they think he's on the other side? Working for the bad guys?"

His arms tightened. "He wants to find his sister and protect his best friend."

"So why don't Alice and Fred work *with* him?"

I loved to stay in his arms and listen to the rumble of his voice in his chest. I felt his shrug as he said, "That's just not their way. You know how public safety organizations are. They're territorial. They have structures and rules. Kinsman's got rules, too, but he's an elite, improvise-in-the-field actor."

It still didn't make sense to me. It seemed like Kinsman and these government agents would be allies. There was something in Andre's voice, though, like he didn't get Alice and Fred either. Almost as if he was talking like they could overhear. We were standing by the door. I remembered what he'd said earlier—to be patient, he was checking something out. They didn't feel right.

"I didn't want you to invite them to dinner."

"I know. But if I were working in a strange place, one of my colleagues had been killed, and a local connection invited me home for a meal, would you think that was a bad thing?"

"I always want you to be fed and cared for. Them? Not so much."

I lifted my head. Studied his face. And thought I got it. He didn't want them here either. He was keeping them here so he could watch them. If they were here, they weren't looking for Charity and weren't threatening her brother. Wasn't there something about keeping your friends close and your enemies closer?

"Okay. I think I've got it."

He nodded.

"I'll try to be hospitable." Before the grill pulled him away, I added, "Did you get a chance to hear about Lindsay's day, or shall I fill you in?"

"Better fill me in. I think I scare her."

"I understand. You used to scare me, too."

He raised an eyebrow. "Really? I thought you just hated me."

"That, too."

We met when he was the detective investigating my sister Carrie's murder. He was brutal. I was defensive. Somehow we fought our way to something better.

I quickly gave him the basics of Lindsay's assault. "I didn't want her going home alone and brooding about it. Wondering what she'd done to provoke him. Which she'd do. And she'd done nothing. I'm also a bit worried that despite what the officers said, this kid will get out on bail and the first thing he'll do is try to get her to withdraw her complaint. Hold on."

I got out my phone and queued up the video. "This is what I saw when I walked in to work this morning."

He watched the brief video without speaking. Handed the phone back. "The poor kid. She's lucky you came in early."

"She's lucky that it didn't get any worse," I said. "She's not lucky. Having a guy press you against the wall, hold you there with his body, and stick his fingers inside you, none of that is okay or easy to get over."

He ran a warm hand gently over my cheek. "I meant she's lucky to have you. So. You have your waif, and I have my annoying government agents. Let's go outside and start our lovely evening."

"Don't forget Jonetta," I said.

"I don't believe anyone who's ever met her can forget Jonetta."

Which was pretty much the truth.

I picked a lot of lettuce, and found tomatoes and a cucumber and made a salad. So far, this garden was keeping up with us. I've heard, though, that a summer garden could drown you in produce. That was hard to imagine.

We sat around in comfortable chairs and shucked the corn while Andre presided over his grill. When he gave me the word, I went inside to start cooking the corn. Lindsay came with me, wanting to know if she could help.

"This is so great," she said. "You inviting me home, I mean. I've got a bunch of friends who have internships this summer, and none of them have been to their boss's homes like this. Just being here, and meeting Jonetta and Andre, makes me feel so much better." She shifted from foot to foot, embarrassed. "I thought I'd be scared of him, but he's so nice."

"Unless you're a bad guy. Or gal," I said, handing her a stack of plates, "he's absolutely the best at making people feel safe."

I got out a fresh stick of butter, just in case some of those present were "roll the corn in the butter" types. I've become so much more domestic since we got the house. Normally, Andre and I work so much dinner is a slipshod thing. Left-overs. Take-out. Something quick and simple or meals skipped altogether.

I don't have ESP and I'm not connected to the psychic network, but something—maybe an instinct for danger honed by life-experiences which in a cop would be the famous cop gut—made me go upstairs to the gun safe. I brought my handy little Barbie special down to the kitchen and slipped it into a drawer. Pretty soon, any such action would have me wrestling with child-locks. For now, I felt safer knowing it was within reach. I expected Fred and Alice were also armed, and of course Andre had a gun.

I wondered what my new neighbors would think if they knew a casual summer cookout Chez Kozak-Lemieux was such a gun party. Probably nothing. This was Maine. People had guns for hunting and for shooting that damned woodchuck that kept eating the garden.

True, there were a few asshats who liked to show off their handguns, but most of them were so overweight or unfit that in a real gunfight, they'd be on the floor in seconds.

Why was I thinking about all this when I was standing in my sunny kitchen, waiting for the corn to boil, about to sit down to dinner with a couple of my favorite people?

Because I was also about to sit down to dinner with two unpleasant federal agents and a traumatized sexual assault victim. And two people had been killed at the house across the street. No wonder I felt like there was a dark sheen over everything, however blue the sky and green the grass.

Lindsay had set the table and put a handful of bright flowers in a small blue vase in the center of the table. Andre came in carrying a platter of delicious-smelling chicken. Everyone came in to wash their hands while I put the corn in a bowl.

As the guests headed for the table, Jonetta stayed behind in the kitchen. "Hey, girlfriend," she said. "What's bothering you?"

An astute reader of people, my friend Jonetta. I shrugged. It was so nebulous. But she would understand. "This feeling that something bad is about to happen. Crazy, I know. But it's so strong."

She nodded. "You've gotta trust those feelings. They happen for a reason."

I'm a competent grownup who shouldn't need it, but I was relieved at how validated I felt.

"Thanks."

I grabbed the corn and followed her into the dining room.

It should have been a strange and strained meal, but the summer afternoon and good food seemed to be working some kind of magic on Alice and Fred. I didn't expect they found themselves invited to dinner very often. It was nice to see some of the stiffness fall away. Partly it was Jonetta. She has a kind of magic that she brings. She has created it—her school and the amazing success of students no one else has expectations for—and yet she's always grateful for it. Gratitude is something we're told we're supposed to practice. Most of us don't. Jonetta does.

Having someone at the table who was grateful for the food,

delighted to be having a vacation, and happy for the company lifted everyone up. Sometimes I think she should be a preacher or a politician, but I know she is meant to the do the work she does. She makes an important difference in young girls' lives. Why would I want her to do something else?

I pushed away the dark clouds.

Andre's chicken was perfect. The salad tasted the way food fresh from the garden does. It was almost laughable the way a tableful of people crunching on corn sounds. MOC was having a quiet evening instead of the usual acrobatics, just enough kicks to reassure me that the kid was still active.

I was in the kitchen, refilling the corn dish, when I heard steps on the deck. It wasn't going to be the postman, or UPS or FedEx at this hour, and we weren't expecting anyone.

We'd had a visit from Nathaniel Davenport, who worked for the dark side. The bad guys might well have someone else looking for Charity who would come knocking on our door. I set the bowl down and slid open the drawer, arming myself.

The screen door burst open, and Jason Barbour stepped into the room. He was sweaty and disheveled and he was holding a hunting rifle. He raised the rifle and aimed it at me. "Where's Lindsay?" he demanded.

I stared at the gun, forgetting how to breathe. It took a few seconds to remember how and to get mad. This guy was supposed to be in jail. They were supposed to notify us—his employers and his victim—if he was released. And he was subject to a restraining order preventing him from coming near Lindsay.

His arrogance knew no bounds. He was breaking so many laws. Obviously, the message of his spoiled upbringing was that laws didn't apply to him. Well, too bad. I didn't know or care what he thought he was here for. He was *not* getting near Lindsay.

With no faith that it would work, I tried reason, giving him a chance he didn't deserve. "Don't do this, Jason," I said. "Whatever you're here for, you're making a big mistake. You're in enough trouble already. Do you really want to add criminal threatening and violating a restraining order to the list?"

"This trouble is all your fault."

My fault that I'd kept him from completing a rape? Why was it that predators always think someone made them do it? And now it was my fault that this idiot had barged into my kitchen with a gun?

"Your fault," I said. "Why did you come here?"

"Her roommate said she was staying with you." A smug and foolish grin, like he was just the cleverest little thing to have tracked me down.

Nothing clever about this. There was an armed and clearly out-of-control man in my kitchen. I should have been cowering in a corner. Instead, I debated: should *I* shoot him or let someone else do it? I was pretty confident I could handle this. A rifle is a very poor close-range weapon. His hands were shaking and the smell of alcohol was coming off him like he was a scent diffuser.

Better to let the professionals handle this. MOC would not like being too close to the sound of gunfire, and anyway, mama was supposed to avoid stress. Oh, if my doctor only knew!

"Andre," I called, keeping my voice calm. "Can you come here for a minute? We have an unwanted visitor."

"What the fuck!" Jason said. "I said I wanted Lindsay."

"You're not getting near Lindsay, Jason. You've done her enough harm," I said. "What part of a restraining order don't you understand?"

He blinked at me like I was speaking a foreign language, like someone saying "no" to him was incomprehensible.

"This is your last chance to avoid serious consequences. Put your gun down on the counter and leave. Now."

I was about to tell him he would otherwise be very sorry when Andre, Alice, and Fred poured into the kitchen. Andre and Alice from the dining room, spreading out quickly in a vee so he could only watch one of them at a time, while Fred appeared from the hall. All three were armed and all three guns were aimed at Jason.

He looked at me, eyes wide, and said, "What the fuck?" again. Whoever had bulldozed his life smooth had made such a big mistake. They'd created an entitled monster who couldn't believe he'd ever face consequences instead of a responsible citizen.

"Detective Andre Lemieux, Maine state police," Andre said. "Drop the gun and put your hands on your head."

Jason stared.

"Police. Drop the gun!"

As Jason stared at them without complying, I slipped past Andre and into the dining room, where I put an arm around Lindsay, and Jonetta and I escorted her into the living room, away from the commotion in the kitchen.

She got as far as "Is that..." before dissolving in tears.

There was another sharp command from the kitchen.

A single explosive gunshot.

Breaking glass.

A scream.

So much for dinner and gratitude.

THIRTY

I wanted to run to the kitchen and see what had happened, but Lindsay was clinging to me and weeping. Jonetta had planted herself between Lindsay and the door. I was worried about my nice new kitchen and seriously pissed off that our pleasant dinner had been disrupted. One shot didn't mean the situation had been resolved.

"This is all my fault!" Lindsay said. "I never should have told my roommate where I was going. She's such an idiot. I should go."

"Let's wait here until we're sure the situation has been resolved," I said. "You go out there now and you could make things worse."

I wasn't worried about Andre being hurt. Maybe I should have been. Maybe I have too much confidence in my husband. Drunks with guns were volatile and dangerous. But there had been three armed and trained people in the room. If anyone was shot, it was Jason. Far more likely, the shot had been a warning when his thick head was unable to process a command to put the damned gun down.

"You can put *that* thing down now," Jonetta said.

I realized I was still holding my gun in the hand that wasn't wrapped around Lindsay. The poor girl would be lucky if she recov-

239

ered from this day's events in her lifetime. "I'll put it back upstairs," I said. "I didn't mean to scare you."

"You aren't scaring me," Jonetta said. "I just don't like being around them if I don't have to. Guns have a habit of going off, especially when the person holding them is distracted."

She was right. I was distracted. And Lindsay was staring at me like I was a dangerous stranger she'd never met. I shifted my gaze to Jonetta. "Maybe you can explain this to Lindsay while I put the gun away?"

"Oh, sure. Give me the hard job," she said, but her calm, and her smile, had returned.

"I guess the corn is going to be cold."

I took my gun upstairs and locked it in the safe.

My phone rang.

Usually, if a call comes in at dinner time on a Friday, it means a client school is in trouble. I looked at the screen. A number I didn't recognize. I was so tempted not to answer. There were enough emergencies on my plate already, and I had company.

That feeling I'd had of imminent danger hadn't gone away when I left Andre in the kitchen dealing with the Jason debacle. What if this was Charity Kinsman? If it was, she definitely needed help. While I was making up my mind whether to answer, the caller hung up. When I called back, there was no answer, and I didn't go to voicemail.

Darn it! Something else that would be like a splinter in my mind. This whole day made me want to scream in frustration. I figured if I screamed at this point, I'd have three people dashing at me with guns, so I passed. I sure wanted to, though. Being tough and waiting things out were what I'd schooled myself to do. Discipline, discipline, discipline. It worked well when I was dealing with other people's crises, or facing down bad guys. I didn't want to have to exercise it in my own house, when someone had threatened me and MOC with a gun.

Stay calm. Avoid stress. Those were my doctor's orders. I liked my doctor, but so often, her advice was utterly unrealistic. I wondered how she'd respond if I asked her how I was supposed to avoid stress when there were drunken gunmen in my kitchen, and a pregnant woman who needed my help was being stalked by a Mexican cartel?

MOC decided that it was time for gymnastics practice, and the first few warm-up kicks left me gasping. I dropped onto the top step and folded myself around my crazy child. Would this kid be more peaceful if mom lived a more tranquil life? It didn't help to tell the little mite that I hadn't sought out any of this. MOC and I were still stressed by it.

I heard Andre down in the living room, his calm voice reassuring Lindsay and Jonetta, then asking where I was. When he saw me bent over at the top of the stairs, he flew up to me in a total panic. Rock calm dealing with a gunman in our kitchen, unnerved by the possibility I might be in labor.

"It's okay," I said. Or gasped. "Just the little acrobat kicking up a storm."

He dropped onto the step below me. "Thank goodness." He put a warm hand on the basketball. "Wow. I never knew babies did this. It's crazy."

"You ought to be on the receiving end of those kicks," I said, resting my head on his shoulder. "So, is everyone okay? And is the kitchen still standing?"

I didn't mean Jason. I didn't care about him.

"We're all fine. Dad's going to have to replace a pane of glass over the sink," he said. "Otherwise, it's fine."

"And that idiot?"

"I'm afraid he resisted arrest after we disarmed him, and some force was needed to subdue him."

"I'm so happy to hear it."

Actually, I wasn't happy. Yes, I wanted Jason arrested and gone, but this was another case of unwanted people bringing in violence and polluting our new house. It looked like I was going to have to get someone in to smudge the place and drive out the evil spirits.

"But you are okay? Fred and Alice are okay?"

He nodded. "How's Lindsay?"

"Not good. You saw her. She's traumatized. You know better than I how it is with a victim who gets revictimized."

"Jonetta is fixing her a stiff drink, and Fred and Alice have taken the idiot outside to wait for the sheriff's patrol to pick him up."

"They let him out of jail this time, and I'll shoot him myself."

"Only if I don't beat you to it. We do our job. The cops. Then the justice system lets these people out."

"His daddy is connected."

"If his daddy can get him out of this, it's his daddy who needs to be shot."

"You'll get no argument from me." I grabbed the railing and hauled myself up. I'm plenty fit, but MOC was distorting my balance. "Do you think anyone is interested in finishing dinner?"

"Oh, I think so. Once the idiot kid is gone. I hear there is pie."

Outside, the wail of sirens announced that our unwanted visitor was about to be collected. We went downstairs, I to the living room to comfort Lindsay, Andre outside to speak with deputies.

Lindsay was sitting in my favorite chair, a big comfortable armchair with an ottoman. Even though it was a warm night, Jonetta had wrapped her in a cozy cream-colored throw. She was clutching a glass of some brownish liquid—either bourbon or Scotch—and looking more relaxed.

I sat on the sofa next to her chair. "How are you doing?"

"Better. I mean, I've been thinking about how it would have gone if he'd come to the apartment, drunk and with a gun. It's not a…uh…lucky situation." She sighed. "But under the circumstances, I'm awfully lucky I was here. With you and Jonetta and Andre." She took a sip of her drink. "I do feel protected."

Well, that was something. "I'm glad we were here to protect you. We'll have to do some safety planning, going forward. For tonight, a bracing drink, maybe some pie and ice cream, a long, leisurely bath, and a good night's sleep."

"Yes, Dr. Kozak," she said.

"Dr. Kozak is going to find out whether people want to finish their dinners," I said. "If not, I'll clear and we'll have pie." I paused in the doorway. "You do like pie, don't you?"

She smiled, looking so young in the big chair, wrapped in all that white fake fur. "I love pie. Haven't learned to make it yet, but that's something I plan to do soon."

"Well, don't worry. I didn't make these. My pie-making skills generally involve a credit card."

Lindsay laughed.

I left her sipping strong spirits under Jonetta's watchful eye, though I'd noticed that Jonetta had a glass of wine in her hand and was looking awfully relaxed for someone who'd just been close to a gun party. I figured she found herself in that situation fairly often.

Andre, Alice, and Fred were outside, chatting with a deputy. I could see Jason in the backseat of the deputy's car, his head bowed. I stepped out into the gathering dark and approached them, surprised at how loud the night sounded, as desperate insects poured their mating cries into the warm night air.

Andre did introductions and the deputy said he'd be on his way.

"Don't let that kid out again," I said. "We're just getting this kitchen finished. I don't need any more windows broken."

The deputy, an older man with a smart face and tired eyes, said, "Ma'am, if only it were up to me."

That wasn't very reassuring. Andre put a solid hand on my shoulder and kept it there as the car backed down the driveway and disappeared. "Don't worry," he said. "That kid isn't getting out anytime soon. However much juice his family may have, generally, when the charge is taking a shot at a public safety officer in his own home after threatening his pregnant wife with a rifle, the courts will not be inclined to release him. The test is whether he presents a danger to himself or others. It's pretty clear he's dangerous."

I looked at the others. "Did you all want to finish your dinners? I can warm things up. Or we can move on to pie."

"Pie?" Alice said brightly.

Even Fred, whose demeanor was that of someone who drank vinegar all day, brightened.

I took the executive decision that we were moving on to pie.

"I'll help," Andre said, and dropped his hand. We all headed inside. We'd mostly finished eating anyway. I'd been about to offer seconds on corn when Jason arrived. Andre cleared the plates and scraped them while Alice rinsed and loaded the dishwasher and I impressed Fred into service putting out dessert plates and forks.

I cut each pie into eight pieces so none of the kids could fight about not getting some of each, and there would still be pie left for Andre's breakfast. He is normally a healthy eater, but he has a soft spot for pie.

I got out ice cream and a scoop and put those on the table. Then I called everyone back. Jonetta came in by herself, holding a finger to her lips. "The poor girl has fallen asleep," she said. "Best thing for her."

I peeked into the living room. Lindsay was curled up in a chair, sound asleep.

The rest of us sat down to pie, and no one was shy about a piece of raspberry and a piece of key lime. I love to see people eat, and enjoy eating, and that was definitely happening here.

When we were done and were clearing the plates, I picked up my phone to tuck it in my pocket. There was another missed call from the same unfamiliar number. Again, I called it back. Again, there was no answer.

It was not how I wanted to end this roller-coaster of a day, worrying about some mystery person out there who wanted to speak with me but wouldn't make it easy. Was it Kinsman, looking for my help in his efforts to locate his sister? Was it Charity, hiding out somewhere and in labor, needing my help? Or was it whoever was trying to find her for the cartel, hoping to trick me into giving away her location?

Nothing I could do, though, if the person wouldn't leave a message. Right now, the ups and downs had left me so tired I could have slept in a chair, like Lindsay.

Alice and Fred finally left for our local B&B just as I was beginning to worry that I'd need to find them someplace to sleep as well. By the time they were gone, I was dead on my feet.

I would settle Jonetta and see if we could get Lindsay to her room. I hated to wake her, but also didn't want to leave her alone down in the living room. If she was tired enough, maybe Andre could carry her up without waking her.

It turned out that he could.

I finished putting things away. He was in the office, on the phone, talking so quietly I couldn't make out the words. Then I heard the high-pitched whine of a fax arriving.

That dark, unsettled feeling I'd had earlier returned with a vengeance. No surprise there. It had been a day full of ominous feelings and bad events. I hoped it wouldn't keep me awake. I have issues with nightmares that only curling up next to Andre can help, and even that doesn't always work, no matter how tired I am.

Now, all we needed was the unwanted return of Malcolm Kinsman, looking for a bed for the night.

Let it be someone else's problem, I thought, as I climbed the creaky stairs. Jonetta was singing softly in her room. Lindsay snored gently in the baby's room. And MOC, unwilling to be ignored, was learning to breakdance.

THIRTY-ONE

A ndre spoke to MOC, who immediately settled down. I hoped this boded well for the future. He didn't tell me about the call, and I didn't ask. Right now, all that mattered was that he was here and nothing had called him away. Except for its usual creaks and groans, the old house stayed silent. No ominous creaks suggested Malcolm Kinsman had returned. My phone didn't ring. No one knocked or barged their way in.

Magically, I fell asleep almost immediately and didn't wake until three-thirty, when I made a quick trip to the bathroom. When I came back, Andre wrapped himself around me and I fell back asleep.

I woke to birds singing and sunlight streaming in. The intensity of the light told me it was late, and I was shocked to find that despite guests in the house, I'd slept until nearly ten. I was definitely shirking my hostess duties.

Grabbing a robe that barely tied around me, I padded down to the kitchen. Andre, Jonetta, and Lindsay were at the table, the crumbled remains of a coffee cake on their plates. The air smelled of bacon and the box of eggs was still sitting on the counter. There was the delicious scent of coffee in the air.

Andre got up when I entered and headed for the stove. "One egg or two?" he said.

"Three." Cholesterol be damned. For some reason, I was starving. Maybe because it was so late.

"Toast?" Lindsay said.

I nodded. Maybe this was what I'd needed all along—a staff to wait on me. I settled in a chair and Lindsay brought me coffee.

"Everyone sleep okay?" I asked.

Lindsay looked sheepish. "Like a rock," she said. "When I didn't think I'd sleep a wink.'"

Jonetta grinned. "Those damned birds woke me up," she said. "Can't remember the last time I was woken by birds. I got coffee, went back to bed, and read for an hour. Can't recall when I last did that, either. I could get to like vacations."

No one seemed rattled by last night's gunman.

I ate my eggs and bacon and toast. Drank my coffee. I'd been tired for so long I'd stopped noticing. Being rested finally made it clear for me. We sat around, drinking more coffee, no one in a rush to go anywhere or do anything. We talked about a trip to the coast for tomorrow, maybe a swim in the lake today. It felt so normal, even if I did keep one ear tuned to the driveway, expecting a disruption that would force a change in plans.

My phone was upstairs, silenced for the night. Now curiosity drove me up there to get it, wondering if there might be more calls from my mystery caller.

There were two, one at one-thirty a.m. and the other at four a.m. Neither time had the caller left a message. If it hadn't been silenced, those calls would have kept me awake. But why keep calling and not leave a message?

Andre's father and cousin showed up even though it was Saturday. While their schedule is somewhat erratic, his family prefers tinkering to taking days off. He excused himself and went to join them. They wanted the barn workshop and garage space finished before winter. Winter felt very far away right now, but they didn't agree. People in Maine seem to think about winter all the time, and anyway, I never argue with a man holding a hammer. While I might like sitting around eating a leisurely breakfast, Andre liked to be working on his space.

I went back upstairs to dress while Jonetta and Lindsay cleaned up. It was like having a big family, with the added pleasure of having one that got along, unlike my actual family. Relaxed and pleasant as this day was, I couldn't shake that ominous feeling. Yesterday's drama with a gunman in the kitchen should have been the answer, if the feeling was predictive, yet it lingered. With MOC constantly reminding me that oh, yes, I was pregnant, I couldn't stop thinking about another pregnant woman on the run. It was crazy how much one seemingly innocuous knock on the door had altered my life.

When my phone rang this time, I almost didn't answer it. But I am a slave of duty, even on a leisurely summer Saturday. It was Emmett Hampton, who also should have been enjoying his Saturday. I said, "Hello?"

"Thea. So sorry to disturb you on the weekend. I just wanted to tell you that the video is brilliant. We're thrilled. That intern who made it? If you're not going to keep her, we'll hire her."

"Thanks, Emmett. She is a treasure, for sure, and we're keeping her."

"Well, just wanted to say thanks. Yanita and Arleigh are delighted. Tell your intern thanks. And of course, we'll be in touch once we've shared this with the boy's attorney. I think this should settle things down."

"It wouldn't hurt to give the student body a look, and have a conversation about using social media responsibly," I said. "If we can find this, so can colleges, and later on, their future employers. Kids who live in a social media-centered world don't always think about these things."

"Good idea. I'll pass it along." He hesitated. "Unless you want to? Does EDGE do these kinds of programs?"

We didn't, but we could, so that's what I told him, already getting excited about a new way we could help client schools. I'd share it with Suzanne when she and her family came to dinner tonight.

Then I wiggled my feet into flip-flops and went back downstairs.

Jonetta and Lindsay were on the back deck, an umbrella pulled over to shade their Adirondack chairs, reading. Jonetta was deep into a Barbara Ross clam bake mystery while Lindsay was reading Down East. Beyond them, bright petunias in pots were a pop of purple and magenta, and then there were my raised bed gardens and the rolling green lawn. It was almost too perfect.

What a pessimist I was. I was sure something had to happen to spoil this lovely day. Almost like that character in Shakespeare who could call spirits from the vasty deep, I heard tires crunch on the gravel. In Shakespeare, Hotspur asks whether, when summoned, they would come. It was my bad luck that too often they did. I stepped around the corner of the house to see what I had summoned. Whatever it was, I didn't want it.

Malcolm Kinsman, looking shabbier and more worn-down than ever, stepped from his little silver car and hurried toward me. I knew that look—it was the hopeful anticipation of someone badly in need of good news. I didn't have any for him.

I led him into the kitchen, pointed to a chair, and said, "Coffee?"

"Please."

"Toast and eggs?"

He smiled faintly, and nodded.

I got out the eggs and fired up the frying pan while I put some bread in the toaster.

He hadn't asked his question but I knew what it was. "I haven't heard from her," I said. "Though there have been a few calls from a number I don't recognize." I handed him my phone. "When I call back, no one answers, and there doesn't seem to be a voicemail box set up."

He scrolled through the phone like there were secrets there only he could find while I cooked his eggs, put a few slices of leftover bacon and the toast on a plate, and gave him a fork and knife. Now all we needed were Fred and Alice to make the morning complete.

"I don't know this number," he said.

"Maybe it's a burner phone the Marshals Service gave her."

"You think they know where she is?"

"After the inspector in charge got killed? I doubt she'd trust them again. And anyway, if they knew where she was, why would Fred and Alice keep hanging around here like we know something. What do you think?"

I put the eggs on his plate and set it in front of him. He began eating automatically like it was instinct and he didn't know he was doing it.

I refilled his coffee and put more bread in the toaster.

"I checked out the places in that brochure," he said. "No joy there."

I wished he hadn't shown up, because there had been some joy here this morning, a peaceful, in the presence of good friends joy. I almost told him that, but he already knew his visit was unwelcome, and anyway, it didn't help. He was still anxiously searching for his missing sister and clung to the belief that I could somehow help her. Find her. Or that she'd reach out to me because I'd met her and we'd connected. I couldn't deny the fact that I'd come close to finding her.

Honestly, I wished she would reach out, because I would try to help her, and there were people here—like Andre—she genuinely could trust to keep her safe. But when two people are murdered in the house where you've been stashed for your safety, you naturally become distrustful. And she didn't know about Andre.

As I was pulling toast from the toaster, my phone rang. Kinsman was holding it, so he answered. He said, "Charity. Don't hang up. It's Malcolm," and waited. Then he said, "Sorry. She's right here," and passed me the phone.

"Who was that?" Suzanne said, when I answered.

"Oh. Guy who's here for breakfast. He thought you were his sister."

"I don't think I want to hear this story," she said.

"You don't. So what's up? Don't tell me one of the kids is sick."

"Nope. Alive and raring to go. They can't wait to visit you and see Uncle Andre. Paul, Jr. wants to know if he can see Andre's gun.

The little one isn't talking yet, but when I say 'Thea' she grins, so I guess you've done something right."

Suzanne's little one was a perfect Gerber baby, wispy blonde hair and china blue eyes and chubby cheeks and an infectious grin. Even her name, Emily, was perfect. I figured MOC would be tall and rangy, with impossible hair like mine, and probably born with cold cop's eyes and a cynical world view. From birth, such a child would scare delicate Emily. But I could be wrong. For all I knew, MOC and Emily would be best friends forever, and Suzanne and I would share sleepless nights and calls to the principal's office.

"Just calling to see what I can bring?" she said.

"Well, we've got steak for the big people and burgers and dogs for the little people and lots of corn and brownies and ice cream."

"Sounds like you've got it covered, but if you don't mind, Paul is dying for a homemade potato salad."

"Like anybody ever says no to that."

"Sure they do. There are the vegans and the keto folks and the gluten-free crowd, never mind nuts and…" She paused. "Food has gotten really complicated."

"Here at Chez Kozak-Lemieux, we are omnivores."

"Delighted to hear it. It's no fun to make a decent meal and then have people push food around on their plates."

"We'll eat, I promise. See you at five?"

"With bells on."

I put down the phone. Kinsman looked so dejected he could have appeared in one of those ads where you can adopt some waif for only pennies a day. He'd probably bristle at the notion that he was a forlorn waif. After all, he was one of America's finest, most highly trained, deadly soldiers. But I saw what I saw.

"I don't know how I can help you," I said.

"I know."

"Yet, you keep coming back here."

He nodded. "You're my only lead."

"Pretty frustrating," I agreed.

"There's no place left to look?" he said, his tone accusing, like I was hiding something from him.

I thought of that isolated A-frame Jeannine the librarian had mentioned. It had been empty when I checked it, but what if it had been a place of last resort?

"There's one place," I said reluctantly.

Instantly, he was on his feet. "Let's go," he said.

I made a "slow down" gesture. "I've got company, Malcolm, and more coming this afternoon. I can't just take off. I can tell you where to go…"

"No. You have to come. What if she needs you? What if those phone calls were because the baby is coming? What if…"

I made the gesture again. "If it were an emergency, she would have left a message."

I got a local map from a drawer and spread it out on the island. "Okay, so we're right here, and…"

I thought of how odd it was that he'd been able to follow me to those cottages when I was looking for Charity. "Do you have a tracking device on my car, Malcolm?"

"Of course."

"Can those devices be hacked?"

He looked embarrassed and didn't reply.

"Do you have one on Andre's car?"

He shook his head.

"What about your car? Have you checked?"

Another embarrassed silence.

"Malcolm, you're supposed to be smart about this. You're supposed to be protecting your sister, not leading bad guys to her door."

He didn't say anything, but body language said all. Give him a team and a mission, and he was an expert. Send him out on his own in friendly territory, without the gadgets, the weapons, or the intel, and, well, he wasn't lost, but it was all a lot harder. It should have been easy. Just call Charity, connect, and take her somewhere safe.

"What I don't understand is why she doesn't just call *you*. She has your number, right?"

Another long silence. "She…uh…she's not speaking to me," he said.

Seriously? The man screws up my peaceful summer days with his damned mission, and he's without the necessary information because he's fighting with his sister? This was ridiculous.

He sighed and sat back down.

I breathed more easily when he wasn't looming over me with that desperate intensity. I retreated a few steps and waited for his explanation. Just steps away, Lindsay and Jonetta read and chatted. Out in the barn, a saw buzzed and hammers banged. Here in the kitchen, things felt far from normal.

"She thinks I should be down in Mexico, rescuing her husband. She doesn't believe me when I say I was sent here. That David asked me to protect her. She thinks I'm a coward who's shirking my duty. Even after that Marshals Service inspector, Jessica Whitlow, was killed, she still doesn't realize how much danger she's in, and how she puts David in greater danger if she's not safe somewhere." He threw out his hands in a gesture of frustration. "If I could find her. Sit down with her, talk to her, I could make her understand. But not over the phone. So you see…if I can bring you with me, maybe you can convince her?"

How many times had people asked me to take on impossible missions like this? And no, I didn't want to think about my successes. Too many of them had come at a high cost. I lacked his training or experience, but life still sent me on dangerous missions. This felt like another one, just when I was supposed to be reforming.

"Take Andre," I said. "Sweep his car for trackers and then use it. I'll give you directions."

Kinsman sighed and rose, heading out to the barn like a man going to his execution. I didn't understand his certainty that I was necessary to convince Charity of his sincerity. They were twins, with a lifelong connection, and her husband was his best friend. Besides, if there was any danger there, I'd be no help. I was not putting MOC at risk. We'd already lost years off our collective lives yesterday with that dumbass Jason and his gun in the kitchen. I could have used some of Kinsman's skills there. Or not. I had had Andre, Fred, and Alice.

I wondered what Fred and Alice were doing today and whether

they'd already located Charity, mooting this entire conversation. Located her and, of course, failed to let me and Andre know. We were just more tools to be used. There were a heck of a lot of unreciprocated acts in my world. Not that I was keeping score or anything. Mostly I was just happy they weren't here.

I got some coffee and went outside to join Jonetta and Lindsay. In the short time they'd known each other, they seemed to have become good friends. Of course, Jonetta is an earth mother, and Lindsay was in need of some mothering.

They lifted their heads from their reading material and looked at me in such perfect synchrony they might have rehearsed it. "Everything okay?" Jonetta asked.

"Kinsman wants me to join him on another search for his sister, and I don't want to. I suggested he take Andre."

"They make a pretty awesome pair," Lindsay said.

"Yeah," I agreed. "They both have chests that are bigger than mine."

They burst out laughing. Then Jonetta said, "I've got 'em both beat."

Which made us all giggle. I don't giggle very often, and it reminded me of my shopping trip with Charity and how silly we'd both gotten. I wanted her to be okay. I just didn't want to go on any more rescue expeditions.

We lounged in our chairs and watched Andre and Kinsman leave the barn, get some things from Kinsman's car, put them in Andre's, then come over to us. More particularly, to me.

"Can you show us where this place is, on the map?" Andre asked.

"I've got the address in my phone, if you want to use your map program," I said, getting out my phone. "And you can take the topo map to get the lay of the land."

Andre loved maps, which is why I had this particular map in my kitchen drawer. Andre put the information in his phone, then he and Kinsman bent over the map. Evidently, they were plotting approaches and looking for places to park the car. Fine with me. They could guy bond over operation strategies and I could sit in the sun and read. I'd be reading client work, it was true, but this was an excellent place to do it.

I left them to it and went back outside. I settled in a chair in the shade of the umbrella and pulled out some work.

"Do you ever just relax and read for pleasure?" Lindsay asked.

"Sure."

Lindsay looked at Jonetta. "Is she telling the truth?"

"Lindsay girl, when you do something you love, and something that matters, it's not a hardship to work long hours."

"That reminds me, Lindsay," I said. "Emmett Hampton called. They love your video and think it will go a long way toward diffusing the situation. Now they want us to work up a presentation on the dangers of using social media. You up for that?"

She smiled. She had a lovely smile. "You'll help me?"

"Happy to. You'll probably be mostly working with Bobby."

"That's great. He's so nice to work with."

Once again, I repressed the desire to beg her to skip that last semester and come right to work. It wasn't likely that she'd work for us forever. She'd need her degree.

"Uh, would it be okay..." Lindsay hesitated. "If I invite my boyfriend for the cookout? I told him what happened and he's in kind of a state."

"Sure," I said. "The more the merrier."

My phone rang. Lulled into a sense of contentment, I didn't check before I answered. "Thea? Is that you?" A panicked woman's voice.

"It is."

"It's Charity. I'm all alone and the baby's coming. I need your help."

Her voice was so faint I could hardly hear her. I sat up, pressing the phone to my ear like that could make her speak up. "Where are you? How will I find you?"

"Up on Morse Mountain. Don't know address. Look for my car, it's..."

And she was gone.

THIRTY-TWO

Andre and Malcolm came out, clutching the map and heading for Andre's car. I jumped up and ran after them. "Wait!" I said. "That was Charity…on the phone…just now. She needs help. She's in labor."

They stopped and turned, staring at me like I'd gone mad.

Then Malcolm said, "Where?"

"I don't know. Her voice was very faint and she said she didn't know the address, just that it was on Morse Mountain. Then the connection failed. When I called back, she didn't answer."

"Morse Mountain," Andre said, spreading the map on the hood of the car. "Is that where we were heading anyway?"

"I think so. She said to look for her car." I realized they might not know what she was driving. "It's a gray Volvo with Virginia plates."

I studied the two big men bent over the map and tried to imagine them delivering a baby while fighting off bad guys. In truth, Andre, being a cop, probably had delivered a baby or two. It happened. But I felt as though she should have a woman with her. I also worried that her directions were so vague that it would be a challenge to find her at all. Maybe she'd call my phone again. I could just give it to them, but then I'd be here without a phone in case something happened on this end.

"Wait," I said. "I'll come with you."

I looked at Andre, our limited expert here. "What should I bring?"

"Scissors. Blankets." He shrugged. "Do you think she has baby gear?"

"She does. She bought it when we went shopping that day. Except a crib. The crib is still in the cottage."

"Anything will do. Even a cardboard box."

I had a Moses basket I'd gotten as a shower gift. I gathered up the other things, put them in the basket, and gave them to Andre to put in the car. I took a moment to tell Jonetta and Lindsay what was happening.

"There are cold cuts and a corn and black bean salad in the fridge. And if you two would like to go to the lake and swim, our family swim pass is tacked to the bulletin board in the kitchen. Beach towels are on top of the washing machine, and there's a beach blanket on the shelf above the dryer."

Malcolm was shifting impatiently from foot to foot like a kid who needs the bathroom. Then his phone rang. He listened, and when he was done looked more distressed than ever.

"The operation's underway to rescue David," he said. "They wanted to know if Charity was secure." He shook his head in frustration. "Dammit. Let's get going!"

My gun was tucked under baby blankets in the Moses basket. I slid into the backseat beside it. I was not getting into a gunfight, but I also needed to be able to defend myself and MOC.

"Should we contact Alice and Fred?" I asked, as Andre drove out.

His sharp "No way" was a conversation stopper, so I didn't ask why we could invite them to dinner but not on a mission to rescue Charity. I was sure he had some logical reason. We'd both sensed something off about them, and hadn't he said he was checking some intel? Maybe last night's fax had given him some answers. God. Cops could be so cryptic.

I rarely see Andre when he's mission-driven like this. Between my husband and Kinsman, the air in the car felt electric. Charged. All edges and intensity, a sharp contrast to the soft summer landscape we were driving through. Andre and I are so intertwined it was jarring to see him like this, so focused and intense, with the kind of unspoken communication between him and Kinsman he usually has with me.

Neither man had to say that they didn't want me there, nor that I would be a huge distraction if anything bad happened. What I didn't know was whether they understood that I was on a mission, too, an ancient mission of sisterhood that neither of them could truly imagine. Running and hiding might have been poor decision-making on Charity's part, but now there was another life involved—that of Baby Amy.

I had pulled up the map I used once before to find the A-frame that Jeannine at the library had mentioned, and whether they wanted my help or not, I gave them directions. It was kind of a maze and I'd driven it before.

Ridiculous, right, me, giving directions to a member of the state police SWAT team and man who could find his way through the mountains of Afghanistan in the dark? I couldn't leave it alone, though. That's not who I am. I am as used to being in charge, albeit of different situations, as they are.

My stomach was in a knot. Those Braxton-Hicks contractions had given me some sense of what Charity was going through. What if something went wrong and no one was there to help? What if the bad guys managed to find her? What if she wasn't at the A-frame and we ended up driving endless backroads on Morse Mountain, looking for a gray Volvo? It was hot in the car but I felt clammy, gripped by a sense of urgency and unable to make things happen faster.

From time to time I glanced out the back, looking for one of those menacing black SUVs, or someone else following us. The road was empty. Morse Mountain wasn't where people wanted to be spending a hot August weekend day.

Fine with me. I wasn't looking for a fight.

"Turn here," I said, though the side road was so shielded by trees it was nearly invisible.

Andre swung onto the smaller road and we wound our way uphill on a road badly in need of repair. I watched their heads swivel as they scrutinized the houses along the road, a lot of broken down trailers and some optimistic new construction that had never been finished. No gray Volvos. Fancy new houses tended to be built on the tops of these hills, so the owners could look out over the land below like lords in their castles. We hadn't gotten to the top yet.

We went on, following a seemingly endless uphill stripe of worn gray road, with thick woods gradually giving way on the right hand side to open blueberry fields, recently harvested and still lined with rows of white string.

"Slow down," I said, "it's on the left just around this curve."

Andre slowed and crawled around the curve, stopping when the little A-frame, isolated in its bedraggled lot, was just visible through the trees. So was the gray Volvo, tucked in beside the house. No other cars and no signs of life. He went forward and pulled into the driveway. He and Kinsman were out of the car in a flash, moving toward the house, guns up and ready, checking the surroundings like they'd worked together all their lives.

Anxious as I was, I chose to play the "little woman" and wait until they told me it was all clear, kind of foolish since I was a perfect sitting duck here in the car as well. From a bad guy's point of view, shooting me would be a perfect distraction.

They checked all around the house before trying the door. Unlocked. I watched them disappear inside. After they'd cleared the tiny house, Andre came back to the car to get me. He looked grim but said nothing. I gathered my basket and followed him back to the house, a short walk that felt surreal.

I've done some scary walks in my time. Once in my underwear in front of a lot of cops and an armed bad guy. That one, to my eternal humiliation, made the paper. Another on the night I actually shot someone. Once to an isolated cottage to see a man I thought I knew—and didn't. Those memories piled in on me now, coming at me out of the blue summer sky like meteors bursting into my brain.

By the time we reached the door and I stepped inside, I was breathless and shaking.

Charity Kinsman was lying on the couch, her knees drawn up, red-faced and sweating. Her brother knelt beside her. Despite the pain of her labor, she was yelling at him, and he was answering her in a calm, if shaky, voice.

"You weren't supposed to leave him," she said. "Isn't that your credo? Don't leave someone behind? So how did that happen?"

Her question trailed off as she gasped her way through another contraction. I wondered if she'd had a chance to go to birthing classes. How long her husband had been gone and whether she'd gone to them alone.

Kinsman's answers were calm as he explained why he was here. He wasn't getting drawn into an argument. His calm was not making a dent in her anger.

I figured she needed the anger to keep her fear at bay. Who knew how long she'd been here, knowing her baby was coming and with no one to help her? Had she been in labor since last night, when someone made those mysterious calls to me?

This argument wasn't helping her. We needed to know how advanced the labor was and whether the best course was to move her to a hospital.

I stepped up to the couch and knelt down, nudging Kinsman out of the way and taking her hand. "How long have you been in labor?"

"Feels like forever," she said. "It started last night. For a long time, it didn't feel like I was making any..." She grabbed my hand, and together we breathed through the contraction.

I looked at Kinsman. "Let's start timing these."

"...progress," she gasped.

I realized Andre wasn't in the room. "Where's Andre?"

"Outside."

I decided not to ask why. She held my hand and we waited.

"Oh no. Here's another one," she said.

Her grip on my hand was like a vise. For months, I'd been imagining being where she was. Now I tried to recall the advice Andre had been given as my coach. I looked sideways at Kinsman. "How long?"

"Two minutes," he said.

That wasn't good. Intense contractions, lasting a minute, only two minutes apart. I was no expert, but it sounded like she was getting close. I didn't know how to decide whether we should try to get her to a hospital or if it was too late.

"Get me a cool cloth," I said, "and if there's ice, bring me some ice chips."

Kinsman unfolded from his crouch beside me and went to the kitchen. He was back a moment later with a wet dishtowel. I wiped her face while he went to see if there was ice. I heard some banging and then he handed me a cup full of ice. I sensed, rather than saw, him going to the window and looking out. Then he went outside to join Andre.

"What's going on?" she asked. "Why are they outside?"

"I don't know," I said. "If there's anything to worry about, they'll handle it. Let's focus on you and your baby, okay?"

"Okay."

We breathed our way through another contraction, this one bad enough to make me wish I would never have to go through this. I was too busy to be scared, though. I was trying to recall my baby lore. Labor lore. I really was going to have to read up. And soon.

"Did your water break?" I asked.

"Yes. A couple hours ago."

That was one thing I did remember—if your water breaks, go to the hospital.

Outside, there was a gunshot.

I looked around. Basically, we were sitting in a flimsy wood and glass box. Not the safest of places. "Does this place have a bathtub?" I asked.

Gritting her teeth, she nodded. We held hands and breathed through the contraction. Then I said, "We're going to put you in the bathtub. It's the safest place until we can get you to a hospital."

I helped her to her feet and we managed the short distance to the tub. I lined it with a blanket and some towels and eased her in.

Then I went back for the Moses basket, my bag, and the ice chips. The basket took up what little floor space there was. I perched on the edge of the tub, wiped her face, and gave her some ice. The next contraction arrived, and after that, there was little time between them. No way we were going to make it to a hospital, at least not before Amy arrived. I tried to concentrate on the business at hand and not worry about what was happening outside.

Charity clung to me like I was a lifeline, using some pretty unladylike language as we breathed our way through what seemed like one long, endless contraction.

"Oh my God! Thea! Oh my God! I've got to push."

Oh hell. Most of what I knew about pushing came from watching "Call the Midwife," which hardly qualified me as someone to assist at a birth. On TV, they had a whole protocol of when to push and when to breathe, and magically the baby's head would emerge and then the rest of it, and everyone would be full of joy and tears except when things went wrong. None of that was helpful now.

"Okay," I said. "On the next contraction, you'll push. You'll rest and breathe and then push again." I had to ask, "Do you have any idea what to do here?"

Her laugh became a scream as I held her hand and she pushed until it passed. I figured I was supposed to look and see if I could see the baby's head, so I flipped up her dress. Yup. I thought that was the baby's head. Thought being the operative word.

"All right. I think I can see the top of her head, so next contraction, you'll push again, and let's see if we can get this little girl born."

She pushed.

We breathed.

The little head appeared. It was flat out the most amazing thing I'd ever seen.

"There's her head!" I said, grabbing another towel from the basket and getting it ready to receive a baby.

Another contraction. Another huge, screaming push. The rest of the baby appeared. I wrapped it in a towel, cleaned off the tiny face, and waited. Right on cue, Amy screwed up that face and wailed.

I got my scissors, wiped them with alcohol, and cut the cord. Then I handed the wailing bundle to Charity. I knew we had to wait for the placenta. For this, my PBS tutorial wasn't very helpful, though I thought it could be a long time.

Meanwhile, I helped Charity sit up and watched her meet her daughter. Her face was rapt with amazement as she traced the outlines of tiny Amy's face. "Oh, my, Thea. We did it. We did it."

Tears poured down her face.

Amy's great dark eyes stared up at her mother.

"This is amazing," Charity said.

It was.

Outside this tiny room, things had gone scarily quiet. I needed to know what was happening out there. I didn't dare leave this room and wasn't sure whether I could safely leave Charity. I veered from elation—we'd actually birthed this baby—to terror. What if something had happened to Andre and because we'd helped Charity, MOC would be born without a father?

"I'm going to leave you for minute. See what's happening out there."

She nodded, though I wasn't sure she'd heard me. She was wrapped up in the baby in her arms.

I got my gun and stood, a little unsteady from crouching so long, from the emotional impact of what had just happened.

I opened the door and stepped slowly out, looking around. The room was empty. As I stood there, trying to decide whether to approach the windows, the door opened and a man stepped in.

I raised the gun. "Stop right there," I said.

He took one step closer, then stopped. Put up one hand. The other hung loosely by his side. I waited. He'd moved into the light where I could see him better. Malcolm Kinsman. Blood stained his sleeve and dripped off his hand. He looked ravaged, barely able to stay on his feet, yet held himself erect. I lowered my gun.

"Congratulations," I said. "You have a beautiful new niece. Now, where is my husband?"

THIRTY-THREE

"He's okay. Just making sure there aren't more surprises. There's an ambulance on the way."

"I hope it's an ambulance built for two."

"Where's my sister? And the baby?" He shook his head like he was clearing cobwebs. "Are they really okay?"

"They're in the bathtub," I said. "It seemed like the safest place. As for okay? Midwifery is not my department, but I think we've done this successfully."

He took a few stumbling steps. I crossed the room, put my shoulder under his arm, and led him to the couch.

"You'll see her soon enough. She doesn't need to be scared by you fainting right after what she's been through." I left him there and headed for the door. The outside door. The door between me and Andre.

"You shouldn't go out there," he said.

It felt like someone had poured a bucket of ice water on me. I stopped, turning to him as a wave of dread swept through me. "You said that he was okay."

"He *is* okay. It's just…"

"It's just what?" I think I yelled it. Then I grabbed for some control. I wasn't supposed to upset Charity. The last thing I wanted was to scare her into coming out here, minutes after giving birth, clutching tiny Amy.

"It's just what?" I repeated quietly. "What is going on out there?"

"Fred and Alice. The Marshals Service inspectors. They're not."

"Not what, Kinsman? They're more fake federal agents?" Like Davenport had claimed to be.

He nodded.

"And they have Andre? They've taken him?"

"Not exactly. Uh…" He leaned back against the couch and closed his eyes.

"Dammit, Kinsman, don't fade on me now. Not exactly what?" I was forgetting to use my indoor voice again. "If he's in trouble, why aren't you out there with him?"

Me in a nutshell. Guy gets shot, he's bleeding on the couch, and I stand there and yell at him.

He mustered the energy for two more sentences. "He's not alone. Tommy and Norah…"

"Are with him?"

He nodded.

How on earth had it come to this? A woman knocks on my door, introduces herself as my new neighbor, and suddenly everything about my life and plans keep getting turned upside down. It was a relief that Andre had Tommy and Norah with him. He didn't need me and my gun out there, too. But I wanted this over. I wanted to be at home, barefoot and pregnant and having a cookout. Instead, I had just delivered a baby, and now I had to deal with a bleeding man. And last night, I'd invited a pair of bad guys to dinner. Well, Andre had. Said he was suspicious and wanted to keep them close. At least he'd hinted at that. Had he known?

I'd like to take Suzanne's advice and avoid situations like this, but I don't understand how I'd do that. It would involve some basic things like never answer the phone, never answer the door, and never, under any circumstances, care about other people's well-being.

I opened the bathroom door. Charity looked half-asleep and baby Amy lay quietly on her chest. For now, that situation was under control. I grabbed the last towel from the basket and headed toward Kinsman, using it to protect the couch while I got gauze and bandages and adhesive tape from my bag. I'm practically a full-service pharmacy. I used my scissors, freshly sterilized, to cut away his shirt sleeve, then pressed pads on the wound and wrapped it with gauze and tape. A very temporary fix. For someone who doesn't like the sight of blood, I was seeing a lot of it today.

Sirens wailing in the distance announced the arrival of the ambulance. It pulled into the yard in a blast of light and sound and two men and a woman in blue shirts headed for the door. Ordinarily, I would have stepped back and directed them to their patients, but after several encounters with people who weren't who they claimed to be, this time I checked IDs at the door.

They were local. They were licensed. I gladly handed Charity and her baby and her injured brother over to professionals, then collapsed on the couch. Now that babies had been delivered and wounds tended, I was limp as cooked spaghetti.

So much for avoiding stress. If my doctor knew about this, she'd probably put me on bed rest. Or in restraints.

I should clean up the bathroom. Figure out what could be washed and what to throw away. I should pack a bag for Charity and Amy.

Ignoring those shoulds, I stayed on the couch, waiting for Andre to reappear.

Outside it was silent.

Inside it was silent.

I put my hands on MOC, who was being very quiet, and said, "I promise you won't be born in a bathtub."

MOC gave my hand a reassuring kick, kind of a "Yo, mama, I get it. So chill." Smart kid seemed to know that mama was done in.

I tipped my head back and closed my eyes.

The door burst open. I jerked upright and raised my gun. Andre was in the doorway, sweat-soaked and disheveled. "Don't shoot," he said. "I've had enough of guns today."

I crossed the room. He wrapped his arms around me. I burrowed into my happy spot and stayed there. He was hot and wet and smelled of sweat. I didn't give a damn.

After a while, I said, "So, Fred and Alice are bad guys, huh? Did you know?"

I felt his chin on my head, nodding an affirmative.

"Took some time to track down the truth. Government, you know. Not particularly forthcoming. A bunch of back and forth. I had to send them pictures of our Fred and Alice before they finally confirmed we were dealing with imposters. The real Fred and Alice are…were…Marshals Service inspectors. The Fred and Alice we met are imposters."

"When did you know?"

"I'd suspected. Last night I finally got confirmation."

"Yet you invited them to dinner? And didn't tell me who they were?"

"I got confirmation after dinner. Before that? I wanted to keep them close and unsuspecting. You would have tossed them out and then followed them and beat the crap out of them."

"True."

"While we were keeping our eyes on them." He nuzzled me with his chin. "So how'd it go in here?"

"Oh. I delivered a baby and then bandaged up Kinsman. All in a day's work."

His arms tightened. "Really? You delivered a baby?"

"I did. Bet you have, too."

"Nope."

"It was amazing. You should try it some time."

"Planning to."

Time stood still. We stood still. Finally, curious, I said, "Did you have Norah and Tommy following us?"

"I did. They were behind Fred and Alice."

"Practically a parade. And you were able to organize this on the spur of the moment on a Saturday?"

"Not quite. I kind of had them on alert after we confirmed that Fred and Alice were fakes."

"Where are they now?"

"Tommy and Norah? They've taken some prisoners to the jail."

"Fred and Alice?"

"Yup. And cowboy boots. Shall we go home? Someone on this team badly needs a shower."

"He does."

He helped me gather things from the bathroom and then pack a bag for Charity and the baby. We carried it all out to the car and headed home. I should have been bursting with questions about what happened outside and how Malcolm Kinsman got injured. Instead, I fell asleep.

THIRTY-FOUR

J onetta and Lindsay were just back from a swim when we
pulled in. They were hanging beach towels and bathing suits
on the line and chatting like they'd been friends forever. Andre
said a quick hello and headed for the shower. I kicked off my
sandals and dumped myself in a chair on the deck. I waved my
hand like a princess directing her staff. "Could someone please
bring me an Arnold Palmer?"

"With vodka?" Lindsay asked, laughing.

"Just a splash."

She stared at me for a moment, debating whether to object, then
read my face and went inside.

"Bring me one, too, please," Jonetta called, "with more than a
splash."

She arranged herself in the chair beside mine and said, "Guess
your day hasn't been as restful as ours?"

"I may have broken my record for eventful." I remembered a
professor with a gun and said, "Maybe not. There was a gunfight. I
delivered a baby. And bandaged up the wounded. It's nice to be
home."

"Whew!" she said. "You doing okay?"

"Don't know yet. Waiting for the delayed shock, I think. But Charity and the baby are okay, and her brother will be, and the bad guys have been caught—though that's been kind of like Whack-a-Mole."

"Alice and Fred?" she said.

"There was something about those two," I said. "I took an instant dislike to them, while Andre kept urging me to be patient and cooperative. I hate to think, though, that people who ate at my table later were shooting at my husband and threatening that poor girl in labor."

"The world is not a kind place, Thea. I see examples of that every day."

"And yet you toil on, always working for your girls. Protecting them. Fighting for them. How do you do it?"

She shrugged. "However hokey this sounds, I think I'm called to do it. We do what we're drawn to do. Otherwise, girlfriend, you would be doing some nice safe job, like Suzanne thinks you should be doing, instead of going up against bad guys time after time."

"You make me sound a lot more heroic than I really am."

Lindsay had returned with our drinks and was listening curiously.

Jonetta smiled and stretched. "I call it like I see it. So how was it, delivering a baby?"

"Amazing. Astonishing. Terrifying. I don't know what I would have done if something went wrong."

"Then, thank goodness it didn't." She tasted her drink and looked at Lindsay. "This is pretty heavy on the vodka, isn't it?"

Lindsay grinned. "You're on vacation."

My drink tasted like ice tea and lemonade. I leaned back in my chair and looked up at the sky, the same sky that earlier had been flinging meteoric bad memories at me. There was something about being home, with everyone safe, and in the company of Jonetta, that was keeping the shock of events in that little A-frame at bay. Fine with me. I wanted to sit out here and relax and feel the soft summer air.

Andre appeared in jeans and tee-shirt, his feet bare, his hair wet and spiky. He looked delicious.

He pulled me to my feet and kissed me, never mind that we had an audience. "What time is Suzanne's crew coming?" he asked.

"Around five." It was a little before three right now. Plenty of time to veg out.

"I have a question about the unfinished guest room. I need your opinion on something," he said. He gave Jonetta and Lindsay one of his patented disarming smiles. "Can you spare Thea for a few minutes?" Maybe Jonetta knew what was up, but Lindsay certainly didn't.

We went upstairs and closed the bedroom door. "How are you really?" he asked, gently tucking a wayward curl behind my ear. He was so close I could feel his body heat. Smell the particular scent that was him, the one I'd recognize in a dark room.

I walked the last step forward so we were touching. "Shaken," I whispered. "Glad it's over."

"You're supposed to be avoiding stress." It was just a whisper in my ear.

My clothes came off. So did his. We gently and quietly offloaded some of the day's horrible fear and tension. My stress levels were lowered so much that I fell asleep right after. I didn't wake up until he knocked on the door, leaned in, and said that Suzanne had arrived.

"Oh, and Malcolm's here, too. I hope that's okay? And Lindsay's boyfriend. He seems like a nice kid."

"As long as it isn't Fred and Alice."

"No chance of that."

I splashed cold water on my face and went downstairs. Suzanne's daughter Emily was sitting in her little plastic seat on the deck, conducting the crowd with a large plastic spoon. Paul, Jr. was at the deer fence, studying the hungry fawn at the edge of the woods and keeping up a litany of chatter to it. Jonetta and Lindsay and Lindsay's boyfriend Sean were shucking corn, and Suzanne and Paul were talking to Andre and Malcolm by the grill. Malcolm's arm was in a sling and he looked pale, which wasn't good, but his intensity level was considerably lower. Maybe he'd taken some meds.

My medicine had been a healthy dose of Andre.

Suppressing a wicked grin, I said hello to everyone, settled into a chair, and smiled at the happy commotion. In the past two days, I might have faced down a bad guy with a gun and delivered a baby, but this was how I loved spending a warm summer afternoon: Andre grilling, MOC kicking, Emily cooing, and my good friends enjoying each other's company. Andre and I had looked for a place to call home for a long time. Finally, despite some bad guys' efforts, we'd found it.

Everyone stayed for dinner, a spectacular feast of platters and bowls piled high with steak and dogs and burgers. With corn and potato salad. I loved the idea of a family assembled from friends. Found myself attentive to everyone and wanting them to eat. For what seemed like the first time since Charity knocked on my door, I wasn't tense. I expected no strangers at the door and no worrying phone calls. It was lovely. Perhaps sensing the loveliness, MOC chose a leisurely stretching instead of an acrobatic routine.

In the middle of dinner, Kinsman got a phone call. He excused himself from the table and went outside to take it. We could all hear his heavy steps as he paced back and forth. He was gone so long I was sure he was getting the bad news that the operation to rescue David Peckham had gone wrong and Charity's joy at Amy's safe arrival would soon be crushed. Or something had happened with Baby Amy.

Instead, when he came back in, his beaten-down look was gone.

He sat down at the table with the first genuine smile I'd seen from him.

"It's over. David is safe. He's okay. He's flying up tomorrow."

It was such wonderful news the whole table burst out with applause, and little Paul said, "Hooray."

Later, when Suzanne and company left and Jonetta and Lindsay and Lindsay's boyfriend had gone to bed, Andre and Malcolm and I sat in the living room, both men holding glasses of bourbon, and they caught me up on the fight at the A-frame. Andre and Malcolm outside, securing the area. Fred and Alice firing from the woods. Malcolm getting shot just as Norah and Tommy arrived and Fred and Alice, outgunned, surrendering soon after.

"They tried to bluff their way out," Andre said, "not knowing we'd finally established their credentials were faked." He sighed. "There's so much talk about interagency cooperation, but when it's feds and locals, things don't always work so well. We still might not know for sure if the bodies of the real Fred and Alice hadn't been found."

Cowboy Boots—I never learned his name and didn't care—arrived late to the gun party and never got a chance to get out of his car.

"I don't like all this death and dying," I said, "even if there was the miracle of a new life in the midst of it."

I looked at Kinsman, who was drooping in his chair. "Are you allowed to tell us what the mission was that you and David were on?"

"Not really. Let's just say we were helping to locate and shut down some drug smuggling tunnels along the border."

"The army does that? Not Homeland Security?"

Kinsman's smile was ironic and amused. "Ma'am," he said, "Special Forces do all kinds of things folks never hear about." The subtext was that was all he was going to say.

Andre shot me one of his "don't press it" looks and leaned in. His mission-driven, male-bonding, take each other on faith world was different from my need to understand the whole picture. This time, he didn't need to worry. Vagueness was fine with me. I really didn't want to know. I wanted to see all of this in a figurative rearview mirror.

In the silence that followed, everyone thinking their own thoughts and processing the day, Kinsman suddenly laughed. "Uncle Malcolm," he said. "Wow. A whole new chapter. I can't wait to see David's face."

He stood. "I hope you don't mind if I borrow your guestroom one more night?"

"It's just a mattress on the floor," I said.

"Right now, I could sleep on a bed of nails."

He left us, and we heard his tired feet climb the stairs.

I moved from my chair to Andre's lap. "Can we stop answering the door?"

"Stop answering the door? Soon as Dad and Ronny are done in the barn, we're building a tower and I'm locking you in there."

I snuggled into his shoulder. "Only if I get a tower to lock you in as well. And who will take care of MOC?"

"A moat, then," he said.

"Dragons to guard us."

"Guard dogs. Bite-trained."

I sighed. "If this were TV, someone would stop by now to assure us that Jason has been convicted and sent off to jail."

"Even on TV," he said, his voice rumbling in his chest, "they'd have to knock on the door."

I think I fell asleep then, ridiculously secure against his chest. In his arms. In a romance, we would have ended there. But I'm no small woman, and before I cut off the circulation to his legs, he nudged me to my feet. He led me upstairs, past all our sleeping guests. We climbed into bed, Andre curled around me. As I drifted back to sleep, I thought of Baby Amy, her tiny, red, squinched-up face and wise, dark eyes.

Sleep, I told myself. Soon my own nights would be interrupted by those tiny cries, those wise eyes, and someone new figuratively knocking on my door. Only this time, it would be life that came knocking.

DEATH SENDS A MESSAGE

A THEA KOZAK MYSTERY, BOOK 11

It was a clear and sunny late summer day, the kind that makes me feel good to be alive. MOC was tucked up in a baby wrap, small and warm against my chest, sound asleep. I was searching through a discombobulated bin of clearance baby things, trying to find a summer hat small enough to fit a tiny head. In all my hasty and interrupted prep, I'd forgotten to get one, and I'd been scolded for my negligence by an elderly lady who thought I was committing child abuse. Trying to find a summer hat at the end of August was impossible. I kept striking out. This was my third store and my temper was as worn as the meager supply of summer goods I was perusing.

At last, almost at the bottom of the bin, I found it, a small yellow embroidered number with a tipsy-looking duck. Hat purchased, I headed back out into the late summer sunshine.

On my way into the store, I'd passed another new mother—at least I assumed she was a new mother since the infant in her expensive carriage was tiny. She was sitting on a bench outside the shop, eating an ice cream cone.

The sight had inspired me and made my next planned stop the ice cream stand. Black raspberry with chocolate chunks. I could almost taste it. Almost feel the sticky warm-cold as it dripped toward the edge of my hand and I caught it with my tongue. I realized that my choice was risky. I didn't yet know how MOC reacted to chocolate.

When I came out of the air-conditioned shop into the bright sun, the woman, well, a girl, really, was standing beside the carriage, waving her arms, screaming like I have honestly never heard anyone scream in the real world.

She was young and skinny, with pale arms and legs that had somehow missed the summer sun. No substance to her except what I took for nursing-mother breasts and a tiny post-delivery belly. Her nearly waist-length hair was thick and blonde and wavy. Magazine cover hair. Model hair. Hair that required time and money to create such a carefree look. She wore a blue striped sundress that came no more than halfway down her thighs, not quite long enough to cover some purple bruises. Elaborately strappy sandals in a matching blue. Her lips were puffed with filler and shone with gloss. She wore more eye makeup than I've worn in the last ten years. The noise she was making was so loud it blurred whatever she was screaming about.

For a moment, I thought it was theater. Some street thing staged to grab tourists' attention. Her panicked expression said no.

I didn't want her screams to wake my sleeping baby. Sleep was a rare enough thing that I cherished these quiet moments when I could enjoy the small, soft body without also having to deal with misery and unhappiness. Without pacing the floor in a darkened room. Still, I was concerned. She was another new mother, and something had set her off. I waited for someone to stop, approach her. Ask her what was wrong. There were plenty of people about who could have helped her besides me.

Plenty of people around who evidently didn't give a damn. They flowed around the screaming girl and her huge baby carriage like she was a rock in a stream. Averting their eyes or pumping up conversation as though volume proved its importance and excused a failure to offer help to someone in trouble. Obviously, someone needed to help. I just didn't want that helper to be me. I have done my share. More than my share.

I stood and watched the scene like it was something in a movie. The drama. The fear she was projecting. The absolutely hateful, shameful way people were ignoring her.

Damn them all!

If anyone had been with me, anyone who knows me, they would have said "Thea, don't!" and dragged me away. But except for MOC, I was alone, and the kid may be good at using noise to manipulate me but hasn't learned "don't" yet.

I took a step closer. Near enough to see into that elaborate carriage. Near enough to see something that would make any mother scream. The carriage that had held a small, sleeping infant when I went into the store—a boy, if all that blue was true indicator —was empty, and the screaming girl wasn't holding a baby.

Available in Paperback and eBook from Your Favorite Bookstore or Online Retailer

ALSO BY KATE FLORA

The Thea Kozak Mystery Series

Chosen for Death

Death in a Funhouse Mirror

Death at the Wheel

An Educated Death

Death in Paradise

Liberty or Death

Stalking Death

Death Warmed Over

Schooled in Death

Death Comes Knocking

Death Sends a Message

———

The Joe Burgess Mystery Series

Playing God

The Angel of Knowlton Park

Redemption

And Grant You Peace

Led Astray

A Child Shall Lead Them

A World of Deceit

ABOUT THE AUTHOR

Kate Flora's fascination with people's criminal tendencies began in the Maine attorney general's office. Deadbeat dads, people who hurt their kids, and employers' discrimination aroused her curiosity about human behavior. The author of twenty-one books and many short stories, Flora's been a finalist for the Edgar, Agatha, Anthony, and Derringer awards. She won the Public Safety Writers Association award for nonfiction and twice won the Maine Literary Award for crime fiction. Her most recent Thea Kozak mystery is *Schooled in Death*; her most recent Joe Burgess is *A Child Shall Lead Them*. Her new crime story collection is *Careful What You Wish For: Stories of revenge, retribution, and the world made right.* In 2020 there's a romantic suspense, *Wedding Bell Ruse,* a story in *The Faking of the President* and one in *Heartbreaks and Half-Truths,* a new Thea Kozak mystery, *Death Comes Knocking,* and a new Joe Burgess, *The Deceits of the World.*

Flora's nonfiction focuses on aspects of the public safety officers' experience. Her two true crimes, *Finding Amy: A true story of murder in Maine* (with Joseph K. Loughlin) and *Death Dealer: How cops and cadaver dogs brought a killer to justice,* follow homicide investigations as the police conducted them. Her co-written memoir of retired Maine warden Roger Guay, *A Good Man with a Dog: A Game Warden's 25 Years in the Maine Woods,* explores policing in a world of guns, misadventure, and the great outdoors. Her latest nonfiction is *Shots Fired: The Misconceptions, Misunderstandings, and Myths about police shootings* with retired Portland Assistant Chief Joseph K. Loughlin.

Flora divides her time between Massachusetts and Maine, where she gardens and cooks and watches the clouds when she's not imagining her character's dark deeds. She's been married for decades to an excellent man. Her sons edit films and hang out in research labs.

www.kateclarkflora.com

 facebook.com/katecflora
twitter.com/kateflora

CPSIA information can be obtained
at www.ICGtesting.com
Printed in the USA
LVHW100717160423
744479LV00012B/63